DEAD AIR

A HENRY & SPARROW NOVEL

A D FOX

SPARTILLUS

PROLOGUE

For a man who always had a great deal to say, Dave Perry was pretty quiet at the end.

The journey through the dark had been terrifying. His jeans were soaked, and not with rain or spilt tea. He had tried to plead with his captor; tried to understand what drove the lunatic to do this.

His voice - so highly regarded by many thousands of listeners for its deep and authoritative tones - was querulous and feeble as he'd said: 'OK... let's talk.' If he was hoping his breakfast show catchphrase, emblazoned below his wryly grinning face on a hoarding outside the BBC Radio Wessex headquarters, might help, he was wrong. His captor merely glanced at him in the rearview mirror, snorted, and said nothing.

He coughed and tried again, marshalling decades of BBC gravitas and reminding himself that he was someone. *Someone* to be reckoned with. He had left senior politicians floundering with his incisive grilling; had confronted cheating businessmen; disarmed world-class celebrities with his quick wit - all on live radio; no edits here, thank you.

'What do you want? Where are we going? Look... you've got to see this is madness!'

He got no reply, so he rested his forehead against his tightly taped wrists, which were anchored to the base of the front passenger seat headrest, and tried to think. He wasn't a strong man. He'd spent way too many hours sitting in a studio, exercising his jaw and his faders; not nearly enough in the gym. He'd never felt the need to work on his physique; he was a local celebrity and got plenty of female attention whenever he appeared at outside broadcasts or charity events. He was nearing his mid-50s but he still had all his hair and if he was perhaps slightly doughy and average looking, his radio voice made up for it. He'd talked an impressive number of young women into bed over the years, and then, when he'd grown bored or stifled, talked them neatly out of his life again with his famously acerbic put-downs.

But his voice was pretty useless now. He needed to get himself out of this car; out of the bonds around his wrists and ankles; out of this crazy situation.

He wondered, briefly, if this was a stunt. Those two new guys on mid-morning, Spencer and Jack, they fancied themselves as edgy and funny, with their endless stupid 'memes' and piss-takes. They'd targeted him before; trying to make him look like some fuddy-duddy boomer or whatever. Maybe this was their work. There could be hidden cameras in this car relaying his desperately 'sad' attempts to get control while they rolled about laughing and live-streamed him on Facebook.

But he doubted that even they would sanction the blade which had cut right through his leather bomber jacket and into his side as he'd been jumped in the shadowy corner of the BBC car park. His attacker had forced him at knifepoint, gasping and shocked, into the back seat of his own Audi, then made him wrap up his ankles and knees with yards of tight gaffer tape. When *that was done he'd had to sit still while his wrists were efficiently bound to the headrest. There had been no time to react or resist.*

The car park barrier had risen automatically after scanning the number plate. There was no chance anyone would notice anything had gone amiss. Unless the attack and abduction had been caught on security camera, and given that the lighting on the lower level had failed - he'd had to use his phone torch to walk safely down the ramp - he would guess there was no telly feed to alert the one sleepy guy at the security hub.

'I have kids, you know,' he whimpered, after a long time silent. It was quite a claim. He did have kids; three of them, the fruit of two long defunct marriages, all now in their twenties. Only one of them still spoke to him and that was just at Christmas. He'd not been much of a provider since he'd left their mothers and each of them had no doubt been poisoned against him over time. Even so, he was a father.

'People... depend on me,' he went on.

His abductor snorted again. It made him angry.

'They fucking do!' he snapped. 'I am The Voice of Wessex! I keep tens of thousands of people company every day; fight their corner; look out for the little guy. Is that what this is about? Were you someone I brought down?'

There was a hoot of laughter. And then, muffled a little by the black face mask: "Jesus. You really do believe your own publicity, don't you?'

He caught his breath. He knew that voice. But where from? Because, in his position, you met so many people. It was hard to remember everyone's name. He had a producer and a researcher to do that for him.

'Who are you?' he demanded, getting angrier and more right-eous now that he'd heard that voice. 'What is all this about?'

The only response was a sudden and sharp turn into a narrow country lane. They'd been travelling for maybe twenty or thirty minutes now. It was late and dark and very few other vehicles were on the road. A minute or two later there was another right turn up a short gravel drive; high hedges and trees on either side. Dave began to shake as the car came to a halt. Outside it was perfectly dark, apart from a gleam of metal picked out by the front headlamps - a wide five bar gate.

The driver got out, scraped the metal gate open across the tarmac, and came around to the back. The door opened with a cold gust of air. Sharpened steel glinted in the weak courtesy light and Dave heard himself whimper again, but all the knife cut though this time was the gaffer tape around his legs, releasing him in a burst of pins and needles. Next his wrists were freed.

'Get out.'

'Where are we?' he croaked, stumbling out of the car. He could smell that it was rural - right out in the sticks. There was next to no light pollution and very little noise, but he could make out a low electrical hum. The car sidelights cast a dim glow, revealing tarmac underfoot and some kind of metal structure up ahead. He felt the blade in his side again, and a strong grip pinching into his shoulder. He still couldn't make out the face inside the hoodie but he knew his captor was younger than him... and fitter. Wiry rather than brawny, but with undeniable strength. Fighting back or trying to run was going to be useless. His only hope was reasoning himself out of this.

'What do you want from me?' he babbled as they moved through the dark. 'I've got money. Not much... but I can go to a cashpoint and get you a couple of grand. You can take the car too.'

He was spun around and slammed against the metal structure, its cold criss-cross struts digging into his shoulder blades. 'Go up,' his captor ordered. Dave turned and grabbed hold of the struts, finding the horizontal ones with his numb feet and scaling the structure until he was maybe a metre up.

'Turn around.'

He turned carefully, flattening his back against what felt like a giant climbing frame. It fleetingly occurred to him that he might leap out, like Spiderman, land on the other side of the hooded figure below and then race away into the dark. Then his ankles were grabbed and held tightly together against some kind of girder while the reel of gaffer tape was handed up again. 'Tape yourself to it.'

He considered kicking the guy in the face. As if reading his mind, his abductor said: 'Try it. Just try it. You'll be on the ground with a knife through your neck before you can say "OK - let's talk.".'

He couldn't move his ankles anyway. He was too afraid; too weak.

He taped up his legs and then his kidnapper climbed up next to him, blade in one gloved hand, and taped each wrist, outstretched, to a separate metal strut, so that Dave was tightly held in a T shape.

In the midst of his terror he finally realised where he was. He still had no idea why. The taping ended and the kidnapper jumped down and stared up at him, flashing a mobile phone torch beam into his face.

'Are you going to..?' whispered Dave.

There was a burst of energy and then something was shoved deep into his mouth. It was only as it was taped into place, silencing him forever, that Dave realised what it was. Dense, thick sponge. More of it was shoved into his nostrils. Quality material; Neumann, probably. Too expensive to breathe through.

He was going to make the morning news. But not in a way he'd ever expected to.

As his chest began to hitch and spasm in a hopeless quest for air, The Voice of Wessex reflected that his last words had been pretty lame.

'And now,' said his killer, 'back to the studio.'

1

'So, tell me, does your dowsing help with your art?'

Lucas Henry sat back in his seat, raised both palms, and stared across the blond wood edifice that separated him from Louella Green and her desk of buttons and faders. She shrugged at him and raised her palms too, mouthing '*Sorry!*' In her mid-30s, black and pretty, he suspected she was used to charming her way out of awkward situations live on air.

Lucas sighed. He wasn't surprised. He might have known it would go this way.

'Well,' he said, at length, adjusting the heavy headphones and leaning back in to the microphone which hung from an adjustable angle-poise style bracket. 'I guess it doesn't hurt. Dowsing is all about patterns and energy... and I guess you could say my paintings are too.'

For the first five minutes of the interview the mid-afternoon presenter on BBC Radio Wessex had behaved perfectly well, discussing only his very successful art exhibition in an independent Salisbury Gallery. But they both knew that she was *dying* to get to the real meat - the *reason*

why an obscure abstract painter from the back-end of Wiltshire had suddenly caught the attention of the art world.

In his return email to Louella's producer, Lucas had
initially said no thanks. But the producer had come back,
pointing out that the reason he'd been asked was that there
was a big push across the Wessex region's schools to inspire
the artists of the future, and somebody like him - homegrown and now slated for an exhibition in London - was
going to be *massively* inspirational. Lucas had tried to
decline again but in the end the producer had worn him
down and he'd agreed to come in and talk.

He should have known better.

'Of course,' said Louella. 'Dowsing helps you to find
inspiration... but many of our listeners will also know that it
helped you to find quite a bit more than that a few weeks
ago.'

'Will they?' asked Lucas, although he knew the battle
was lost. He could have wrenched off his headphones and
stormed out of this soundproofed cell, and been quite
within his rights. He'd specifically said to the producer that
he didn't want to talk about the events of early September.
He had hoped the nature of his involvement would stay out
of the news but of course it had eventually filtered through.
The producer, though, had assured him that Louella was
only interested in the art.

'Lucas... you were a *wanted man,*' Louella said, grinning
at him cheekily. 'You were arrested and charged with kidnap
and murder... and you might be languishing in prison even
now if you hadn't used your dowsing powers to find the *real*
killer - saving the life of a Wiltshire policewoman *and*
another of the killer's intended victims along the way.'

'Um,' said Lucas. Because... what *could* he say to that? *Yes
- I'm a hero! Do they sell capes on Amazon?* 'It wasn't just *me*,'

he added. 'DS Sparrow saved that woman, really. I just helped.'

'Well, obviously we can't comment in great detail before the inquest,' said Louella. 'But it's pretty much public knowledge that between you both, you made Wiltshire a much safer place for female runners. And as I'm one of them, I just wanted to say... *thank you.*'

'O...kay,' said Lucas, feeling intensely uncomfortable, not least because he'd just name-checked Kate on air and he had a feeling she would hate that kind of thing even more than he did.

'So... how does it work?' Louella went on. 'The dowsing? Can you really find water and lost things?'

'Lots of people can,' said Lucas. 'It's not magic. It's an innate ability in all of us.'

'Really? So... if I lose, say, my mobile phone or my car keys, I can just close my eyes, turn around in a circle with a couple of twigs, and dowse my way to them?'

'In essence, yes,' he said. 'But some people are better at it than others - and anyone who tries it has to practise. It takes a bit of work to get yourself into the dowsing state.'

'But if I practise,' she went on, breathlessly, 'I can find my keys or my phone?'

'Um... yes,' he said, tempted to add *and bodies, too, if you're not careful.*

'SO!' went on the presenter, joyfully. 'I've asked Daryl, my producer, to hide my phone. It's somewhere in or around this building, but I have no clue where. Can you find it for me?'

Lucas gaped at her. *What a total fucking ambush!* He wanted to say as much but she was the one in control of the faders and he didn't like to think about how much of his tirade would be relayed across three counties.

'I mean... I don't want to put you on the spot,' she said. 'Listeners should know that we *didn't* plan this beforehand. It's a bit of an ambush.' She had the grace to look a little sheepish.

Lucas shook his head at her, mouth compressed and then gave a tight smile as he replied: 'Fine. Let's do it. But you might need to go to The Carpenters if I've got to search the building.'

'Oooh yes!' she squeaked. 'How did you know I've got *Top of the World* cued up next? You must be able to dowse for top tunes!'

'Evidently not,' he grunted. It was just an unlucky guess. But he dipped into his shirt and pulled out a small blue glass pendant - an old bottle stopper he liked to call Sid. With his free hand he reached across to her.

She stood up, pulling her mic up with her and giving him her fingers. 'So - you take my hand,' she said, commentating for her listeners, 'and that gives you a connection, yes? Although... shouldn't it be Daryl's hand you're holding? He hid my phone.'

'Either will do,' said Lucas. He didn't add that he might be tempted to break the producer's wrist for all the out-and-out lying.

'Are you feeling the... what is it... vibrations?' she asked.

'If you like,' he said. 'OK, got it.' He let her hand drop. 'You'd better get that top tune up.'

'This is SO exciting,' said Louella, bringing up the syrupy opening chords of the *Carpenters*' hit beneath her voice. 'We're about to find out whether Lucas Henry really can dowse... right here and now on BBC Radio Wessex!'

As soon as the ON AIR light had gone off he tilted his head and raised his eyebrows.

She pulled her headphones down around her neck and

looked theatrically guilty. 'I know, I *know*... I'm sorry! But I just couldn't help myself. I mean - you're an actual bona fide *hero,* Lucas! People should know.'

'They really shouldn't,' he said. 'Now... let's go and find your bloody mobile.'

She let her producer take over the knobs and faders, with an instruction to segue into another track if they weren't back in time, and then she led him out of the studio, into the lobby outside the newsroom, and stood, breathlessly, looking at him.

He sighed, shook his head and closed his eyes. Getting into the zone was always harder in situations like this. He didn't do party pieces... not for many years anyway. It was hard to know whether just going home right now would make him a bigger twat than staying and finding her phone. He suspended Sid between his fingers and let the stopper swing to a halt on its strong stainless steel links. The necklace looked a bit like a slender plug chain and could have been prettier in silver, but its strength had saved his life more than once. Sid began to slowly spin clockwise before moving into a figure of eight dance and then, finally, the pendulum rocked back and forth along a single plane.

Lucas followed the patterns his mind threw up; whirls and eddies in a dimension he could never fully describe to anyone else. Other dowsers he'd met - the good ones, not the performers - had said the same. Some things were just beyond describing. Some things were just a *knowing.*

'OK,' he said, snapping Sid into his palm. He had a clear direction. He set out along the corridor, back to the reception area. Louella trotted after him, holding out a small recording device.

'We're heading down the corridor,' she said, her voice full of excited reverence. 'OK - hang on, Lucas, we need my

ID card... OK... so now we're in reception... *Hello, Moira! Just passing through!* Now - ID card again - we're out the other side of reception and in the corridor to the back end of the station. Lucas seems very certain about where we're going. Now we're heading for the back stairwell... I wonder if we're going outside. Down we go, and again, another flight... and left... and... OK, ID card again... this is the post room and...' She faltered into silence.

Lucas, after another quick consultation with Sid, had reached up into the top right of maybe thirty name-tagged pigeonholes. The name on this one was Kelly Tyler. He slid his hand under a padded envelope and found a small, slim Apple mobile. He held it up to show Louella, who was gaping at him in shock.

'Not yours?' he asked, disingenuously, turning to replace it.

'No!' she squeaked. 'I mean... yes... that's... that's mine.'

She stared at him in a moment of awed silence. 'You *really can do this!*'

'Well, like I said... it's not magic,' he replied, finding himself impatient to be away now that he'd proved himself, pointlessly, to a radio presenter. He looked at his watch. 'You can run that without me, yeah? I've got to get away now.'

'Oh really..? Can't you stay until the end of the show?' She bobbed up and down and gave him a *pretty please* face. 'We could get people to call in about things they've lost and maybe...'

'No... sorry... got to go,' he said.

She looked crestfallen, but she nodded. 'OK... let me get you back to reception and signed out,' she said. 'And thank you - that was mind-blowing. I'm just gobsmacked!'

'Sure,' he said. She certainly *deserved* to be.

'I'll make sure I tell everyone about your exhibition!' she said as they headed back to the reception.

'Thanks,' he said.

In reception he was signed out, handing in his ID card. *Top of the World* was winding down to its ending and the producer had just segued into *Cracklin' Rosie*. Lucas really had to get out of here.

'He's just *found* my phone,' Louella told the grey-haired lady behind the reception desk. 'With *dowsing*. It's the coolest thing I ever saw! I was gobsmacked. *Gobsmacked!*'

'Well, fancy that,' said Moira, smiling warmly. She raised an eyebrow. 'Maybe you should get him to find Dave Perry!'

'He hasn't turned up yet, then?' asked Louella, in hushed tones.

'Nope... not for three days.' The receptionist leaned in towards Louella and spoke in a low voice, which Lucas still heard clearly. 'They think he might have gone on a bit of a bender.'

'Oh my,' said Louella. Then she turned back to Lucas, beaming. 'Thank you *so* much, Lucas. Will you come back again? Will you?'

He beamed back. 'Not a chance.'

She pouted. 'I know... I was naughty! Forgive me..?'

'I'll think about it,' he said, heading off to the revolving door. The presenter rushed away to share her recording and her gobsmackedness with her listeners.

All in all, it was not a great day's work. He should have stayed at home and got on with another painting.

He walked into the revolving door, noting someone else coming in on the other side. Two people, in fact, each taking a quarter pie slice of travelling glass and air. Lucas glanced through the glass just as a fair-haired woman glanced through her side. Both of them drew in a short, sharp breath.

DS Kate Sparrow was arriving as he was leaving. Behind her, if he wasn't mistaken, was her sidekick and admirer, young DC Michaels. Michaels, remembering recent events, glared at him. Lucas exited the door and walked down the steps. He was tempted to look back; to see if Kate had looked back at *him*. But like a teenager trying to impress a crush, he squared his shoulders and walked on, face front. Kate didn't want to see him. She'd made that clear. So *he* didn't want to see Kate.

Sid thrummed against his chest, not fooled for a second.

2

'DS Kate Sparrow and DC Ben Michaels,' said Detective Sergeant Kate Sparrow, flashing her ID. The BBC receptionist looked politely alarmed and reached for her phone. 'Mr Larkhill,' she said. 'I have a lady and gentleman from the Wiltshire Constabulary here to see you.' She glanced at them both, nodding. 'He'll be right through,' she said. 'Can I sign you both in, please?'

After signing in, Kate settled on one of the low chairs by a drinks machine.

'Please - help yourself to coffee or tea or hot chocolate,' the receptionist called across, sweetly.

'Thanks,' said Michaels. Her detective constable made a beeline for the drinks machine. 'What's it to be, boss?' he asked. He'd taken to calling her that recently, with a bit of a twinkle, which she did her best to ignore.

'Hot chocolate, I think,' she said. 'Thanks.'

It was cold outside and she was glad to warm up after the trek from the car park to the reception area. She'd only been back on active duty for a week. After her last brush with the man she'd just seen leaving she'd needed to take a break. Not really for her mental health; more to preserve her career. Bringing Lucas Henry into her last investigation had very nearly cost her her job. She couldn't really pin that on the dowser, though - her boss wasn't narrow-minded about occasional use of fringe talents. It was much more to do with the way she had mishandled evidence and used it to help further her absurd conviction that Lucas could help the case.

Absurd or not, it had turned out she was right. But that didn't change that fact that she'd behaved... well... illegally. So when Chief Superintendent Rav Kapoor had suggested she take some time off to recover from her injuries and the trauma of the Runner Grabber case, he'd laid it heavily on the line. Either she take a break... or he would suspend her for her misdemeanours and thereby *force* her to take a break.

Coming back had been a big relief. She needed to have focus in her life. Time without focus left her way too much opportunity to brood. She didn't want to dwell on what had happened to her and she really *hated* having to talk to a counsellor about it. She would have been lying, though, if she'd said she was unaffected. She had come within a whisker of a very unpleasant death; a future graphically laid out in front of her in a basement where one long dead woman lay in a corner and another one was dying right in front of her. Her dreams were still full of it and she felt tense whenever she was out of her house, especially when a blue van of any kind drove past her.

But work hadn't really been a problem. It was good to get back to some kind of normality. It had all been a bit dull and pedestrian, though, so even if she was a little nonplussed to be here, she was glad to be getting out and *doing* something. She and Michaels were only putting in a visit because the super had asked them to. Normally a misper case for a grown man with no documented mental health issues or criminal record would be logged and, if it was at a low risk level like this one, a PC would attend to it in the next 24 hours. This kind of thing was hardly high on the priority list of a busy city station and certainly not within the remit of the CID.

But Chief Superintendent Rav Kapoor had a high regard for community relations, and a good relationship with Rob Larkhill, managing editor at BBC Radio Wessex. A call from Larkhill had been routed directly through to the super. So, half an hour later, after sending a couple of PCs to Larkhill's home address and getting a report back that there was no reply and no car in the drive, she and Michaels were on their way to BBC Radio Wessex. The newsroom and studios were in a purpose-built red brick building in the lower end of the town, close to the many braids of the River Avon which constantly threatened to flood the A36, and a few minutes away from the cathedral, the square and other tourist spots.

'My mum loves all these guys,' said Michaels, holding his waxed paper coffee cup and nodding up at the many portraits artfully suspended against the reception walls on clips and wires. 'She's always got them on. She knows more about Sheila Bartley's life than she does about mine.'

'Probably just as well,' said Kate, arching an eyebrow. Michaels was a few years her junior and a bit of a ladies' man if the gossip was to be believed. Gossip was as close to her DC's off-duty activities as she ever intended to get. She knew, from her own observations and from the same sources of gossip (DC Sharon Mulligan mostly) that he had a bit of a thing for her. She did everything she could to discourage it; a lovelorn sidekick she did *not* need.

'It's your own fault,' Sharon had said to her in the ladies' toilets just last week. 'If you *will* go around being all blonde and beautiful and kick-ass, what do you expect?'

'I *don't!*' Kate had exploded. 'Look - not a scrap of make-up! Hair that hasn't seen a salon for six months. And it's not like I dress to impress, is it?'

Sharon, black, plump and gorgeous in her own style, had folded her arms and rolled her eyes. 'You don't need to, boss. The townie boots and the jeans and the jackets... it may be practical but you look like a hottie, like it or not. If you want to damp down little Ben Michaels you'll have to tell him you're a lesbian. Oh wait... no... that won't help.'

She smirked and Kate had been compelled to flick tap water at her and say 'A bit more respect for your senior officer, please!' before departing.

'Josh Carnegy,' Michaels went on, pointing to a twentysomething guy with tufty fair hair and a wide grin. 'My gran is nuts about him. She once queued for two hours to get him to sign a postcard at some summer fair. There were about ten other grannies doing the same thing. I don't get it.'

'He's there for them,' said Kate. 'Even in the wee small hours. I get it. Kind of.'

She scanned the other portraits, all taken in a professional studio with white backdrops, doing her best to disregard an involuntary shiver that passed through her when she recalled her own visit to a photographer's studio a few weeks back. *Stop it. Focus.*

Judy Goodson was an elegant, auburn-haired lady who, according to the note at the base of the picture, did the traffic and travel. Next along was their misper and after him was a photo of the mid-morning team, Spencer and Jack.

The younger guys - late 20s she would guess - were in a studiedly 'wacky' pose; one pretending to strangle the other, who was holding a trumpet and pulling a perplexed face. What they were doing here on a station with a demographic of 50+ she couldn't guess. Perhaps they had a thing for The Carpenters or Neil Diamond. Whenever she stumbled across the Radio Wessex frequency on her car stereo it seemed to be The Carpenters or Neil Diamond. Or Lighthouse Family if they were feeling edgy.

Neighbouring Spencer and Jack was a pretty black woman, probably around thirty, who presented the mid-afternoon show. Louella Green was broadcasting now through the PA system which piped the station feed through to reception.

Before Kate could study any more of the line-up a mousy-haired man arrived in reception, looking professionally stressed. He held out a hand to her. 'DS Sparrow?' he asked. The swinging BBC staff lanyard badge read *Robert Larkhill.*

She nodded. 'And this is Detective Constable Ben Michaels,' she said, indicating her colleague.

'Thank you both for coming. Please - come through to my office,' said Larkhill. 'Do bring your drinks.'

They were led along a carpeted corridor, past heavy, soundproofed doors with glass panels. Through the first of these she glimpsed a newsroom filled with desks and six or seven people seated at them, staring at monitors and bashing away on keyboards. Through the second she saw a serious-looking young man attending to a small console of buttons and lights, apparently handling calls for a live phone-in. And through the third she saw what had to be Louella Green, headphones on, talking animatedly into her microphone.

Larkhill's office was just beyond this studio; a magnolia room with one burgundy wall covered in the artfully scrawled names of towns and villages across the BBC Radio Wessex patch. The window behind his desk had a view down to the car park and a small garden with some wrought iron benches and a wooden gazebo for the station's banished smokers to shelter under. The plainer walls were hung with Sony Awards certificates and press cuttings featuring the presenters.

Larkhill invited them to sit on a couple of chairs in front of his desk.

'Well,' he said, running his fingers through thinning hair and giving them a tight smile. 'I certainly wasn't expecting to have *this* kind of meeting today.'

Kate nodded. 'You're concerned about a member of staff who's gone missing,' she stated.

'Yes - my breakfast show presenter,' said Larkhill. 'Dave Perry. He hasn't been seen since Friday. Of course, he's not a weekend presenter, so I only noticed he wasn't in on Monday. Now it's Wednesday and we still can't get in touch with him.'

'You've tried his family?' asked Kate.

'He lives alone,' said Larkhill. 'He's divorced... twice. His children are grown up now and he doesn't see a lot of them. We have got in touch, though, as far as we could. We have the second Mrs Perry's number. She hasn't heard anything from him and nor has her daughter.'

'Has he been having any... problems? At work?' asked Kate. 'That you know of?'

'No, I don't think so,' said Larkhill, rather too quickly, she thought. Didn't even stop to ponder. 'I mean,' he went on, 'the presenters can all be rather... tricky, shall we say? At times. Highly strung. They need a fair bit of TLC.'

'And Perry - how needy is he?' asked Kate.

'Oh - about the same as the rest. He's an important part of our output,' said the manager, glancing up at the wall where at least two Sony Awards held the name Dave Perry - *The Voice of Wessex.*

'He's got a big poster all to himself out front,' observed Michaels. 'Must be doing well with the ratings.'

'Well, RAJAR figures go up and down,' said Larkhill. 'Our listenership is very loyal, though. Dave is a well-loved presenter. And he loves his listeners too... and that's why I'm so concerned. It's completely out of character for him to miss a show. *Three* shows is unheard of!'

'But he has missed a show before..?' Kate asked.

'Well, yes, a year or so ago, he didn't show up but that was because he was... ill,' said Larkhill.

'Ill... how?' she prompted.

'Well, he'd got a bit low,' said Larkhill. 'And he'd drunk rather a lot. Some kind of relationship issue - a break-up, I think. It was before my time, so to be fair I can't be sure. I've only been running this station for eight months. I was down at Radio Solent before then.'

'Has he got a drink problem?' Michaels asked, with his usual bluntness. It was warranted on this occasion, though, thought Kate.

Larkhill looked uncomfortable. He squirmed in his chair and then pressed an intercom button on his desk. 'Donna,' he said. 'Can you pop in here?'

Donna, it emerged, was his PA. She arrived from her office next door in a matter of seconds. A tall, middle-aged woman with hair cut in a dark bob, she didn't look surprised to see two representatives of the Wiltshire Constabulary and Kate guessed she was well aware of the reason for their visit. She closed the door with a swift glance into the corridor and then turned to them all, eyebrows raised.

Larkhill said, without preamble: 'Donna, between you, me and these two officers, does Dave Perry have a drink problem?'

Donna considered. 'Not exactly... I mean, he's not an alcoholic if that's what you mean. But he has been known, every so often, to go on a bit of a bender. When he's had an upset.'

'So... has he had an upset? That you're aware of?' Kate asked.

Donna looked at Larkhill and then back to them. 'Not that I know of, no. But it's not like we're best friends. We get on well enough but I'm not sure I'd know if anything was wrong. He seemed just the same as usual when I saw him on Friday.'

Kate sensed they were getting nowhere fast. She had a dozen more important things to do back at the station; so did Michaels.

'We'll need a good, recent photo of him,' she said. 'And contact details for him, his family, any friends he might be staying with, if you know of any.'

'Donna will get those for you,' said Larkhill. He gazed up at the nearest framed cutting - a photo of Dave Perry at some kind of fun day event, dressed as an old gramophone, its trumpet curving around his head, and a sash reading "The Voice of Wessex" across his chest. 'I do hope we find him soon. I do hope, if you'll forgive me, that I'm wasting your time.'

3

L ucas had taken the opportunity to visit an art supplies warehouse within walking distance of the radio station, leaving his motorbike - a Triumph Bonneville he'd inherited from his late aunt - in the BBC car park. It was only as he went to pay for some new soft pencils that Lucas realised he'd left his backpack behind. It was still in the studio with Louella Green.

Cursing, he left the art suppliers and retraced his steps to BBC Radio Wessex. He found the receptionist - Moira, he remembered her name was - doing a word search. 'Sorry,' he said. 'I left my bag in the studio with Louella about half an hour ago.'

'Oh,' said Moira, putting the puzzle book aside and giving him a twinkly smile. 'I thought you *found* things! Didn't think you *lost* things.'

'Ah, well,' he said. 'I've lost a lot of things. My marbles, mostly.'

She laughed and buzzed through to the producer. 'He'll be out with it in a couple of minutes,' she said. 'Do take a seat - have another hot drink if you like.'

Lucas didn't like. He wanted to get out of here. He had a prickly, creepy feeling, knowing Kate Sparrow was somewhere in the building. Of course, she might have left already, but his instincts were telling him otherwise. If she came back through reception and he was still here, she was going to wonder *why*. She might think he was hanging around to speak to her, and although they had plenty to talk about, he most definitely was *not* here to speak to her. Until today he hadn't seen her for weeks - and didn't expect to see her at all until the inquest into the death of one very sick killer the pair of them had helped to despatch.

It wasn't just that they each probably needed to process the trauma of that day in their own way; there was more to it than that. Lucas had only recently discovered that they had an unhappy shared history; one that neither of them took pleasure in revisiting. Kate probably didn't want to go there. Neither did he.

He wandered the reception area and idly picked up one of the many postcards of the station's presenters. A chubby-faced middle-aged man peered out from it, posed across a broadcasting desk, his headphones around his neck, one eyebrow arched quizzically beneath an artfully tousled lock of greying brown hair. Beneath the image were the words: DAVE PERRY - *THE VOICE OF WESSEX*. Dave Perry had autographed it in thick black felt tip, with the legend: *OK - let's talk!* Lucas recognised the slogan from the hoarding out front and remembered that this was the breakfast presenter who hadn't shown up that day. Or maybe for a few days.

He felt buzzy. Wired. It wasn't just about the proximity of Kate and the chance of being caught waiting here; he suddenly, *really, urgently* needed to get out of here. At that moment the door to the corridor which led into the studios and newsroom was flung open and Louella's young producer - Daryl - stepped out with Lucas's brown leather backpack in one hand.

'Sorry,' said Lucas, reaching for it.

'No problem,' said Daryl. 'Thanks for coming in today. Loved what you did.'

Lucas nodded and then saw, over the young man's shoulder, three people walking along the corridor towards reception. One of them was Kate. The other was DC Michaels. Lucas grabbed the backpack, turned around, and virtually ran for the revolving door, goosebumps washing the back of his neck. As he spun himself out of the building he glimpsed Kate emerging into the reception area. *Damn!* He just had to hope she wouldn't recognise the back of his head.

He ran back to his bike, realising, as he did so, that the signed postcard of Dave Perry was still in his hand. He shoved it hurriedly into his leather jacket pocket, slung his backpack over his shoulders, and put his helmet on. He straddled the Triumph and throttled up. It took some effort to stop himself roaring off to the ring road. That would attract attention and he just *bet* that DC Michaels would recognise his number plate. Kate and her DC were exiting the revolving doors as he rode away, and he told himself she hadn't noticed him. She hadn't.

He should have gone straight home. He absolutely should have. But Sid thrummed against his chest and told him to take a different route, up to the north. Lucas cursed his little glass helper. He didn't want to do this. He absolutely should NOT do this. He passed his turn-off point and kept on riding, wishing he could stop but pulled along like an iron filing to a magnet.

When we get home, Sid, he said in his head, *you are going back in that sock. I don't know why I'm even wearing you these days, you little stirrer.* But in truth, he knew it wasn't the inanimate lump of glass that dictated situations like this. The dowsing talent was within him; Sid was just a focal point, even though the pendulum seemed, very often, to be a living entity in its own right.

He travelled on for twenty minutes, under the A303 and up towards the plain, taking a left instead of a right and neatly avoiding any Stonehenge traffic, although he doubted many people would be haunting the stones on a late, darkening November afternoon. No. Onward. Further north. The patterns in his dowsing mind were guiding him towards something tall; something metal.

He reached a small village, passed through it, found himself on a road which was barely more than a farm track. He could sense the magnetic field of the transmitter long before he saw the top of it, gleaming in a shaft of setting sun. A little further along he pulled over, climbed off the Triumph and rested it on its kickstand at the side of the lane. There was nobody about. Well, almost nobody. He pulled off his helmet, put it on the bike seat, took a deep breath, and made for the metal five bar gate a short walk away. It was possible he was wrong. It was *always* possible. Just, in twenty years of experience, not probable.

He stopped before he reached the gate and had a little word with himself. *Seriously, mate... why don't you just get back on the bike and go home? Right now?* And he agreed with himself. That was absolutely the only sensible thing to do right now. Above him a magpie chakked noisily in the tree and then subsided, leaving no sound at all except a slight whispering of leaves and the ever-present, sub-bass hum of electromagnetism sent out by the transmitter. He felt a deep, deep chill sink through him. *Go. Go now.*

He stepped forward and reached the gate, which was

ajar, its steel tube base marking a perfect curve of scraped concrete. He sidled through the gap, walked past a couple of boxy metal units housing electrical circuitry, and on towards the mast.

It wasn't a huge structure but it was still a good twenty metres high. This was just a booster to the bigger masts and sported no satellite dishes or massive aerials, only a spindly antennae on each of its upper limbs. A vertical ladder ran up through the centre of the basic criss-cross structure, with dire warning notices to ward off thrill-seeking kids (clearly posted in the days before Xbox was a thing). Although the top of it could be seen for a few miles around, the four-footed base wasn't visible to passing traffic. You would need to make a point of coming in and looking. Which might explain why nobody had noticed the body gaffer-taped to it.

Lucas took a long, slow, steadying breath. 'Fuck,' he said, not unreasonably.

He stepped across, pulling the postcard from his pocket for another look. It was hard to be sure, because most of the man's lower face was wrapped in grey gaffer tape; the same tape which also held his body up in a T shape, about a metre above the ground. The eyes were open. They looked as if they had been pecked, probably by the same territorial magpie now chakking away again in the trees. Lucas guessed the corpse was several days old.

And now what? He didn't need to get any closer to know this was Dave Perry. Although there wasn't much to recognise beyond the thick thatch of greying dark hair, every vibration surrounding the deceased breakfast presenter screamed its truth to the postcard in Lucas's hand.

And, to repeat himself, *now what?* The very LAST thing he needed was any further involvement with a murder case. Because he was pretty sure it wasn't suicide, unless Dave

Perry was a magician at self-bondage. Someone had done this to him. Someone who was clearly wanting to make a bit of a statement. Maybe a listener had been pushed over the edge by one too many spins of *Cracklin' Rosie*.

Lucas walked back to the road, helmeted up, got on his bike, and went home.

4

There was a mountain of admin waiting for Kate when she and Michaels got back to the station. It was normally the very least favourite part of her job. It always felt like homework... and as it was a decade since she'd left school, some part of her always resented it. But it was a necessary evil. She understood the importance of doing it properly; more than one otherwise watertight court case had been thrown out because a copper had been sloppy with their admin.

She logged the details of the waste of time missing persons file first. She could get Michaels to do it but he had other stuff to get on with and her roster of work was still fairly light as she got back into the flow of full-time hours. Dave Perry would probably show up at work tomorrow, sheepish and fragile after a four or five-day pub crawl. It wasn't difficult to gather, from the tactful phrases used by Donna the PA and her boss, that a bender was definitely what they were thinking. They were worried, though, she guessed, that he was in a ditch somewhere. Of course, his car not being on the drive also meant he could have driven

off for a little unsanctioned downtime somewhere. Maybe
he'd met someone. She'd also picked up that he liked the
ladies... a little indiscriminately if the two divorces were
anything to go by.

She put some calls in to the local hospitals and quickly
established that nobody fitting his description had passed
through any A&E department in the county. She could call
the numbers for his second ex-wife and daughter too, but
made a decision to wait a day before she did so. This was
just not waving enough red flags at her to start spooking
relatives.

A vibration in her pocket reminded her that it was time
to spook herself. 'Bugger,' she muttered, logging out of the
system and acknowledging the note on her phone which
read: **Joanna C in ten minutes.**

'I'll be back in an hour,' she told Michaels, grabbing her
bag. He raised his eyebrows, expecting more information
and then lowered them and gave a slow, understanding nod
when she didn't offer it. Kate gritted her teeth. Having to see
the counsellor every week was aggravating enough without
her colleagues knowing all about it. They did know though.
In a small station like Salisbury it was pretty much impossible to keep anything like that a secret. It wasn't as if she
could get out of it, either - continuing to see Joanna Cassidy
was one of the conditions of her phased return to work.

She hurried the five-minute walk to the counsellor's
small practice, determined to spend no more than forty-five
minutes in the building. Joanna Cassidy welcomed her with
the easy professional warmth Kate had got used to over the
past couple of months. 'Come on in,' she said, leading the
way through to her office. The room was designed to relax
her clients, with pale green walls, elegant potted plants and
soft lighting. It also held an oak desk and chair and wall-to-

ceiling shelves full of books on psychology, sociology and psychiatry. Kate sometimes wondered if the whole wall was a fake edifice, which, when you pressed the spine of a certain leather-bound tome by Freud or Jung, would spin around and reveal a hidden dungeon. She'd obviously played way too much Resident Evil with Francis in their teens.

'How have you been?' asked Joanna, settling herself in the comfortable leather armchair which mirrored Kate's. 'It's your first week back, yes?' She smiled and Kate was struck by the lack of lines in her pale golden skin. Considering the levels of stress that must be bouncing around in the ether of this room, Joanna didn't seem to be absorbing too much of it. She looked barely older than Kate, although her evident experience suggested she was a good ten years her senior.

'I've been fine,' said Kate. 'It's great to finally get back to work. Honestly, I could have done it six weeks ago.'

'Hmmm,' said Joanna. 'Can you remember how you were feeling when we first spoke?'

Kate didn't miss the hint. She sighed. 'I was a wreck,' she said. 'But... wouldn't anyone be?'

Joanna nodded. 'Your experience back in September was very traumatic. You've coped very well but I really think you did need that time off; time to recover.'

'Well, sitting around in a onesie watching Homes Under the Hammer was an absolute tonic,' said Kate, slapping her knee.

Joanna smiled again. 'I do think you're probably ready to be back at work, but be careful about the way you use humour as a shield, Kate. Are you aware how often you deflect questions about how you're feeling? Or make jokes about it?'

Kate rolled her eyes. 'Look - have you ever walked through CID and listened to the talk? It's just the way we are. We deal with the shittiest end of the human nature stick; we have to laugh about it.'

'About half my practice is with police officers in some degree of distress,' said Joanna. 'I know exactly what you mean, but here, with me, is not the same as being in CID. You've already shared a lot with me.'

Kate thought back to the first session when she'd arrived, brittle and wise-cracking and left having used up every tissue in Joanna's box. Yes, she'd shared a lot. She just didn't want to *keep sharing.* It didn't feel normal.

'How are you sleeping now?'

'OK.'

'Any more nightmares?'

'Only a couple of times a week now.'

'Have you had any more panic attacks?'

Kate shrugged. 'A couple of *moments*,' she said. 'Nothing major.'

'Tell me the most recent one.'

'Well... I was out on a visit today and... I saw some photos. Proper professional photos of BBC presenters, you know, on a white backdrop, well lit.'

Joanna nodded. 'And that reminded you..?'

'Yes,' said Kate. 'Yes it did. But I didn't go into a melt-down. When I'm at work it's easier to control. It's when I'm just me... walking somewhere crowded maybe... that's when it can really kick off. Sometimes I just have to go home.' She looked up at the counsellor, quickly. 'But not at work. Never at work.'

'There's something you can try,' said Joanna, getting up and going to her desk. She opened a drawer and withdrew a brightly coloured cardboard package, about the size of a book. She handed it to Kate who accepted it with some bafflement. There were pictures of crocodiles and lions on the front and a cellophane window revealing grooved stripes in muted rainbow shades.

'Um... plasticine?' she queried.

'Plasticine,' confirmed Joanna. 'Take it home. Play with it. Make some things. And keep some in your pocket.'

'You want me to go around with a lump of modelling clay in my pocket..?'

'I do. At work and out and about generally. Try it. Whenever you feel a sensation of anxiety, squeeze the plasticine in your pocket and send the sensation into it through your fingers.'

Kate stared at the packet, enjoying its weight and fleeting memories of days in pre-school. She gave a low chuckle. 'All those years getting your doctorate and... plasticine!'

'Well,' said Joanna, settling back into her chair with a grin. 'I do have *some* other techniques up my sleeve, but I'm just saying... give it a try. It might help when you're struggling to sleep too. Make something. If you use it all up, get some more.'

'Well, thanks...' said Kate, sitting up and tucking the packet in her satchel. 'Can I-?'

'No you can't,' said Joanna, rolling her eyes. 'We have thirty-five minutes left. I want to hear more from you. About what happened in September... or maybe about what happened sixteen years ago. Whichever you like. I think there's still a lot to work through.'

Kate sighed and got the packet out again. 'Can I make crocodiles while we work through it?'

'If it'll keep you talking, you can make a scale model of a Tyrannosaurus rex,' said Joanna.

After the session, Kate walked back into CID with the not unpleasant scent of plasticine all over her hands, half a packet of unused strips in her bag and a lump of mixed up colours in her jacket pocket which had recently been crocodiles.

'Um... Sarge,' said a voice as she settled back at her desk. She turned to see Sharon Mulligan loitering behind her. 'There's something you might want to listen to on the tape.'

Kate got up, dumping her bag, and followed the DC to the corner of the room where an old-fashioned answering machine sat, taking calls on the CrimeStoppers line. It wasn't so old that it had tiny cassettes in it, like a nineties Dictaphone, but it was a very early pioneer of digital record-ing, in a beige plastic housing. Replacing it wasn't high on the agenda because most of the calls that came through to it were complaints about vandalised bus stops, dog mess in the streets or teenagers being... teenagers. It earned its keep once a while, though, with a genuinely helpful tip-off. The point of it was to offer anonymity and occasionally this paid off.

Sharon pressed the clunky brown PLAY button on the machine and a voice, slightly muffled, began to speak.

'There's a body. I just saw it on the Shrewton mast,' said the voice - male, mature, no noticeable accent. 'You need to get down there.'

And that was it. The caller hung up.

'What's the Shrewton mast?' asked Sharon, who'd only come to Wiltshire three or four years ago from her home-town of Rotherham.

'Well, I guess it's one of the TV and radio mast sites,' said Kate. 'Must be one near Shrewton village.'

'Do you think this is for real?' asked Sharon. They got

plenty of prank calls and hoaxes on the beige box of wonders.

'I guess we'd better find out,' said Kate.

'Me! Take me!' said Sharon, bouncing up and down on the balls of her sensibly-shod feet. She was usually partnered with DS Sharpe, but Sharpe was off on leave and Sharon had been office-bound for several days.

'Sorry,' said Kate, laughing. 'Ben gets first dibs. But if it's for real, you'll be joining us.'

An hour later, Kate and DC Michaels stood in a pool of arc light, Sharon at their side, staring at the gaffer-taped effigy on the Shrewton mast. Kate and Michaels had pulled into the farm road, found the mast site and clocked the whole, unlovely truth of their anonymous call in an instant. For a moment Kate had fostered the hope that it *was* a hoax - a leftover Guy Fawkes dummy, perhaps, put there for a laugh.

But a few steps closer and there was no doubt, from the smell, what they had here. If the past few days hadn't been so cold it would have been a great deal nastier and the buzzing of legions of flies would surely have alerted the locals much sooner.

The forensics team had quickly arrived on the scene to cordon it off, photograph it and comb it for evidence. DC Sharon Mulligan arrived around the same time - and it was she who got to do the big reveal. Staring up at the body, held up in a T shape but sagging, Christ-like, against the tape, she said: 'It's Dave Perry. You know... the BBC Radio Wessex breakfast show guy.' They had found an abandoned Audi a little way down the lane and she'd just got the DVLA trace on the number plate.

'Bloody hell,' said Kate, feeling her scalp prickle. Her waste of time misper had just morphed into big news.

'I always thought he'd be better looking than that,' the detective constable added.

'He's dead, Sharon,' said Kate. 'And his eyes have been pecked out. Cut him some slack.'

He *was* cut some slack as soon as the photographer, forensics and pathologist had done their thing. It was a small site, offering up no clues, and the Audi had been collected and taken back to the police pound for further scrutiny. The gaffer tape was sliced through and Dave Perry's remains were carefully detached, lowered to the ground and put into a body bag.

'He was stabbed in the ribs,' said Bryan De'ath, the pathologist. Everyone called him Death. He knew it. He didn't even roll his eyes any more. A small, plump man of around forty, nominative determinism had had its way with Bryan; he was *always* destined to be either a pathologist, an undertaker or a serial killer. Kate was glad he'd gone for pathologist; she liked Bryan, even more for his stoicism in the face of that curse of a name.

'Was that what killed him?' she asked.

'No,' said De'ath. 'There are only superficial wounds. To get him to do as he was told, I would guess. I can't be certain, of course, before I get him back to the mortuary, but I would hazard he died of suffocation. The material in his mouth and up his nose is dense grey foam. It looks very much like the windsock of a microphone.'

They took that in, wordlessly, for a beat and Kate realised she'd be seeing a lot more of BBC Radio Wessex from now on. It seemed likely one of their mic socks was missing.

'Doesn't look like a spur of the moment thing,' said Michaels. 'Gaffer tape... choking... Could it be a sex game, gone wrong?'

'He's fully clothed,' said Kate. 'And taped up like that, *he* wasn't getting his rocks off. Can't imagine anyone else was, either. I mean... in a hotel room, with a lubed-up root vegetable and some stockings on, maybe... but this isn't that. It's a show, though, isn't it? Whoever it was, they wanted him found like that.'

'Better get Yankie-boy on the case,' said Michaels.

Kate nodded. This did seem like a job for Conrad Temple, their occasional guest criminal psychologist.

'We need to let the super know too,' she said. 'Radio station manager is a friend of his,' she explained to Sharon and De'ath. 'Kapoor sent us round to talk to Robert Larkhill, the managing editor, just this morning because he'd reported this guy missing. I thought it was just a bit of time-wasting.'

'We'd better get a trace on that CrimeStoppers call too,' said Sharon. 'I mean... that could be the killer, couldn't it?'

Kate nodded. She was well placed to understand that killers sometimes did it for attention. And bumping off a well-known BBC presenter was definitely going to get that. It was a regional Jill Dando situation. God, how wrong she had been about this one. She rubbed her face, embarrassed at herself. She should have better instincts after all this time. Still, she wasn't psychic.

She closed her eyes as an image of Lucas Henry flashed through her mind. *Stop it.* She squeezed the plasticine. Lucas Henry wasn't psychic either. He'd be the first person to point that out. He was just a dowser. A practical, normal, everyday, perfectly average killer-tracking dowser.

And possibly a practical, normal, perfectly average everyday killer.

5

Gemma Henshall got herself a coffee with lots of sugar and gave Moira a guilty smile. Staff weren't meant to help themselves to the reception hot drinks. There was a coin operated machine in the lobby outside the newsroom but the coffee in that tasted like dead dog. Or what she imagined dead dog might taste like if roasted, ground up, diluted and dribbled through a plastic nozzle with a lacklustre squirt of UHT milk.

Moira wasn't a big stickler over the occasional indulgence, though, especially when she could see a staffer had put in a very long day. And Gemma *had* put in a very long day. Well over twelve hours. As researcher on the breakfast show she was contracted to work from 5am until 1pm but, like many young, keen broadcast assistants, she put in far more than that, unpaid. If you wanted to make your mark in broadcasting, you put in the free overtime; got ahead of the competition. Alongside James, the producer, it was down to her to keep the breakfast show lively, relevant and exciting, simultaneously appealing to the mum on the school run, the businessman on his way to the office and a couple of retirees in their sixties, known as *Phil and Sue*.

Phil and Sue represented the station's heartland; loyal and committed after years of listening; the mum was a replenisher, in her thirties or forties with kids at school, beginning to appreciate community, the businessman was in his fifties and interested in local politics and the DowJones index. In regional radio nirvana they'd be scoring twentysomethings too. Teens were a lost cause but kids would be listening because parents and grandparents were.

That was the task set out for Gemma, James and - when he was there - Dave Perry. It was down to Gemma and James to find the topics, jack the guests and set up the talking points to the satisfaction of EVERYONE. It was, as any sane person in radio would know, totally fucking impossible. The more you tried to please the replenishers, the more you'd piss off the retirees. The more business you put into the mix, the more the mums on the school run would switch off. The more six-year-olds you lined up to sing the jingles in *Jingle Singer of the Week*, the more you sickened that share index obsessed businessman. The more you played 21st century hits, the more the over seventies would clamour for rock-'n'roll. And so on. An ever turning wheel of discontent chasing satisfaction chasing disengagement chasing loyalty. It was utterly exhausting, but still she tried.

She tried and tried, because she *loved* radio. Like nearly everyone else she worked with, she just *loved* it, despite the relentless way it consumed her life. It had never occurred to her to walk away from it, not even since the Dave Perry *situation* had arisen a few weeks ago.

Having him off work for the past couple of days had been pretty pleasant, even if running the show with Sheila had been hard work. Sheila, in her sixties, wasn't really cut

out for the breakfast show. Jack and Spencer would probably have been a better fit, and they were gagging for it, of
course, but Sheila had been drafted in at the last minute
because she was already in the station, grudgingly - and
bafflingly - working on the What's On bulletins at 6.15am
when Dave had still not shown up.

Sheila had been the mid-morning host until four weeks
ago, when she'd been unceremoniously bumped off it to
make way for Jack and Spencer. After decades working for
Wessex she was, perhaps understandably, pretty aggrieved.
But she'd swallowed it and relocated to the *What's On* corner
with an outward show of grace. Being in the building when
the urgent call went out for a swing jock, she'd stepped in
with a swirl of chiffon scarf and Estée Lauder, opened the
fader on the dot of 6.00am, and nobly steered the unwieldy
ship of breakfast across the morning rush hour.

Gemma liked Sheila but knew she was totally wrong for
breakfast. Far too gentle in her dealings with local council-
lors and phone-in guests who waffled on for way too long,
she overran the news junction three times and crashed the
pips at the top of the hour twice. When it came to politics or
current affairs she was about as incisive as a Labradoodle.
Yet Sheila wanted the slot, clearly, and thought she had a
shot at it. She was wrong though; she had never been cut
out for it; her whole personality shrieked mid-morning or
mid-afternoon or radio roadshow meet and greeter. The
listeners loved her but they wouldn't tolerate her for long on
the fastest, busiest show of the day. It was like trying to work
your way along the fast lane of the M25 and getting stuck
behind a daffodil-yellow Morris Traveller doing 45mph.
Charming... but fucking annoying after two minutes.

Still, at least Sheila hadn't yet tried to grab her
researcher's tits. Gemma sighed into her coffee as she took a

seat in reception. It was 5.40pm and she should be home in her tiny flat by now, having an early dinner and getting ready for bed at nine. The daily crack of sparrow-fart clock-ins pretty much wiped out all hope of a social life but this was entirely normal for radio station wannabes. She went nowhere and met nobody. The only action she'd had in months was the unwelcome attentions of The Voice of Wessex.

She cringed when she thought about it. She'd really looked up to Dave when she first arrived on staff six months ago after nearly a year of casual shifts. Getting the breakfast researcher gig had been so exciting and she later heard that Dave had put a word in for her. Or so he said. After a while it became clear *why*. He was always checking her out and making suggestive remarks, which he liked to wave off as blunt-speaking and being *anti-PC*. 'I call it as I see it,' he liked to say, which, in her case, meant, 'If I like the look of your arse, it's only honest of me to tell you.'

She ignored his honest appraisals of her backside and, in due course, her breasts, hips, legs and face, because she just didn't want to think it was important. She didn't want to think he was one of those 70s throwback jocks who thought this kind of thing was just normal. He was only in his 50s, for god's sake - young enough to be better acquainted with the dos and don'ts of workplace interactions with a colleague young enough to be his daughter.

He was smart enough never to say any of this stuff when James, his efficient and rather monosyllabic producer, was in the room. It was always when it was just the two of them in Studio A that he would take the opportunity to squeeze past her, resting his hands on her hips and brushing himself along her bum.

'Alright, my little Gem,' he liked to say, as he went. No

matter how much she pulled away, abruptly, from him, he refused to get the message. She suspected this was all part of the game for him; he liked the chase. Had anyone else had experiences like this with Dave? She didn't want to ask. Didn't want to be *that girl*.

Until last week, when he'd really pushed it too far. He'd found her in an editing suite, recording some links for his promo trailer. He wandered in on some thin pretext, and started rubbing her shoulders. She'd stiffened immediately and said: 'Dave - really - I don't need a massage. I just need to get on, OK?' But instead of backing off, he'd just lowered his mouth to her ear and his hands to her breasts, having a little play as he whispered: 'Come on, little Gem, you know you want this. You're as tight as piano wire. I can loosen you up.'

She'd got to her feet, ripped off her headphones and told him to fuck off.

Even then he'd just laughed. 'Lighten up, Gem!' he'd said, holding his palms up as if she was being hysterical. 'We're just having a bit of fun here. You're way too young to be so uptight! Jeez - is it your time of the month or something?'

She had gaped at him; fury and mortification cutting her throat just when she needed a good comeback. He'd carried on laughing as he opened the soundproof door, allowing the busy atmos of the newsroom to flow in. 'Don't worry about it, Gemma,' he said, loudly. 'It's no problem. I'll see you in the morning.'

Then she'd sat down at the desk, heart pounding and hands shaking with fury. How could that have just happened? It was then that she'd noticed her screen where the track was still visibly rolling; the red RECORD light glowing above a series of seismic spikes. Gulping and trying to regulate her breathing, she'd saved the track and spooled it back. There, on the screen and in her headphones, was the full interaction between herself and Dave. She pressed her hands to her mouth, realising what she had here. What she might do with it. His whispering was hard to make out but her reaction to it was loud and clear... as was his comment about her being uptight and pre-menstrual.

Think. She needed to think. Taking this to Rob Larkhill could be the answer to her problems... but did she really want to? Sexism and harassment claims at the BBC had peaked in recent years and although many of the complainants had won compensation an awful lot of them saw their careers sidelined not long after. Did she want to get a reputation as a 'complainant' before her career had even started?

So she'd saved the file in one of her private folders, marked TBC (to be considered) and had thought about not much else since. That had been two weeks ago. More comments had followed since, more unwanted contact, but as yet no more tit-squeezing. The stress of it all was telling on her, though. Last week she'd begun to think of leaving; maybe getting work at a sister station like Solent or Berkshire.

Friday had been the worst. He'd brought chocolates from a fan into the tele-in area and, right next to James, had popped one into her mouth while she was on the phone to a listener, sliding his fingers in with it and stroking her lower lip as he withdrew them. At that moment, as Elsie from Wilton guessed at that morning's *mystery noise*, she had gagged on a strawberry creme and felt such rage. Rage that could only end in some kind of action.

Today she was calmer. She had an appraisal with Rob. Things seemed brighter.

So, here she sat, a USB key in her pocket containing the WAV file of Dave's assault, and waited for her appointment to come around at 5.45pm, wondering whether she would ever actually share it, whether she really needed to. She had drained the coffee and was just about to get up and buzz her way into the corridor and along to Rob's office when the revolving door spat out Finley Warner.

Oh dear. He made a beeline for her, carrying his usual Radio Wessex branded tote bag over his skinny shoulder. What could be in it today?

'This is for Mike,' he said to her, without preamble. He knew she was staff; she'd helped out on a station tour a couple of weeks ago. He dug a Marks & Spencer biscuit tin from the bag and handed it to her. She lifted the lid and found a doughy looking fruit cake.

'Well, that's lovely, Finley,' she said. 'Thank you. I'm sure he'll love it. I can drop it in to him now - I'm just passing his studio.'

'I could come with you,' said Finley, his wide brown eyes lighting up.

'Sorry, Finley,' she said. 'I can't take you in now - you'll need to wait for another station tour. It's the rules, you know?' She smiled at him and patted his shoulder.

Finley sat down on the sofa, sighing heavily. Despite being only in his twenties he was a long-serving superfan of BBC Radio Wessex, having become utterly fixated on all things radio from the age of nine. His parents had indulged his obsession by bringing him in to BBC Radio Wessex at every opportunity; on air for every quiz the kid was awake for, skipping in for all the open day tours and outside broadcasts. It was rumoured they even took him for picnics at the foot of the Rowridge transmitter masts on the Isle of Wight during summer holidays. She had learned all this from her colleagues who had forewarned her that Finley was a regular and mostly harmless. '*But NEVER eat the cakes!*' they had all said, knowingly.

'You probably won't get to see Mike today, Finley,' she said, going in to bat for the drivetime presenter in a way she hoped he would for her. 'I know he's got to dash straight off at seven.'

Finley looked disappointed but not surprised. His usual jock-bothering success score was probably below twenty per cent. 'Sheila crashed the pips,' he said as he got to his feet, looking slightly to the left of her.

She smiled at his accurate broadcasting vernacular. 'She did,' she said, in a conspiratorial whisper. 'But everyone does once in a while.'

'Dave hasn't,' said Finley. 'Not for three years, six months and five days.'

She blinked. 'Well... I'm sure you're right,' she said. 'Um... I'd better take this cake in!'

'I'll bring one for Josh next,' said Finley, backing towards the revolving door. 'Josh is my favourite. I go to bed with Josh.' He gave a loud cackle, as if he'd learned this phrase - and the appropriate follow-on reaction - from the many other fans of the overnight presenter who routinely trotted out this weak gag.

'See you later, Finley,' she'd said, smiling brightly and heading for the inner sanctum with her ID card at the ready.

It was only as she glanced back that she noticed the two people walking into reception as Finley reluctantly mooched out. A pretty blonde woman and a slick-looking dark-haired guy with her. They both wore a grim expression which made her shiver. She buzzed herself through and got into the corridor, heading for Rob's office.

'Ah - Gemma, come on in, take a seat,' he said, as soon as she knocked. 'Sorry I couldn't see you sooner - you've had a very long day.'

'Thanks,' she said, sitting and taking a deep breath.

'Bit of a week,' said Rob. 'Can't be easy without Dave.'

'Well...' she said.

'Sheila's all wrong for breakfast,' Rob went on, 'between ourselves, of course. But until Dave's back I haven't got much option. Everyone else is flat out with their own shows - I don't want to create a great big domino effect by moving Jack and Spencer in... or Mike.'

'Sheila's doing really well,' said Gemma. 'Do you know when Dave gets back?'

'Hopefully tomorrow,' said Rob.

Then the phone on his desk went and he picked it up, waving his apology at her. 'OK,' he said, his face suddenly very serious. 'OK... well... you'd better send them through.'

He ended the call and glanced at her, looking a little discombobulated. 'Sorry, Gemma... I know you've waited all day... but something important's come up.'

'Oh,' she said, standing up and fingering the USB key in her pocket. 'Maybe I can-'

But the door knocked and, never properly closed, was pushed ajar by the two people from reception.

'Ah,' said Rob. 'I see you found your own way.'

'We need a few minutes of your time,' said the woman who - Gemma was suddenly quite certain - was a police officer.

'It's fine - I'm gone!' she said, walking past the woman and the younger guy who smelled of heavy hair wax usage.

'Sorry Gemma,' Rob called after her. 'We'll catch up tomorrow.'

She got into the corridor and leant against the wall,

suddenly exhausted. She wasn't the kind to listen at doors. Rob's door, though, had a dodgy catch and it had once again not quite closed. She could hear what was being said and somehow, her ears sharpened by high adrenaline, she could not drag herself away.

'It's about Dave Perry,' the woman said.

'Have you found him?' asked Rob.

'We have,' said the woman. 'But it's not good news. Dave Perry is dead.'

Gemma knees gave way and she sank to the floor.

6

The transistor radio was old but once he'd put some fresh batteries into it and found a high point in the kitchen to perch it on, the aerial picked up the strong frequency of BBC Radio Wessex's drivetime show.

Listening to someone called Mike Tierney, Lucas heated himself some soup on the electric stove he'd had delivered a couple of weeks ago. While it was still pretty bare, the kitchen of his late aunt's bungalow... now *his* bungalow, he reminded himself... was slowly shaping up to something usable. He'd got a proper fridge and a microwave too. A washing machine was to be delivered the following week. He had Mariam, his friend and mentor, to thank for all these luxuries. The owner of the Henge Gallery in Salisbury city centre, she had run an exhibition for him recently and - thanks to some unplanned publicity around that murder case he had blundered into and helped to solve - there'd been a lot of interest. As touched upon by Louella Green, he'd become a person of some considerable interest to first the police, then the public and then, more profitably, some art collectors.

All his paintings had been snapped up within his two week exhibition slot - and at several times the prices he and Mariam had first discussed. This meant he could finally get the electricity back on and then some white goods into the dilapidated bungalow, along with a sofa and an armchair in the front room and a decent mattress for Aunty Janine's old bedstead. He'd considered something new from IKEA but the old wrought iron rather spoke to him these days. Dark and twisted. Yep.

Mike, on drivetime, had been discussing bike lanes and tree-planting and even done the weather, but he so far hadn't mentioned that his breakfast show counterpart had been crucified on a transmitter mast. In fact Mike had just run a trailer for the breakfast show featuring The Voice of Wessex along with a series of clips of people saying how fabulous The Voice was and why they never missed a show, concluding with the man himself and his irritatingly smug catchphrase: 'OK... let's talk!' This all suggested that nobody yet knew about the gaffer-taped effigy on the Shrewton mast. Maybe nobody at Salisbury nick had even bothered to check that CrimeStoppers tape.

The thought made him a little queasy as he poured Scotch broth into a bowl and sawed off a large hunk of granary loaf to butter. Should he actually have called Kate?

FUCK NO! yelled his reason. JEEEEZUZ!

And of course, his reason was right. After getting haplessly caught up in not one but *two* murder investigations in his life, Lucas really didn't want to make it a hat trick. Three hours earlier he had walked away from the crime scene, climbed back on his bike, and got the hell out of Dodge. But he'd stopped in another small village on the way home. It was the kind where nice upper middle class locals kept their old phone box in a state of loving restoration. The glass panes were shiny, the paint gleaming scarlet, and there was a little shelf for a book exchange, featuring everything from Danielle Steele to Christopher Brookmyre. Amazingly the telephone was still there and it actually worked - with coins too. More amazingly, he couldn't see any security cameras trained on it.

So he'd done a quick search on his mobile to find the CrimeStoppers number and then punched the digits in on the retro metal keypad. Should he try an accent? A growl? Maybe impersonate his mother..? In the end he didn't; he just pulled his soft jersey biker's buff up over his mouth and delivered his intelligence in a muffled way.

'There's a body. I just saw it on the Shrewton mast,' he said. 'You need to get down there.' Then he hung up and got out of there fast, as if the Wiltshire Constabulary could reach through the receiver and grab his collar there and then.

It was the right call. Literally. He'd done what needed to be done - informed the authorities - and he had not compli-cated their case by involving himself in it. If he was identi-fied as the caller the first question would be 'Why did you suddenly visit the base of a remote mast in the middle of nowhere?'

'Because my little glass bottle stopper told me to,' was never going to be a helpful reply. Some of them would understand what he meant but others, who weren't yet privy to the full details of the Runner Grabber case, would merely assume he needed arresting and/or sectioning.

Also, the ones who knew about his talent really didn't love him for it. He and Sid had massively helped to end their last big investigation but he'd seriously pissed them off along the way; not least for leaving them stranded in a bog at one stage, while he did a runner. It was safe to say there weren't many Lucas Henry fans at Salisbury Central Police Station. They'd tasered him twice and he reckoned they'd be quite happy to do it a third time just for the hell of it.

He was all needles and pins *now* - jangly from that afternoon's encounter, not just with a dead guy but also, fleetingly, with Kate. What were the odds, eh? Sid seemed to give a little thud against his chest and Lucas sighed, put down his spoon and pulled the chain over his head. 'You,' he said, letting the stopper dangle in front of his face, 'are just messing with my mind.' He got up and took the pendulum and chain into the bedroom, where he found an old woollen sock and shoved them both deep inside it, balling it up and burying it deep in his well-travelled rucksack. Then he chucked the rucksack out of sight under the bed.

Back in the kitchen he finished his soup and bread and butter and then switched off the radio before opening a bottle of red wine. He took it, and a glass, to the front room and the new sofa. If he got himself agreeably sloshed he might drown out the insistent pulse of interference from Sid. And thoughts of Kate too, if he was really in luck.

7

L arkhill held his head in his hands, staring at his desk and taking long, slow breaths. 'I can't believe it,' he said. 'I just can't believe it. You're... you're sure it's him?'

'Well, obviously the body will need to be formally identified, but he looks like the publicity photo, the car registration checks out as his... and...' Kate exchanged a glance with Michaels. '...the material in his mouth and up his nose appears to be... the foam sock off a microphone.'

'Jesus,' murmured Larkhill, looking pale and sweaty.

'We'd like to know what kind of microphone socks you use here at the station,' said Michaels. 'And if there are any missing.'

Larkhill was mopping his brow with the back of his sleeve. 'I'm pretty sure they're all Neumann mic socks in the studios, but I'd need to check with our chief engineer. All presenters carry their own mic socks these days, for hygiene reasons. They have them in small vinyl cases and keep them in their bags or pigeonholes, usually. Then they put them on the microphone when they arrive in a studio. Of course, they leave them behind sometimes... I'm always telling them off for that. Jesus...' His face flushed and then paled again. 'With his *mic sock*..?'

'Would you like a colleague here with you?' asked Kate. She didn't want to have to call in a first aider if the guy started hyperventilating. Sometimes having another person present was stabilising.

'Yes,' he said, and then pressed his intercom and summoned Donna Wilson.

The PA dropped by in her trench coat, carrying a bag. 'I was just heading home, Rob,' she said, and then stopped when she spotted his visitors. 'Oh. What's up?'

'Come in - close the door,' said Rob. 'You'd better take a seat.'

She sat on the edge of a low bookcase and took the news with more composure than her boss but she was still shaken. 'Bloody hell,' she said. 'Who would do something like that?'

'That's what we'd like to know,' said Kate. 'Can you think of anyone who might want to do that to him?'

Larkhill shook his head. 'Well... who can guess? He was a big personality, you know? And people didn't always like what he said.'

'Aren't BBC presenters meant to be impartial?' asked Michaels.

Larkhill gave him a pitying look. 'Well, yes, if they're presenting the news - or Any Questions - but local radio presenters are *personalities*. I mean, yes, of course he had to toe the line up to a point, especially around politics, and always give both sides equal airtime, but Dave Perry was a stirrer - a catalyst for conversation and debate. That's what he was best at.'

'So... are you saying someone might have taken issue

with something he said on air?' asked Kate, feeling her energy sag. The station had around 400,000 listeners according to the last RAJAR report; that was one hell of a suspect pool.

'What about colleagues?' asked Michaels. 'Anyone he didn't get on with?'

'Mike got along fine with everyone,' said Larkhill, glancing at Donna as if seeking back up.

'Radio stations - they're like families,' said Donna. 'We have our ups and downs of course, but everyone's very supportive.'

Kate sensed she wasn't going to get far with these two and their managerspeak. She and Michaels were going to have to interview everyone in the building, alone, to get the *real* picture. And get them all to present their microphone socks too, although she suspected this wouldn't help much. A mic sock was probably quite easy to misplace around here.

'Couldn't it be, you know, random?' asked Larkhill, mopping his shiny face with a crushed cotton handkerchief. 'Maybe he was just in the wrong place at the wrong time?'

'So... you think he might have been ambushed by chance?' said Kate. 'By someone who wanted to gaffer tape a stranger to a transmitter mast and stuff shredded mic sock into their airways?'

'Yes, I grant you, it does seem quite... specific.'

'We're going to need to talk to all your staff,' said Kate. 'Who's in now?'

'Um... not many of them,' said Larkhill, glancing at the clock. 'Just Mike and his producer Lewis, I imagine. The rest will have headed home by now.'

'What about - er - "Showtunes Shep"?' asked Michaels,

consulting the schedule print out from the BBC Radio Wessex website.

'That's not local,' said Larkhill. 'It goes out on the English regions opt... Shep doesn't come here, he's the same presenter for most of the stations around the south of England but he's based in Oxford. Cost-cutting,' he added, with a sigh. 'Some of the smaller stations come off air after drivetime and stay off until 6am the next day, but we've still got Josh, our overnight presenter, on between ten and one in the morning.'

'So - the next one in will be Josh?' asked Kate.

'He'll be in around nine,' said Larkhill. 'To prepare for getting on air at ten.'

'And his producer?'

'Josh is self-op,' said Larkhill. 'Um... I mean he doesn't have a producer. He gets himself on air and handles all the calls from his studio. Again... cost-cutting.' He shrugged.

Kate sighed. This could be a very long night. 'We'll wait for your drivetime team to come off air and talk to them right away,' she said. 'And can you call Josh and ask him to get in half an hour early? Then we can talk to him around eight-thirty.'

'I - um - is it fair to talk to him about Dave before he goes on air?' asked Donna. 'I mean... it's going to seriously freak him out. *I* wouldn't fancy having to be here alone, chatting through the small hours to all the old ladies of Wessex, after learning my colleague's been murdered. Especially after...' she paused and glanced at Larkhill.

'After what?' asked Kate.

Larkhill rolled his eyes. 'We had a little... erm... situation a few weeks back.'

'Really?' Kate sat up, pen on notepad.

'It's nothing serious,' said Larkhill. 'It's just one of the fans who doesn't always get the boundaries. He's harmless. But he started coming down to talk to Josh, waiting by the car park exit. Josh got a little freaked out.'

'Who's this fan?'

'He's probably fine,' said Larkhill. 'He's just a fan. His name's Finley Warner. I have his contact details; he's always coming along to station tours and outside broadcasts; a bit of a radio geek, you know?'

'Right,' said Kate. 'Yes, his contact details will be useful. And yes,' she glanced over at Donna. 'I get your point about talking to Josh just before he goes on air. When can we get him during the day?'

'I'll get him to come in tomorrow afternoon,' said Larkhill. 'Of course, the news will probably have reached him by then- oh god!' He winced and shook his head at Donna. '*We're* going to have to put this out, aren't we?'

'Yes,' said his PA, looking sick. 'It'll be going out on *Dave's* show. Unless...' She looked at Kate. 'Are we meant to keep quiet about this?'

'We're not officially naming the deceased until his body has been formally identified,' said Kate. 'I can't tell you when that will be. It's not my job to advise you on what to put out on air - that'll have to be your call. Of course, your competitors may well get the story whether or not you do, so...'

'They might already have it,' said Michaels. 'Word spreads pretty fast and the site was close to a small village... our presence caused a bit of a stir and there were at least a couple of sight-seers. Something is probably already getting out on social media.'

'All we ask,' said Kate, 'is that you do not mention any of the details to anyone else outside this room. Nothing about the gaffer tape, nothing about the mic sock. You can be vague about the location too. It's important that certain details are on a need-to-know basis in a case like this.'

'You won't tell the staff when you interview them?' asked Larkhill.

'We'll be asking questions; not running a briefing,' said Kate. 'Please get a memo to everyone and organise their time tomorrow so we can speak to them all. Can we use your office?'

'Of course,' he said. 'I'll get that memo out.'

'No details,' said Kate. 'Just the request - the time and the place. Now,' she looked at her watch. 'Where can we wait until Mike Tierney and his producer are free? You can let them know their colleague is dead... but nothing else, OK?'

'Fine,' said Larkhill, shaking his head. 'Fine.'

Donna moved across and squeezed his shoulder and he patted her hand appreciatively.

The PA took them back to reception, where Moira had packed up and gone, leaving the revolving door stationary and locked and dimmer lighting over the desk and sofas.

'I need to head off - are you OK here?' Donna said.

Kate nodded. 'You seem to be handling this all very calmly,' she said.

Donna gave a gentle snort. 'I've worked here a long time. You wouldn't believe the dramas I've seen. Radio presenters... it's like a kindergarten! Mind you... none of them got themselves murdered before.' She shook her head.

When the PA had departed Michaels collected all the presenter postcards, including some weekenders - Rebecca on the gardening show, Judy on traffic and Tim on the Sunday god slot - who weren't featured on the big posters up on the walls.

At ten minutes past seven Larkhill brought the drivetime

team out to meet them. Tierney and his producer arrived, looking shellshocked. Tierney appeared older and more thick-set than his promotional photo, with receding grey hair and a single gold ear stud hinting at wilder days in commercial broadcasting. His producer, Lewis Jones, was a thin, black, bespectacled guy in a crew neck sweater and jeans, carrying a vinyl manbag and a cake tin. Larkhill agreed to leave them to talk in the deserted reception area. The interview didn't take long.

'I don't - I mean, I *didn't* - really know the guy that well,' said Tierney, blowing out his lips and staring into middle distance as he processed the news. 'I mean, yeah, we're on the same station, but we're opposite ends of the day. How did he die?'

'Asphyxiation,' said Kate, not elaborating. 'So, you didn't spend any time with Dave?'

'Well, only the occasional station event,' said Tierney. 'You know, he's breakfast, I'm drivetime - never the twain shall meet.'

'What did you think of him?'

'Well,' said Tierney, casting a glance up at the Dave Perry poster. 'He was a bit of a legend, wasn't he? I had a lot of respect for him.'

'Did you like him?' asked Kate.

Tierney blinked. 'Um... I didn't *dis*like him,' he said. 'I mean, like I told you, we didn't see much of each other. He was... a bit of a player; liked the ladies. Two ex-wives, three kids... all grown up now, though, I think. He was, you know... colourful.'

'And can you think of any reason why anyone would want to harm him?'

'Sick of his face on their morning commute?' he quipped

weakly, glancing towards the hoarding outside. His expression clouded. 'Sorry. Not funny.'

'Can we see your mic sock?' asked Michaels.

The presenter blinked and then, shrugging, pulled a palm-sized black case from a pocket in his army surplus coat. He opened the zip and presented an oval of dense grey foam. 'Full of my DNA,' said Tierney. 'I should put it through the wash. Do you want to..?' He held out the sock and Michaels waved it away.

'No - we're good,' said the DC. 'You always have it with you?'

'Yeah, everyone does, if they're on air or making packages. You've got to have it on you, if you're using the mics. We live in a post-pandemical world!'

The interview with Jones, the producer, was no more enlightening and Kate released them both a few minutes later, with instructions to keep what they knew to themselves for now. For all the difference it would make.

'Oh hang on,' said Jones, as he and Tierney made for the staff exit to one side of the revolving door. He turned and tipped the contents of the tin into the bin under the reception desk, leaving the empty tin by Moira's switchboard. 'Listener's cake,' he explained, grinning guiltily. 'A fan brought it in. Home made. Most of them, you just don't chance it.'

'Especially if it's Finley's,' added Tierney, raising an eyebrow.

'Because..?" asked Kate.

'Well... let's just say we think he puts a lot of himself into these things,' said Tierney.

8

A corpse sighting, a brush with Kate Sparrow and four glasses of red wine were not a recipe for a restful evening. Lucas slipped into a doze on the new sofa and found himself in the troubling company of Mabel and Zoe.

They were, as always, just the way he remembered them. Lithe and graceful, Mabel dancing across the heath in her cut-off jeans and crop top, Zoe in her shorts and a knotted check shirt. Laughing, teasing, daring him. For that last sweet summer when they were all fifteen, the sun always seemed to be shining and the grasshoppers singing. Even inside his dream, though, he knew it was all going to go wrong. At any moment. Like it always did.

They were lying in the grass on the edge of the quarry and Mabel was swinging Sid between her fingers, over the drop, the chain wrapped around her pink-painted nails. She was singing that old sixties hit: 'In the summer time... when the feelin' is high...'

'There's a time to go, there's a reason to die,' Zoe finished, from underneath her pile of rocks. Because they had all seamlessly arrived in the bottom of the quarry, Zoe buried, but apparently alive. Sid was back in Lucas's teenage hands now and had changed from a blue glass stopper to a small, bloodied chunk of bone. Skull bone. Lucas knew it was a perfect fit for the hole at the back of Zoe's broken head.

The police were coming. Lucas could sense them just behind him on the cliff above and he was *willing* Sid to stop being a shattered piece of Zoe's skull. It just looked so bad. So incriminating.

'You shouldn't have done it,' said Mabel, so close the tip of her tongue touched his earlobe. But when he looked around she was nowhere to be seen.

Lucas groaned in his half-awake-half-asleep state and wished he'd never come back to the UK. These dreams hadn't plagued him for years... until he'd come back to settle his aunt's estate and take the bungalow. In fact, not even then, despite being so close to the plain and the heath and the quarry of that long-lost summer. No - it was only after Kate Sparrow had strolled into his life to ask him to dowse for a missing woman that the bad dreams had started up again. Dreams of The Quarry Girls, as the press had dubbed them at the time; one found bludgeoned to death, the other vanished and presumed also murdered. Mabel's body was never found.

Yup. It was Kate Sparrow's fault. He turned over on the sofa, rubbing his face and sinking back down to that other-worldly state where dreams tango weirdly with the waking world. DS Sparrow couldn't claim to be innocent either, could she? When she had come to the bungalow and demanded he dowse for her, she must have been well aware of what she might be triggering. If he'd known about her connection to Mabel and Zoe at the time he might never have got involved, but she had deliberately withheld that from him.

Someone was pulling the wool over someone's eyes and sometimes he wasn't even sure which was which or who was who anymore. Little wonder Kate was avoiding him. Little wonder his common sense was screaming at him to avoid *her*. His thoughts were unravelling as he slid back into the dream state, watching Mabel and Zoe walking across the heath again and trying to yell after them: 'STOP! Don't go there! I'm sorry! I couldn't help it!' But the words wouldn't come out because his mouth was full of foamy stuff and tape was across his face.

His mobile burred violently on the surface of the wooden crate beside the sofa, jolting him from his unhappy slumber. He snatched it up, his eyes foggy, without looking at the caller ID.

'I know it was you,' said Kate Sparrow.

'What? *What?*' he burbled.

'Lucas, just tell me.'

He rubbed his face. 'I don't know what you're talking about,' he said. He glanced across at the clock and saw it was just after 10pm.

'The message on the CrimeStoppers tape,' she said.

He let out a long breath. 'Look... I was asleep. I'm a bit foggy,' he said.

'We traced the call to a phone box in Steepleford,' she went on. 'Then we checked ANPR in the area and identified your motorbike in the vicinity around the time of the call. *Then* we checked the cell network data and - who knew? - your mobile number pinged up *right by* that phone box.

'Shit,' muttered Lucas, remembering that quick online search for the CrimeStoppers number. Idiot. Rookie error.

He should have had his mobile switched off the moment he'd decided to follow his dowsing instinct.

'What the hell, Lucas? I mean... what, the bloody *hell?*'

'Alright, alright,' he said. 'Yes. It was me.'

'So why didn't you call me?' she demanded.

'Why do you *think*? I don't want to get caught up in this!'

'But you *are* caught up in it,' she said.

'No... no I'm NOT. I'm just a passer-by. That's all.'

'How could you be passing by out in the middle of bloody nowhere?' she said. She let out a short sigh. 'How did you come to find the body?'

'I was at the station - you saw me there,' he said.

'Yes,' she replied. 'I heard you too, while we were driving in. Thanks for the shout out,' she added, drily.

'I'm sorry - I shouldn't have mentioned you. Anyway...' He took a breath. 'I was in reception when the presenter - Louella, her name is - started talking to the receptionist about this guy not showing up for work.'

'So you offered to wave Sid around again - this time for more than just her phone?' said Kate, snippily.

'Well, *no,* I didn't. I didn't even want to dowse for her bloody phone, as you might have picked up if you were listening.' There was a beat of silence which suggested she had been listening and she *had* picked that up. 'And I wasn't remotely interested in any more missing person searches, thanks very much. I was just going home.'

'Yes... you looked pretty keen to be gone,' she remarked.

'Look, you're the one who's been avoiding *me,*' he pointed out.

'I've been busy,' she said.

'Right. Fine. So have I.'

'So - what happened next? Did the nasty presenter piss

you off so much you fancied bumping off the next radio jock you met?'

'Don't be ridiculous. Sid led me to him.'

'I'm not sure those two sentences really work together,' she observed.

'I left my bag behind in the studio,' he went on, trying to keep his voice even and calm. 'I went back to get it and, while I was waiting for someone to bring it to me, I picked up this Dave Perry's postcard, with his autograph on it.'

'So... something he'd touched,' said Kate, sounding suddenly less accusatory.

'Yes. And I guess I just got something from it, because I should have gone straight home but instead I kept going, following the patterns.'

'Are you telling me Sid took you straight to the murder scene?'

He paused; breathed in and out. 'It's happened before,' he said, at length.

There was another pause, the static between them almost palpable. Was she remembering the time, a few weeks ago, when he'd arrived at the murder scene in time to stop someone killing *her*? Or was she remembering the time, sixteen years ago, when he'd arrived too late to find her sister?

'I think we need to talk,' she said.

'Yes... yes, we probably do. But do you really *want* to involve me in your investigation right now?' he asked. 'I mean... it just makes the whole thing more complicated, doesn't it? You know and I know why I was there - and why I got the hell away from there and left an anonymous tip off. As soon as it goes on record, it's the whole Lucas Henry merry-go-round all over again. You don't need that. And I certainly bloody don't.'

She sighed and he knew she got his point. 'I nearly lost my job last time I kept you under wraps,' she said.

'Yup. Well... it was your call then and it's your call now. Do what you have to do,' he said. She didn't answer and he gently hung up.

9

'I just miss him,' said Daphne from Wilton. 'I miss him so much.'

'I'm sure you do,' said Josh, making shadow play rabbits with his hands as he watched his reflection in the darkened glass of the picture window into Centre Studio. A few months ago the lights would have been on and there would have been a late night producer in tele-in, visible through the other window, grinning across in sympathy and maybe making nob gags into his ear.

'He was always so lovely to me,' Daphne burbled on. 'He used to sing to me over breakfast and he used to rub his head on my chin. Of course, he used to leave a terrible mess on the carpet too, whenever I let him go.'

'Worth all the cleaning up, though, I'm sure,' said Josh. 'I'm sure Joey's looking down from that great budgie cage in the sky and singing to you still. Daphne... I've got to move on, sweetheart - I've got the news coming up!'

'Yes, of course, Josh,' sniffed Daphne from Wilton. 'It's lovely to talk to you. You know, I'm always telling my friends I go to bed with you...' she giggled.

'..and wake up with Dave Perry?' he finished for her. More giggling. He potted the call before she could ask for a Carpenters track. If he played *Top Of The World* one more time he was going to start head-butting the desk until his spilled brains clogged up the faders. It wasn't that he didn't appreciate Daphne - he really did. When he'd arrived five years ago, a newbie, in the overnight slot, he'd been thrilled at the audience reaction. The late night listeners had really taken to him. They were a disparate bunch - lots of pensioners, of course, widowed, lonely and struggling to sleep, mostly women. But also a good number of cabbies and lorry drivers working the small hours. Phoning in to answer his quiz questions or request a track or just to share an opinion about the state of the world seemed like a religion to some of them; the same names in the same locations coming up again and again.

He got plenty of late-night interaction and thanks to the caller ID software on the phone-in system, which he was now required to operate himself during the three minutes a golden oldie track allowed him, he could dodge away from the repeat callers from time to time; make sure they didn't get to dominate. Some of them were great - really funny and bright and witty. Cabbies, in particular, were excellent at writing acceptably rude limericks and texting them in while waiting for a fare. Other listeners had different reasons for tuning in through the night; they came up with achingly sad stories about their lives and he had to be careful not to let that kind of thing dominate his output; you could only depress your audience so much. A dead budgie was the worst of it tonight and he hoped it would stay that way.

'And now... at just coming up to midnight... it's time for the news,' he said, cross-fading to the news ident, closing his mic and wheeling the chair back for a stretch and slurp of

Coke. Somewhere in Manchester a late-night news presenter was now reading out the headlines for regional stations all over the country, saving each of them the expense - and the company - of someone else in the building with the overnight jock.

Josh did not like being the only one here. Until six months ago it had been him and Lewis, his producer, but then Lewis had been moved to drivetime and Josh had been told that cuts across the corporation (blame the govern-ment) meant an overnight producer was a luxury that BBC Radio Wessex could no longer afford. So now he was the only person in the building at night. There wasn't even a security guard to talk to - just a load of CCTV cameras which routed to some security hub somewhere in Wiltshire. Fat lot of good that was if an axe murderer showed up at the back door, hacking his way in.

To be fair, he hadn't started thinking this way until last Friday when Finley fucking Warner had shown up at ten past one, lurking at the back gate in his BBC Radio Wessex fleece and suddenly leaping out from the shadows, waving a bloody *jumper*. Josh had nearly wet himself with the scare. The guy was bloody *obsessed*. It wasn't enough to phone in on every show, turn up at every OB, and continually drop in with questionable home bakes... now he was branching out into knitwear.

'Jeeezuz!' he had squawked, hands to his throat as the tall iron security gate clunked shut and locked behind him. 'Finley! What the hell?'

'I got you this!' Finley had said, joyfully. 'You said you like jumpers!'

Josh had agreed that, yes, he did like jumpers, and it was really kind, but that it was best if Finley dropped his very thoughtful gifts into reception during business hours. 'Or...

just *don't*, Finley,' he'd said. 'Honestly... I don't need this stuff. I'm just happy that you like the show, OK?'

'But I made it myself,' said Finley, his face shadowed under the hood of his quilted anorak and his voice cracking.

'You knitted.. this?' Josh queried, holding the thick burgundy woolly up to the white glare of the streetlamp.

'No... I put that on the front.'

Which was when Josh had noticed the image of Finley and himself posing together at an OB during the summer, screen-printed onto a cotton panel and stitched onto the burgundy jumper (M&S if he wasn't mistaken).

It had taken him five minutes to get rid of Finley and then, when he'd walked on home he had the distinct impression the guy was still following him. He couldn't see him but he just *felt* it. It was creepy. He didn't want fans knowing where he lived. People said Finley was harmless but Josh wasn't so sure. There was something seriously odd about him. What kind of grown man got so fixated on a radio station that he convinced himself that every presenter was his best friend? Even when they were blunt with him. He'd heard that Dave Perry had recently told Finley to go and get himself a life. Dave, of course, had always prided himself on his plain speaking; code for being a rude bastard.

Not for the first time, Josh felt that sour burn of bitterness. He felt like John Tracy, stuck up on Thunderbird 5, doing his duty in the endless dark of space while the rest of the Tracy boys got all the action and the glory by day, back on Earth. He had proved himself long enough on the nightshift. It was about time he got his shot at breakfast. Dave had ruled that roost for fifteen bloody years and it really was time for fresh blood.

'Just a short stint on overnight,' Chris Kinson - the

manager back then - had said. 'Earn your stripes. Then I can
see breakfast for you in the not too distant.'

That was five years ago and he was still hanging on a
promise. The new manager, Rob Larkhill, had also hinted
that breakfast might be his next move. But months later...
still nothing. Josh felt he'd earned enough stripes to make a
set of deckchairs. The problem was, he'd done it too well.
The oldies loved him. They had taken him to their collective
hearts and although he sort of loved them too, he knew they
were collectively stifling his career in their cardigan-
wrapped, Ovaltine-steamed, Vick-smeared embrace. *'I go to
bed with Josh Carnegy...'*

He'd spoken to Rob again just last week and got nothing
but flannel... *hang in there, Josh... your time will come...*

But when? Because Dave Perry just wouldn't go.

The smug fucker just... wouldn't... go.

And on a station where presenters had a half-life of forty
years, what could make him?

''...two-nil after a penalty shoot out. And that's all from
me for now; I'll be back in an hour.'

Josh pulled himself out of his reverie to opt Wessex back
in and go to the first track of the night. Hey, who knew?
Cracklin' Rosie!

———

'ANOTHER HIT from the fabulous Neil Diamond.' The
presenter was making a good effort at sounding genuine but
Kate suspected he was way too young to be a Neil Diamond
fan. Probably more Radiohead or even Fall Out Boy.

She reached out and switched off the radio. She wasn't
going to get any serious intel from listening to Josh Carnegy
and his harem of octogenarians, clucking the night away.

She'd be better off getting some sleep... but sleep just wouldn't come. It wasn't just Dave Perry on the mast, hanging in her mind's eye like the persistent after-image of a camera flash. It was bloody Lucas bloody Henry. Once again she was finding herself in an impossible position with Lucas Henry.

The last time she'd kept information from Kapoor about Lucas, the super had made it abundantly clear that he wouldn't overlook it the next time. Right now, she was the only one who knew the identity of the anonymous caller to the CrimeStoppers line. Although anonymity was its selling point, the police at no point promised they wouldn't *try* to locate the caller, if it was important enough. And this was important enough. Of course, if Sharon or Ben had picked up the intel on his registration and his mobile number, she wouldn't be in this position - someone *else* could have made the call.

But no, it had to be her. And now she was in turmoil once again, just when she needed to get to sleep. She was going to have to put Lucas back in the frame, like it or not, because she couldn't pretend she hadn't done the work and found the caller. The evidence was right there in the station's computer system. She'd speak to Kapoor first thing and hope she wasn't in hot water for not bringing it to him sooner.

It wasn't only this which chased away sleep, though, was it? Where Lucas Henry was concerned there were altogether too many layers of conflict; personal, professional... psychological. *Sexual*, whispered an unhelpful voice, low in the mix. She pulled the pillow over her head, shuddering with shame. How could she? How *could* she find him attractive? Lucas Henry may have saved her life... and probably the life of at least one victim of a serial killer... but that didn't wipe away the stain of what he *might have done* sixteen years ago.

You need to talk to someone about this. The sensible voice in her head; her mother's, most likely, was right. She did need to talk to someone. But who? Joanna? Oh god, no.

Upstairs her younger brother Francis was probably pulling an all-nighter on some online computer game. She could go up and sit next to him and tell him what she was thinking. Trouble was, Francis barely knew Lucas from back then; back when he was best friends with their sister Mabel and her friend Zoe. Francis had been only seven when Mabel disappeared and Zoe was found murdered in the quarry. His memory even of Mabel was hazy, he admitted these days. They kept her photo in amongst the collection of family shots by the front door, along with pictures of their late mother; they wanted to keep both alive in their memory. You never knew what you'd lose next in this life. This was probably the reason she and Francis had opted to convert the family home into two flats, so they could keep an eye on each other in case death or disappearance threatened again. It was a nice location, too; a quiet street of Edwardian houses with long sloping back gardens that led down to the river. Their mother had bought it not long after she'd accepted her daughter was never coming back; giving them a fresh start in a new home... and a new name to match. No longer Johanssen but Sparrow, her maiden name. They still lived in Salisbury but just far enough away from their old life to give them some respite from the compassionate glances and hushed conversations in the post office; the kind smiles at the school gates.

That name change was the reason it had taken Lucas so long to twig their connection. Because he *had* worked it out, eventually; that Detective Sergeant Kate Sparrow was the little sister of Mabel, the girl he'd dowsed for and never found. It can't have been easy for him to make the discovery. Getting involved again with the Wiltshire Constabulary had been hard enough after what had happened when he was fifteen.

And the kicker was, she felt responsible - partly. She was the one who'd got Mum to call Lucas when Mabel didn't come home. She was the one who'd said that Lucas could dowse for Mabel and Zoe. Mum had begged him to do it, of course. So he'd come over to their place and then got out Sid, his little blue bottle stopper on a chain, and dowsed a path all the way to the quarry.

Kate hadn't seen Zoe's body. She hadn't gone down into the quarry with them. She had been made to wait in the car. She still heard her mother's scream, though. She could hear it right now as she lay staring into the sleepless dark; could see the flock of startled rooks scattering into the sky through the smeared side window of the old Nissan Micra. She remembered the police arriving and then Lucas being put into the patrol car, a copper's hand on the crown of his head. She remembered wondering why.

Of course, it was obvious, when they thought about it later, why the police would suspect Lucas. He had, after all, led everyone directly to the scene of the crime and Zoe's body. Who else but the killer would know where to go? It had been a grim time for him. He was only saved by his mother's insistence that Lucas had been at home with her when the pathologist said Zoe's life had ended. But he wasn't saved. Not really. Although his name had never been printed in the local papers - he was legally still a child and so given anonymity - rumour got out. There were eggs thrown at the car and then graffiti sprayed on the house. The school asked Lucas not to return except for his GCSE exams, explaining that it would be much easier for him to stay away. Lucas's mother, always a little free with the wine, did not cope well. She was sacked from her job at the bank after being found inebriated at her desk.

Soon after, they moved away and that was the last Kate had heard of him for a decade and a half... until earlier that year when a friend of a neighbour mentioned something about his aunt dying and Lucas being the sole heir to her modest estate. Then she'd set out to mess his life up again by dragging him into the Runner Grabber case.

Bloody good thing for her that she had, or she'd most likely be a desiccated corpse by now.

Not so bloody good for Lucas. Especially now that he'd stupidly helped her out again. Why the hell did he have to *do* that? Why put himself on the line again, for someone who had used him and abused him in the line of her work... and then refused to see him. Why?

Did he have something to atone for?

She realised she had been staring at the dark ceiling for a solid twenty minutes or more, her unhelpful mind turning Lucas Henry over and over. There was something he was hiding; she knew it. But what? Even now her mind skittered away from the darkest of her suspicions. Wouldn't quite frame even the thought. But the thought, framed or not, drifted around in the deepest pockets of her psyche, like the hint of a shadow on an X-ray, or the whisper of a growing infestation in the basement.

With a groan of frustration she flung back the duvet and got up to make a cup of tea, switching the radio back on and carrying it with her into the kitchen. With a full mug she sat at the small pine table and found herself instinctively reaching for the cardboard packet. She got the plasticine out and started making snails, rolling fat little bodies out of the brown and then making twisted coils of yellow and green to put on their backs. The unpleasant fizzing inside her began to subside a little and time passed gently.

'I think you need to work on your golden ratio.' She jumped and looked around to see Francis peering around her kitchen door. He held up his key to her flat and smiled apologetically. 'Sorry... just saw your light was on. Was worried.'

She blinked and shook her head. 'I might have been having mind-blowing sex with someone. You'd have needed therapy for life. Anyway... what golden ratio?'

Her brother grinned, leaning in the kitchen doorway, his fair hair messy and definite signs of ketchup on his sweat-shirt. He really needed to get out more. 'The Fibonacci number sequence. A snail's shell perfectly follows the rule of the golden ratio. The divine proportion - sixty-two to thirty-eight - is found everywhere in nature. A snail's shell is the perfect example. Except when it's rendered in plasticine in the small hours by my messed up sister.'

'Hmmpf,' she commented. She was about to say he was just as messed up as she was, but in truth he looked abso-lutely fine. He was pretty much nocturnal, communicating with friends and work colleagues all over the world from his computer set up in the study he'd built upstairs.

'What's the plasticine about then?' he asked.

She shrugged. 'Therapy. A suggestion from Joanna.'

'Is it helping?' he asked, smiling gently. He was very paternal about her these days, which was irksome when he was three years her junior.

'I'll let you know,' she said. 'Bugger off back to your world wide web of wonders. I'm going back to bed... soon.'

He nodded. 'We should go out some time. Like normal people,' he said, as he walked away.

'We should,' she said, smiling. 'We will.' She sighed and then went back to her snails, peering at the undivine proportions of the spiral shells and trying to improve them. She was teasing out their little feelers with her finger tips as Josh Carnegy said: 'I can't believe it, but we're out of time,' over the swell of the BBC news intro music. 'Once again, thank you all for sharing the wee small hours with me. Tomorrow we've got the book of the week review, a brand new Where and When quiz and obviously loads of calls from *you lot*. Nanight folks. Sleep well.'

He sounded like he meant it and she could imagine a lot of lonely wakeful listeners snuggling down and finally switching off for the night.

She just wished she was one of them.

———

Josh slid his mic fader shut and then pressed an assortment of buttons to give control of BBC Radio Wessex's output over to the guys at 5 Live.

Then he powered everything down to stand-by in Studio B and gathered his coat and bag. He noticed a text from Rob on his phone asking him to come back in at midday. Well... that could be interesting. Maybe the boss was *finally* going to talk to him about coming off nights. Maybe everything he'd done would turn out to be worth it.

He texted back: **Sure. See you then.**

Then he headed out through the empty, silent newsroom, lit only by the endless flicker of the News 24 screens, descended the rear stairwell and went out through the garage where the radio car, the VERVs and a couple of pool cars were parked. He was particularly twitchy tonight; he felt like he was being watched all the time these days, like someone was going to slap a hand on his shoulder at any moment.

But there was nobody in here with him and nobody outside either. He wished he'd got a car. He could drive but he'd never got around to buying something; his flat was only a twenty minute walk away from the radio station and BBC local radio pay wasn't really enough to justify the expense. He might have felt safer, though, getting into a car and driving out through the electronic gate, windows up and doors locked.

He took a deep breath and opened the footpath exit. On the other side there was nobody at all.

Just a tin. A Marks & Spencer biscuit tin. On the low wall right by the gate. His own publicity postcard was stuck to it. He stared at it for several seconds, his heart racing, and then leaned over and flipped off the lid. Inside were flapjacks, about a dozen of them, sending up a sickly sweet waft of oats and syrup. Of course. He'd mentioned last night that he loved a nice flapjack.

'What the *fuck,* Finley,' he muttered, putting the lid back on with a shudder.

He took the gift with him to the nearest bin and shoved it inside, wondering how his life had gone so wrong and twisted that he now spent his nights getting freaked out by an empty garage and a tin of flapjacks.

Had it all been worth it?

10

'Sheila, I hate to call you in the dead of night,' said Rob. He pictured her on the sofa, glass of wine in hand, her beloved cat on her lap... or maybe in bed; she had an early start after all.

'What's up?' she said, sounding perfectly bright.

'I was worried I might wake you.' He poured a glass of red for himself, hoping it might steady him, and sat down at his kitchen table.

'Me? Oh no - I was taking a look at Mars. It's a lovely clear sky tonight. Tried to see it up at the Rollestone observatory last night with the Astronomy Society but it clouded over.'

'Oh... only I thought as you'd got an early start in the morning...'

'Oh, I slept this afternoon,' she said. 'Got three hours. I sleep in shifts all the time; especially when I know I'm going out stargazing; it works a treat. Anyway, what's up?'

'You might want to sit down.'

'Oh my,' she said. 'That sounds serious. Are you offering me the breakfast slot?' She giggled and he knew she was only half joking. She'd been angling for the permanent gig for years, clueless to how badly suited to it she was. She didn't even have any journalism training, for god's sake. She'd joined the station as a secretary back when they still edited with razor blades and sticky tape.

'Sheila... Dave Perry is dead.'

There was silence at the end of the phone and then an exhalation. 'Shit,' said Sheila. Not a word often heard from her lips. 'What happened? Did he have a stroke or something? He's always drunk way too much.'

'No,' said Rob. He gulped. 'Sheila, he was murdered.'

Another silence and then: 'What? No! Oh my god. How? Where? Who killed him?'

'I'm telling you this now because it's bound to get out. It'll probably be all over the commercial stations' news by tomorrow morning; I wanted to warn you. I think we're going to have to go with this as our lead story. Just be brave and open up to the listeners - turn tomorrow's show into a phone-in memorial, remembering Dave. Do you think you can handle that?'

'But... I mean... wait a minute. I still don't understand. Who would want to kill him? Was it someone's husband?'

'I don't know. That's what the police are looking into,' said Rob. 'They told me about Dave earlier this evening; I'm still in shock myself. They want to come in and interview all the staff tomorrow. I'm drawing up a rota for them to work through. I shouldn't really be telling you anything but I thought you needed to be prepared. I'll be getting in at five to brief James and Gemma and whoever's on the news shift.'

'But you still haven't told me how he was killed?' Sheila sounded shrill, on the edge of hysteria.

'Asphyxiation,' said Rob. 'That's all I know. We won't be going into details on air, of course. Not unless one of our competitors gets ahead of us. I'm expecting to get calls from the Journal and Spire FM and probably the nationals and network too.'

'Oh my god; he was strangled,' she murmured. 'That's it then - it's got to be a husband. Dave always had a thing for the married ones. I told him it would come back to bite him one day. Never thought it would end like this though. A punch-up, maybe, but...'

'Well, nobody knows just yet,' said Rob. 'Sheila... are you up to this? I can get Spencer and Jack in if you think it's going to be too-'

'No,' she said, 'I'm fine. It *should* be me. I've known Dave longer than anyone else on the station.' She sniffed. 'I can't believe it. When did it happen?'

'They think some time over the weekend,' he said. 'The body wasn't found until today. Out Shrewton way.'

'Oh my god,' she said, 'I was up that way myself on the weekend, with the Society. In fact, I'm pretty sure *you* were too. Didn't I see you near Donna's place?' Despite the gravity of this discussion, a slightly teasing note entered her voice. He knew there were rumours about him and his PA.

'Sheila - you need to get some sleep. We both do,' he said. 'Tomorrow is going to be the day from hell.'

11

Chief Superintendent Rav Kapoor sighed and shook his head. 'You're serious?

'Yup,' she said. 'Lucas Henry. He says he picked up a signed postcard at the station yesterday after overhearing the presenter and the receptionist saying Dave Perry was missing. Then he got... you know... a dowsing thing going. He followed it and found the body.'

'But he didn't call you? Or us?'

She shifted awkwardly on the plastic seat in front of his desk. 'Well... he's not had a great time with the Wiltshire Constabulary over the past few weeks, has he? He got tasered twice, for a start. He wanted to stay anonymous this time. You kind of can't blame him for not wanting to get involved again.'

'Assuming he's *not* involved,' said Kapoor, leaning back and folding his arms across his chest.

'If he's involved, why would he call us at all?' she said. 'And honestly... you don't really think he *is* do you?'

'I don't know,' said Kapoor. 'Do *you*?'

She paused and took a breath. 'I think he's proved, more than once, that he *can* do this whole dowsing thing. It's not some kind of magic trick; dowsing is a *thing*. Look it up online; there are engineering companies and developers who hire these guys to dowse for water before they start building. They pay them for the service. It saves thousands, apparently. Lucas is... just one of them; just very good at dowsing. He was always brilliant at it when we were kids. He found stuff all the time. Watches, keys, toys...'

'...bodies,' said Kapoor. Then he pressed his lips together and said: 'Sorry.'

'No need,' she said. 'He never found my sister's body, after all.'

'I'm going to need to speak to him again,' he said.

She sighed. 'I thought you'd say that. Do you want me to bring him in? I could get him later this afternoon. I've got to get back to the radio station this morning; start the interviews with Michaels. Bill Sharpe's back off leave, yes? Are he and Sharon Mulligan still doing the family end?'

'They are,' he said. 'Perry's ex-wife - I'm not sure which one - has agreed to formally identify the body. But don't worry about Lucas Henry. I'll give him some thought. Get back to the station and crack on with the staff interviews.'

'Thanks,' she said, getting up.

'And Kate..'

'Yes, guv?'

'Thank you for being straight with me about this,' he said.

'No problem,' she said, although it didn't *feel* like no problem. It felt like betrayal. She'd really had no choice, though. And she guessed Lucas knew that. He probably wouldn't *completely* hate her for it.

Back in CID she found Michaels on her desk, eating a flaky chocolate croissant for breakfast and sifting through print-outs from the BBC Radio Wessex website. Helpfully all the presenters had a short bio and photo online. From a staff list sent by the ever efficient Donna, she'd learned there were around a dozen backroom staff too, producers and researchers as well as a handful of news and sports journalists who worked shifts across all the output, but mostly on weekends. There were also a couple of BBC engineers looking after the station's IT, broadcasting desks and radio cars. A cleaner came in every other day. It was a pretty small team for a station which covered the best part of three counties.

Kate had brought her portable radio in from home and now she flicked it on again to catch the latest. It was 7.38am and it seemed the entire listenership of BBC Radio Wessex was in mourning. The breakfast show had become a live, rolling memorial, throwing out all other news apart from a desultory five minute bulletin on the hour and the half hour, and running nothing but clips of Dave Perry's most memorable on-air moments interspersed with his favourite songs, calls from weeping fans and recorded inserts of various local celebs expressing their shock and grief and personal memories. It was all being fairly ably steered by another station stalwart, Sheila Bartley. Sheila said: 'Oh... you're going to start me off again,' roughly every five minutes. Judy on traffic and travel had cried during a bulletin.

It reminded Kate of the outpouring of grief that had followed the death of Princess Diana; news reports of that time showed mass hysteria - everyone jostling to prove that *they* were feeling it more than anyone else. It didn't ring entirely true. Neither did the Dave Perry memorial party. She pulled up the news feeds and found that the murder had made the front page of *The Journal*, albeit their online edition at this hour. It had also scored a mention in the nationals and a couple of paragraphs on the regional section of the main BBC website. Details were sketchy at this point but the poetic nature of Dave Perry's demise - found at the bottom of a radio mast - had caught a lot of attention. As it was surely meant to. None of it should have got out there yet, but once the police arc lighting at the scene of the crime had gone up, several curious locals had been drawn in, like moths to a flame, and caught sight of more than they should have. Rural areas were sometimes hard to quickly seal.

'It's a peach, isn't it?' The accent was warm American and Kate turned around with a ready smile, catching Michaels rolling his eyes.

Conrad Temple, their occasional guest crim psych, was back.

'Didn't take *you* long,' muttered Michaels.

Conrad grinned and shrugged, pushing a floppy brown fringe off his forehead and fixing Kate with his wide brown eyes. 'You know I just *live* for coming here.'

'So what do you make of the death of The Voice of Wessex?' Kate asked, sipping her coffee and checking her watch. 'Make it fast because we've got to get to the radio station.'

'Well, it's not hard to work out that it's been done as a big statement,' said Conrad.

'No, that's not hard,' said Michaels.

Temple grinned at him. What Kate liked most about the guy was the way he seemed to find every dig at him quite hilarious. She had never seen him take offence, even though he took a lot of crap from coppers who thought his lofty theories might take quite a beating if he ever spent time at the policing coalface. They seemed to miss the point that a criminal psychologist's perspective was valuable because he or she *wasn't* at the coalface.

'Go on,' said Kate, switching off the radio and pulling on her jacket.

'Well, the microphone sock in the mouth and up the nose was clearly designed to suffocate the guy... but also, more symbolically, to silence him. So I'm guessing whoever killed him was offended by something he'd said. Also, it wasn't very hands-on. It looks like Perry was made to tape up his own legs and one wrist, presumably at knife point. He didn't make a run for it. Maybe he thought that was all the killer wanted - to shame him; leave him there alive to be found, humiliated, having peed his pants, by some local farmer or dog walker. But no - the final act of the killer was to tape his other arm up and then stuff in the mic sock and tape up the guy's mouth and nose. So... our killer didn't want to strangle the man himself. Didn't want to beat his brains in or stab him. The knife marks weren't deep, according to Death.'

He clasped a cardboard folder to his chest and tilted his head to one side, considering. 'So it wasn't a very physical act and not done in any kind of a frenzy. It was planned; methodical. I would say our killer had a long-held grudge.'

Kate nodded. Forensics were working over the car but nothing had come back yet, apart from traces of gaffer tape adhesive on the passenger seat head rest and rear seat footwell, which suggested Perry was taped up in the back of the car before arriving at the mast site. They'd found a small empty zip-up case on the back seat too, which was almost certainly for Perry's personal mic sock. No prints anywhere.

Kate guessed someone planning a 'methodical' and ritualistic murder would have gloves on and probably a hat and a
face mask too, to minimise the risk of leaving a DNA trail.

'We've got to go,' she said, grabbing her bag and car keys.
'We'll see you at the briefing, yes?'

'With some deeper insights, I hope,' said Temple,
favouring her once again with his boyish smile. She found
him very likeable. Maybe a little *more* than likeable.

'Twat,' said Michaels as they headed out into the
corridor.

'Why?' she asked, although she knew. Her young DC
was probably picking up on the hint of flirting going on
between her and the crim psych.

'*Symbolically silencing him*,' Michaels parroted, doing a
bad copy of Conrad's Boston accent. '*Long held grudge.*' He
snorted. 'He got choked to death with foam and gaffer tape
because some fucker hated him.'

'Well, that's the short version,' said Kate, with a grin.
'And probably just as accurate. Let's see if we can find out
which fucker, shall we?'

They passed DC Sharon Mulligan on the stairs. She
grinned, shaking her head, when she saw them. 'Former
Mrs Perry's just been in to ID the body,' she said. 'Took one
look, said "Yeah, that's him", turned around and left.'

'And that's all she said?' asked Kate. She was surprised.
Sharon - a warm combo of northern lass and West Indian
momma - could normally get anyone talking.

'Actually, no,' said Sharon. 'I walked behind her on the
way out. I'm pretty sure she muttered "*Wanker*".'

'Family all informed?' asked Kate.

'Yep - and all alibied up, too,' said Sharon. 'His sons and
his daughter seem upset and shocked, of course, but

nobody's tearing their shirt. I'm guessing he never won Dad of the Year.'

'Well... at least his listeners loved him,' said Michaels.

"Yeah. All four hundred thousand of them probably flashed before his eyes,' said Kate.

12

Gemma had never been so glad to get out of the station. Nervous, yes, because it was only the second time she'd been out in the old radio car on her own, but so, *so* relieved to get away from the rolling Dave Perry Memorial.

Salisbury Broadcasting House was filled with staff. It seemed everyone had come in, regardless of their shift, to share in the grief, the shock, the sheer fascination. Even Becs off the weekend gardening programme was hanging around, looking freaked out. Gemma wasn't fooled; they weren't purely there to speak to the police, as requested by Rob Larkhill. Most of them had come in way earlier than necessary, just for the traumafest. They were *revelling* in it. Not one of them, in their huddles and tear-stained hugs, had said 'He was such a lovely guy.' Because he wasn't. Dave Perry was not a lovely guy. He was just a man who had somehow found a successful career to go with his unpleasant personality.

In truth, she was mostly glad to be out because she didn't know *what* to feel. Dave Perry was dead. He was gone.

How could she be sad? She should definitely make a *show* of being sad, like all the others, but knowing that she'd never again have to endure his slimy approaches was a blessed release.

She'd got lucky, really - after the first hour on air she'd picked up a call from the stricken leader of a community choir in Wilton, where Dave had gone to school, who said the group wanted to sing something in his memory, on the steps of the local church. Mostly retired ladies, they were planning their ad hoc gig right now and would be ready to publicly sing out their sadness within the hour. James had loved that, especially when he learned the song they were going to finish on was *Everybody Hurts* by REM. 'Take the VERV and get down there!' he'd commanded. 'We want that to end the show. It's perfect. We can backtime them from the nine o'clock news.'

So here she was, leaving James and a hurriedly conscripted Jack from the Jack & Spencer show, to man the Switchboard of Grief, while she headed out to Wilton. She was nervous, though, even in her relief, because it wasn't the modern, easy-to-manage VSAT Enabled Reporter Vehicle that she was driving. Both of the VERVs were unavailable - one because it was being repaired and the other because it had already gone out for a sports fixture up country. This meant the only option was the old radio car. An unwieldy thing, it was basically a converted Ford Focus with a solid column of steel through its back seat area. The column housed the telescopic mast which could be raised to a five-metre height from a console fitted on the passenger side dashboard. Most of these radio cars had been pensioned off years ago, when the BBC bought into a faster, lighter, cheaper fleet of vehicles which could use satellite and mobile phone technology to send live feeds from outside broadcast sites pretty much anywhere.

She had received her official training from Malc, the station's chief engineer, a couple of months ago, on both the VERVs and the old radio car. The VERVs were easy to learn; very high tech, with their own WiFi field and a pretty much seamless connection to the nearest cell. The old radio car was something else. It was a museum piece - quite literally. It was kept in the garage mostly to entertain guests when they came in on tours of the radio station. In the same way they kept a couple of the old Uher reel-to-reel recorders and the massive Studer cut and splice editing machines with their oxide ribbon, razor blades and sticky tape. People loved that stuff. Malc, especially, got a bit misty eyed about it. Maybe this was the real reason why the station hadn't yet junked all the ancient tech.

She'd only used the old car once, since her training, covering a harvest festival event for Becs on the weekend gardening show, when the VERVS were both out for two important football matches. Most broadcast assistants learned to operate the gear this way; ad hoc requests from producers or presenters who were short of help. When you were new in radio you did everything you were asked to do. It was the only way to learn and to move up in your career.

So she'd said yes to Becs, despite her misgivings, and driven the heavy old Focus off to Avebury. She'd nearly totally cocked up the whole OB, forgetting to press a crucial button to transmit via the correct mast tower. She'd also nearly electrocuted herself by starting to put the mast up under a power line; only noticing it as she'd held her finger on the hydraulic button and then freezing in shock before taking the mast down again, moving the car to a safer spot, and starting the procedure all over. All with an audience of two or three hundred agog harvest festival-goers. She still went hot and cold when she thought of it. But today would be better, as long as she could find somewhere safe to park. She wasn't going to cock it up again.

In the event it went smoothly. She found the church and the weepy ladies of the choir and managed to park and get the mast up without incident. Then she linked through to the studio and got the choir on air, having backtimed their song, with a little rehearsal, to run up to the news at nine. The choir was good and their rendition of *Everybody Hurts* was rather touching, as long as she didn't think too much about who it was being sung for. Afterwards, Carol, who'd set up the flash choir, came over to stand next to her as she brought down the mast. 'I can't believe I'll never hear his voice again,' she sniffed, pulling a fresh hanky out of her beige puffer jacket.

Oh, you will, thought Gemma. *They're going to be running his greatest fucking hits for weeks.*

'I mean, it's so shocking,' Carol went on. 'Must be even more shocking for you; I mean, you *knew* him, properly. I'm just a listener. I know he could be quite... forthright... on air, but I bet he was lovely to work with, wasn't he?'

'He certainly was forthright,' said Gemma. The mast had fully lowered now, but as she released the down end of the rocker switch the motor kicked off again and the aerial started to ascend. Puzzled, she hit *down* a couple of times, but it just kept going up. It got halfway to its full height before her insistent jabbing made it drop again. 'Sorry,' she said to Carol. 'Having some technical issues here!' But the mast finally behaved itself; the wires and telescopic sections concertinaing back into place and staying put at last. Gemma made a mental note to mention it to Malc. It clearly needed its wiring looked at.

She got back to the station feeling happier than anyone should on such a day. She'd pulled off a nice radio car opt for a really tough breakfast show and *ding, dong, the shit was dead*. Yes, she felt guilty, but hey, job done. She parked the radio car back in its bay, plugged it in to its charger point, locked up, left the key back on its hook, and then rearranged her face to mirror the de rigueur grief of the day.

It was only when she stepped into the newsroom that keeping the look became a more natural affair. A blonde woman in a dark green cord jacket, black jeans and black boots walked up to her. 'Gemma Henshall?' she asked, consulting a list of names on a clipboard. 'I'm Detective Sergeant Kate Sparrow. Can you come with me please?'

Gemma glanced at Rob Larkhill, hovering nearby, and he nodded. 'Everyone's getting interviewed today, remember?' he said, and she relaxed a little. She spotted Josh Carnegy hanging around the newsroom with a cup of coffee, looking freaked out. It was a rarity seeing him out in daylight hours; he looked odd without night lighting.

She followed the detective to Rob's office where a man in his early-to-mid twenties was sitting to one side of the manager's desk. 'This is Detective Constable Ben Michaels,' said the woman, settling herself into Rob's chair and indicating that Gemma should take the seat opposite. 'We're speaking to all the staff here today to get a picture of Dave Perry's life - in case it helps us understand what happened to him.'

'What *did* happen to him?' she asked. 'Nobody seems to know.'

'How well did you know Mr Perry?' said DS Sparrow, disregarding the query.

'I - um - well, I've only worked here for a few months,' said Gemma. 'So... not very well, really.'

'Did you like him?' asked the guy, pinging a ballpoint pen against his A4 pad and regarding her through slightly narrowed eyes.

'I... um...' Should she lie? 'Well, he was a bit of a legend.'

'So we keep hearing,' said the female detective. 'But that's not what we're asking you.'

'Well,' said Gemma, feeling a flush rising through her. 'I thought he was...' She floundered, trying to find a single adjective which was positive.

'Have you got your phone with you?' asked the woman, in an abrupt change of tack.

Gemma blinked and then rummaged in her jacket pocket, retrieving the iPhone. 'Yes,' she said, holding it up. 'Why?'

'Do you mind if we just take a look?'

She flushed again. 'Um... well, I'm not thrilled about it - but if you must. Are you going to tell me why?'

Again she got no answer, but the woman smiled at her tightly and took the phone. Then she handed it back and said: 'Can you put in the code so I can take a quick look around?'

Gemma did and then waited in tense silence while they started poking around in her apps. After a couple of minutes the pair of them glanced at each other and the guy said: 'It can be checked at the network provider end. And the tech guys can probably retrieve it too.'

'What?' asked Gemma, getting seriously anxious now. 'Will someone tell me what the hell is going on?!'

DS Kate Sparrow put the phone face down on the table, but kept her hand on it. It was only now that Gemma noticed the detective was wearing fine latex gloves. 'We found Dave Perry's mobile under the passenger seat of his car,' she said. 'Our tech guys got into it and scanned his texts and calls. It seems the last communication he had with anyone was a text, asking to meet up for a drink on Friday evening.'

Gemma looked from one to the other and held up her palms.

The detective regarded for a few seconds before adding: 'The text was from you.'

13

Lucas was in the garage, washing down his bike, when a representative of the Wiltshire Constabulary showed up. He wasn't surprised to get a visit - but he *was* surprised to get a visit from Chief Superintendent Rav Kapoor. On his own. No DS Kate Sparrow hanging awkwardly behind.

'Is that a Bonneville?' asked Kapoor, which had to be a better opening than tasering him senseless.

Lucas glanced up and then back at the bike. 'My aunt left it to me. I don't think she'd been on it since her wild child days in the seventies. It was pretty well preserved when I found it in here.'

'Lovely machine,' said Kapoor. 'I used to have a Norton, back in the day.'

'So then,' said Lucas, standing up and rubbing his hands dry with a rag. 'Did you come for motorbike reminiscence?'

'No,' said Kapoor. 'I came because I'm curious.'

Lucas sighed. 'Do you want to come in? I could do with a coffee.'

'That would be very welcome.'

In the kitchen the man settled himself at the table, taking off his cap and laying it on the spare chair beside him. He steepled his hands, leant his chin on them, and watched Lucas put the kettle on and get milk from the fridge.

'Kate told you then,' said Lucas, at last.

'DS Sparrow has a responsibility to inform me of all developments in an ongoing case,' Kapoor said. 'Even when she doesn't want to.'

Lucas sat down and placed steaming mugs in front of them both, pulling a tub of Demerara sugar and a spoon along between them. 'I really didn't want to get involved again,' he said. 'I should have just let someone else find that body and report it.'

'Why didn't you?' Kapoor stirred a spoonful of sugar into his coffee.

'Because I pictured some kid with a dog finding it. I wouldn't want that. Just wish I'd done a better job of staying anonymous.' He sighed.

'DS Sparrow tells me you dowsed your way to the body,' said Kapoor. 'Is that true?'

'Yes,' said Lucas. 'I heard the BBC staff talking about him being missing. I should have shut my bloody ears. But once it gets in there...' He shook his head. 'I picked up the guy's promo postcard and it had his autograph on it; his... patterns.'

'And that's all you needed?'

Kapoor seemed genuinely interested. Lucas couldn't pick up any sarcasm from him. He could pick up other things though. He shut his mind down. None of his business. Sid was still in the sock in the other room and he was bloody well staying there.

'Sometimes a pattern... a frequency... comes through strongly. I just followed it and ended up at the Shrewton mast.'

'I've never seen you do this thing,' said Kapoor. 'I hear tell that it's a talent which probably saved DS Sparrow's life, along with Melissa Hounsome's. The trouble is, Lucas, a career in policing tends to turn you into a very sceptical being. Our world is all about evidence.'

He let it hang there for a while and Lucas felt his jaw tightening. 'I don't do party pieces.'

'Yes you do,' said Kapoor. 'When it's important enough. Now... if I can have evidence of this ability of yours, for myself rather than reported by others, it will make it much easier for me to believe your sudden involvement in yet another murder case is purely down to your rather hapless talent.'

Lucas took a gulp of coffee and sighed. 'What have you hidden?'

'I'd rather not say.'

'Oh right - a blind test to find *something*, somewhere, for some reason.'

'The reason is that I would like to understand,' said Kapoor. 'I find what I've heard very hard to believe. Convince me.'

Lucas put down the mug and left the room, teeth gritted. Once again he was back to unearthing Sid from the balled up sock of oblivion. He felt angry but also a little wired, if he was honest with himself. He didn't want to admit it, but life at the bungalow had been a bit dull of late. The muse hadn't really arrived for his next art collection, despite Mariam's encouragement. He had been feeling dispossessed and disconnected, thinking about Kate and the upcoming inquest too much.

He returned to the kitchen, sat down opposite Kapoor, and suspended Sid between his interlocked fingers, in the triangle formed by his elbows on the table. He looked at Kapoor levelly for thirty seconds, during which the man looked back, his dark eyes giving nothing away.

With a short, impatient exhalation, Lucas got up and walked to the front door, Sid spinning below his palm, sending up little buzzes and coughs of frequency that were beginning to take shape in Lucas's mind map as he moved. He sensed Kapoor following and said: 'Leave the door on the latch. We're not going far.'

Sid guided him along the lane, past Kapoor's regulation BMW, with an assortment of the man's complicated patterns reaching from it like sea anemones waving from a reef; these he disregarded. This wasn't the time or place. He kept walking. There was a rise in the land, about two minutes along the lane, and an overgrown stile on his left, leading to a rambler's access path on the edge of a neighbouring farmer's land. Lucas mounted the stile, glancing back to see Kapoor close behind, his face unreadable.

The man didn't need a hand; Lucas could see he was mostly pretty fit. So he didn't hold back for him but pushed on up the path. He found the first thing pushed deep into a network of roots at the base of an oak tree. A bracelet of yellow gold coin charms. He picked it up and had the satisfaction of watching an impressed smile spread across Kapoor's face. 'Your wife won't be too impressed if she finds out what you did with this,' said Lucas.

Kapoor shrugged. 'I guessed you would want something meaningful,' he said. 'I gave that to her on the eve of our wedding.' He took the bracelet and tucked it into his tunic pocket.

'Right, so... the next thing,' said Lucas.

'There's a next thing?' Kapoor raised his eyebrows in a show of surprise.

Lucas shook his head and turned away to continue up the steep hillside. Another couple of minutes and he reached a pile of logs. He felt around inside the stack and withdrew a clear plastic bag containing what appeared to be a single leather sandal. He turned to look stonily at Kapoor, Sid chilling in his palm and his throat constricting.

'This doesn't look like your size,' he said.

'It isn't,' said Kapoor. 'Don't open the bag, please - it's evidence.'

'Pretty old evidence,' said Lucas. He really didn't want to rise to it.

'About sixteen years old.' Kapoor looked at him, waiting.

Lucas felt a sudden rush of anger. He shook his head. 'Cheap trick, don't you think?' he said. He handed it to Kapoor with some velocity and then headed back to the bungalow.

They didn't speak on the return journey but when they reached his car, Kapoor stopped beside it. 'I'll let you get on with your day,' he said. No thank you. No suggestion that he was in any way impressed. No apology for showing Lucas the footwear of his murdered friend.

Lucas very nearly kept on walking but something made him stop, take a deep breath, and turn back to the man. 'When is your next medical due?' he asked.

Kapoor blinked. 'I beg your pardon?'

'Your police medical - when is the next one due?' Lucas dug his hands deep into his jeans pockets, Sid still bunched up in his left fist.

Kapoor shrugged. 'Not for a few months. Why do you-?'

'Don't wait for that,' said Lucas. 'Go and see your doctor. Tell him to check your kidney function.'

Kapoor looked deeply sceptical.

'And... I think we're done here,' said Lucas, and left.

14

It had been one hell of a day. Malcolm Bright's workload hadn't been lightened by the station suddenly filling up with every staff member on the roster as they all crowded in to share their shock about Dave Perry and attend their interviews with the police.

So many of them in one place meant every single terminal was switched on and being used, even if only for a spot of idle gaming or surfing while they talked in hushed and excited tones about what was going on. The LAN was under strain and he still needed to get down to the garage and do some vital maintenance on the old radio car. The mast motor switch was misbehaving, according to Gemma when she'd got back from that morning's OB. He knew he should decommission that hulk of trouble for good, but it was still a useful back up and, he couldn't deny it, he kind of loved the old beast.

He wasn't immune to the atmosphere, either. Other press had started to show up; the local ITV guys had parked a sat truck right out front. It made him feel childishly territorial, seeing the opposition's vehicle right here on his BBC turf. The staff were in a state of confusion too. Some had been interviewed by other reporters on their way in to work. They didn't know if they should talk - there had been no all-staff email directive against it. Malcolm had some sympathy for Rob Larkhill. There wasn't really a chapter in the BBC handbook on what to say to rival media when the house-hold name you worked with was murdered. *The Journal* had sent a reporter and a photographer who were busy getting a vox pop of grief from maybe twenty BBC Radio Wessex listeners who had gathered on the steps outside to express their sympathy. Flowers were arriving and so many calls were coming in to the phone-in line he'd needed to get them rerouted back to the main switchboard where an extra receptionist had been called in to help.

By lunchtime a book of condolence - bought hurriedly at the local WHSmiths - had been opened, so the listeners could drop in and write their feelings down when they brought flowers. Malcolm found the whole thing bizarre. These people barely knew Dave Perry. If they had known him they probably wouldn't be crying. The man was a five-star twat. Malc wasn't happy he was dead; he didn't think the guy deserved to be murdered. Strangled, apparently. Nobody seemed to know for sure. But he did think that of all the presenters to lose, Dave Perry, self-anointed Voice of Wessex, was one he'd probably miss the least.

He'd spent most of the day keeping his head down and getting on with his duties - trying to avoid the gossip. Even he couldn't miss the shock rumour that Gemma had been marched off to Salisbury nick, though. What the hell? That had to be nonsense. Although, he reflected, if he had to work with Dave Perry every morning, five days a week, maybe *he* might be pushed to murder the guy.

And now there was another problem; with the output. It

seemed something was interfering with the signal. Rowridge was running normally, as far as their guys were concerned, so it wasn't the big transmitter over on the Isle of Wight and he didn't think the more local relay masts were the issue. It looked like something closer to home. Malcolm puffed out some air and shook his head. It was late afternoon and the light was fading fast. He was going to have to check the mast on the top of Salisbury Broadcasting House - and he was going to have to do it now.

He pulled on his anorak; it was getting dark and raining lightly outside the small window of the IT & Engineering room. He walked past Rob's office where the boss was now back behind his desk, the police having returned to base with Gemma. The guy looked knackered, which was no surprise.

Malcolm cut through reception, squeezing past the damp tissue-wrangling queue for the book of condolence and grimacing sympathetically at the harried-looking receptionists pinned to the switchboard. He went on through to the other wing of the building where a locked door presented itself opposite the ladies' toilets. Malcolm pulled out one of a dozen keys and let himself through to the narrow stairwell on the other side. The iron spiral staircase led up to the top of the building and beyond. Its landing was inside a small four-sided cupola, two metres across, with windows on three sides and a door out onto the roof. The access area for the mast was usually thick with pigeon shit, so he was glad of his stout work boots as well as the anorak as he stepped out into the cold drizzle.

The base of the station transmitter was in a brick-built channel, hidden from view of traffic out front and the car park out back by the slant of two sections of grey-tiled roof. This was designed to give engineers a little shelter from the wind when they were required to attend to the mast for maintenance or repair. Of course, once you climbed up a little way, you got everything the weather could throw at you, but the mast was only five metres higher than the roof.

He hoped the problem would be obvious; maybe a deceased pigeon clogging up a crucial working part.

Malcolm stopped dead. Working parts of the mast were indeed somewhat clogged. But not with a pigeon. Something much larger was blocking its signal. Something with dyed blonde hair and a pink jacket. The chief engineer felt himself go hot and cold as he neared the shape; his mind wrestling with repulsion and recognition. The face, above the gaffer tape, was puffy and grey; eyes open and staring, hair uncharacteristically messed up. A toppled over BBC Radio Wessex mug lay just below the taped left hand, a dribble of hot chocolate pooling on the brick. Beside it lay a cake tin with its lid partly off. It looked as if a picnic had been going on up here.

The fingers, bunched up inside the twists of tape, were tipped with glossy pink shellac nail polish. This was the convincer. Although Malc's mind continued to flip around in horrified denial, there was no doubt that the body taped to the foot of the mast was none other than much loved former presenter of mid-morning Sheila Bartley.

Just hours after she'd hosted the on-air memorial for her colleague, she had followed his example and got murdered herself.

15

Of course Gemma Henshall wasn't their girl. Kate had known this just by talking to her back at the radio station. But there was no doubt that a text had been sent from her phone to Dave Perry's, to suggest meeting for a drink. They had no choice but to take her back and get the interview taped.

Gemma said she'd been at home with her parents in the window of time when Perry had been killed; they could verify this up to a point but it wasn't the most reliable alibi. Parents were apt to lie for their offspring in a crisis.

'Who had access to your phone last Friday afternoon?' asked Kate, watching the girl's pale face closely as she and Michaels sat opposite her in the interview room.

'Nobody,' said Gemma. 'I mean... nobody that I knew of. I had my phone with me all the time.'

'Whereabouts?' asked Michaels. 'In your bag? In your pocket? On your desk?'

Gemma bit her lip, searching her memory. 'Probably in my bag,' she said. 'But maybe on my desk for a while.'

'Did you go to the toilet?' asked Kate. 'And leave it behind?'

'I don't know... maybe...' Gemma looked around her helplessly. 'I guess I must have because it wasn't me who sent that text. I mean...' She shuddered visibly. 'Why would I ask Dave out for a drink? I didn't even *like* him!'

Kate saw something in her reaction and leaned in, resting her elbows on the smooth-topped grey table and speaking gently. 'Gemma, was there a particular *reason* you didn't like Dave Perry?' She saw the girl flush.

'I... he... he was just...'

Kate saw Michaels open his mouth and glared him silent.

'He kind of came on to me,' mumbled Gemma. 'He didn't really want to take no for an answer.'

'Are you saying he forced his attentions on you?' asked Kate. It was a quaint figure of speech for an ugly situation, but she didn't want to put words into the girl's mouth.

Gemma studied her hands, clasped tightly on the table top. 'Kind of,' she said. 'I mean - not, like assault, as such. He was a bit grabby. He kind of took advantage, squeezing past me, that kind of thing. He put his fingers in my mouth once. He was giving chocolates out and he just...' She shuddered again. 'So... there was no way he was getting an invitation to drinks with *me.*'

Kate nodded. 'For the record, that *is* assault,' she said. 'Did you complain?'

'I tried,' said Gemma. 'I set up a meeting with Rob Larkhill. I was just about to tell him about it when you arrived.'

'Right,' said Michaels. 'So... we came along just at the wrong moment?'

'I suppose so,' said Gemma. 'Can you, like, dust my phone for prints or something? See who else picked it up?'

'That's happening now,' said Kate. 'What do you think would have happened if you'd had a chance to talk to your boss about Dave Perry's behaviour?'

Gemma sighed. 'Nothing, probably. I mean... Dave was *The Voice of Wessex*. Big doings. I guess I hoped Rob might just have a word with him... but even if he had I would probably have had to move onto another show. It would have been too awkward.' She shook her head. 'And breakfast is the *best* show to work on. It's brilliant experience. I don't want to go, I just...' She paused, as if realising for the first time that the problem had solved itself.

It had clearly been on DC Michaels' mind too.

'So it's quite good for you, in a way,' he said. 'Dave Perry not ever coming back.'

Gemma gaped at him, realisation dawning in her eyes that she had just revealed a whopping great murder motive. If she *was* Dave Perry's killer, thought Kate, she was doing an Oscar-worthy act of dumb innocence. Which left the question... *who* had sent that text?

The interview room door was rapped loudly and Sharon Mulligan put her head round it. 'Um, have you got a moment?' she said, glancing from Kate to Michaels. 'Something's come up.'

———

IT WAS FULLY dark by the time Kate got onto the roof of Salisbury Broadcasting House. SOC had already set up some arc lighting around the scene. Happily, at this height and contained by a pitched roof on either side, there was no need to shelter the body from public view.

De'ath had got there ahead of her and was already finishing up his preliminary findings.

'Is it the same as before?' asked Kate, the wind whipping at her hair and prompting her to pull it back into a ponytail.

'Yes and no,' said De'ath. 'Yes, she's been gaffer-taped to a mast, I think we can all surmise *that*, and no, she wasn't stabbed in the side. I can't be sure until the post-mortem, of course, but I'm betting she was drugged. There's no sign of struggle. The taping looks... neater, as if it was carried out in a more leisurely fashion.'

'Any microphone sock in her airways?'

'Yes,' he said. 'The same make it would appear.'

'Jesus,' said Michaels. 'That's the one who was on air first thing this morning, wasn't it? Sheila Bartley. We interviewed her at lunchtime.'

Kate found herself wondering who was going to get into the breakfast show seat the next morning - running an on air memorial for *Sheila* this time. If radio presenters were a superstitious type she could guess that the rush for the top job might have slowed a little this time around. Back at the landing of the narrow stairwell the station manager and the chief engineer were sitting on the top step in a state of shock. The engineer had discovered the body after investigating a problem with the signal from the mast.

The last time Sheila had been seen appeared to have been mid-afternoon, in the newsroom. How she had ended up on the roof of the building was the key question. Staff didn't normally go up there; not even for a crafty smoke. They went to the sin shelter down in the car park.

Sheila wasn't a small woman; it would have been very difficult to get her up there while drugged or dead, in a fireman's lift. She would have had to walk up the steep steps herself. The mug and the tin of what turned out to be home-made rock buns were a clue. Perhaps someone had suggested a breather... a bit of perspective. A mug of cocoa and some cake up on the roof after a harrowing day. Who, though?

'That tin,' said Rob Larkhill, when Kate went to speak to him. 'I... I think I know where it came from.'

'You do?' Kate raised an eyebrow.

'We get things brought in all the time, for the presenters,' said Larkhill. 'Listeners get very attached. Sometimes they like to bake.'

'They bake?'

'Oh yes... and some are a little more persistent about it than others. Finley Warner - we spoke about him this morning - he drops stuff off maybe two or three times a week. Cakes, biscuits, knitwear...'

'Knitwear?' repeated Michaels.

'Yes, some pretty awful jumpers come into SBH,' said Larkhill with a sad wince.

'Not always awful,' interjected Malcolm Bright. 'Some of them are good; we get some really nice listeners too, you know. Not all of them are bonkers. Some of them, you'd even take a chance and eat the cake. Like Eileen in Old Milton and Maria in East Gower - you get to know them quite well and they're alright. They come along to the OBs and we chat.'

'What are OBs?' asked Michaels.

'Outside broadcasts,' explained Bright. 'We take the show out on the road sometimes and broadcast live from summer fairs, festivals, things like that.'

'So... Finley brings in cakes,' Kate went on, eyeing the tin beside the body.

'He does,' said Larkhill. 'And they're probably fine. He's probably harmless, but...'

———

'A STALKER?' said Kapoor.

It was fresh news for the CID briefing at seven - on a day of so much fresh news it had needed to be delayed from six.

'Possibly,' said Kate. 'Finley Warner is his name. Twenty-three, ardent fan of the station. Maybe too ardent.'

'At twenty-three?' said DC Mulligan. 'Well that marks him out as a weirdo for a start. He should be listening to Radio One on his phone and livin' it large, not cosying up to bloody Neil Diamond by the family wireless.'

'*Sweet Caroline*... played repeatedly by Fred and Rose West as they dismembered their victims,' said Conrad Temple, nodding sagely. It took them all a moment to realise he was joking.

'Is Warner on his way in?' said Kapoor. He looked tired as he stood to one side of a display of photos which had recently been updated with images of Sheila Bartley along-side Dave Perry; a pair of gaffer-taped effigies on metal masts.

'Yes,' said Kate. 'The station has his address on file; he's been on a lot of tours and attended every Radio Wessex carol concert. He lives with his mum and dad. They're coming in with him. He was allegedly stalking Josh Carnegy, the overnight guy. Josh didn't mention it in our first inter-view with him, but he'd stayed in the building so we went through this with him in a second interview. He says Finley Warner has waited for him outside the security gate three times in the past month - at around 1.10am, when Josh gets out after his overnight show.'

'And what has he done?' asked Kapoor.

Michael's consulted his notebook. 'He brought a tin of macaroons on the first occasion, then a tin of, umm, shortbread. And, just last week, in the early hours of Saturday morning, a jumper. With a photo of himself and Josh Carnegy screen-printed onto a cotton patch and stitched onto it.'

'Anything else?' asked Kapoor, with a small shake of the head.

'Um... well he might have left some flapjacks by the back gate last night,' said Michaels. 'Josh Carnegy found a tin there, with his publicity postcard taped to it.'

'Are all these gifts available for forensics?' asked Kapoor.

'Probably not.' Michaels replied. 'Josh says he threw them all away - including last night's offering - in a bin outside the station, on his way home. We checked and there are daily council refuse collections, first thing,' said Michaels. 'But other tins might be knocking around the station. The guy's a serial baker and - what did they call him?' He glanced at Kate.

'Jock botherer,' she supplied. 'So... we're waiting on forensics for the tin of cakes found next to Sheila. Death says the mug of cocoa had Rohypnol in it. So, maybe that's the way she was easily persuaded up onto the roof and then killed without any struggle...'

'So... do we think this *jock botherer* somehow made it into the station and persuaded Sheila Bartley up onto the roof without getting noticed?' asked Kapoor. 'Perhaps drugging her first... or maybe once she was up there? And then suffocated her? All without getting noticed?'

'The building was full of people,' said Kate, thinking aloud. 'All staff and freelancers were in to speak to us and a lot of them just hung around, talking about the murder. Reception was chock-a-block with hysterical Radio Wessex fans, queuing to sign a book of condolence; other press were lurking about too. It was mayhem. So if he was going to pull off another murder, it might have been quite a good time to try it.'

'Security camera footage?'

'We're going through it now, guv,' said Mulligan. 'Although there aren't many cameras. I mean, you'd think there would be in a place like that, but they're only in reception and on the front and back entrances. One in the newsroom too, but it doesn't cover more than half the floorspace.'

'And the access to the roof?' Kapoor went on. 'How easy?'

'The door to the stairwell up to it needs a key,' said Michaels. 'The chief engineer has one on his key ring and another on a hook in a cupboard - it's still there. Another engineer has a key too; he's been away in Italy all week.'

Kapoor sat down on a desk, sagging. Kate didn't blame him; she was pretty exhausted too. It had taken a lot of plasticine mollusc-moulding to make herself tired enough to sleep the previous night and she guessed she hadn't got more than four hours in total. She would love to go home and crawl into her bed right now, but she guessed she was going to have to speak to this Finley Warner first. It made her uneasy just thinking about it. A twenty-three-year-old fixated on a radio station pitched at a fifty-plus audience was already ringing alarm bells; not because he was likely to be a serial killer but because he was likely to be a simple soul who could easily be *mistaken* for a serial killer. She had met the type before. Police had their own share of groupies; usually kids with obsessive tendencies. Kids of all ages.

Obsessions could, of course, drive you to do bad things. To make stupid decisions.

All of a sudden Lucas Henry was back in her mind.

16

Sid should have been back in his sock. Lucas knew he should. And yet here he was, hanging around again, nestled in under his crew neck jumper.

'Hello stranger,' said Mariam, getting up as he made his way to her at their usual table in the Pheasant Inn. She kissed him on both cheeks, her spicy perfume gentle on his senses. In her fifties, with long dark hair and almond-shaped eyes, she still looked fantastic, but although many of his old university mates had madly fancied her a few years back when she'd been running one of the art degree courses, Lucas had always had a different kind of appreciation for Mariam.

His mother was somewhat absent in his life; had been for most of it one way or another. She lived in Spain with her new husband these days but even when they had lived in the same house she had been more interested in reaching the bottom of a bottle than connecting with her only child. So he guessed he must have been seeking a mother figure when he went to university... and maybe Mariam had been after a son figure. All he knew was that she had been caring and inspiring and had not even judged him when he dropped out and threw his degree away in the second year.

Throughout his wandering across Europe over the next decade they had stayed in touch, and when he'd returned to Wiltshire earlier that year, she was the first person he had sought. It had worked out pretty well for them both; the exhibition of abstract paintings she had encouraged from him had sold out - and handsomely.

'You've got that look again,' said Mariam, as they took their seat near the large open fire.

'Please don't break into a Simply Red song,' said Lucas. 'I *will* have to kill you.'

'It would be a kindness,' conceded Mariam, with an understanding nod. 'But no - I mean it. You're wearing that distracted look; something is buzzing around your mind again. And probably around your neck too, if I know Sid.'

Lucas ran his hands through his straggly dark hair and sighed heavily. 'I think I've just complicated my life a bit more.'

'Oh no,' she said, eyeing him over her glass of Prosecco. 'What have you done?'

'You know this BBC guy they've just found dead?'

'Everyone in Salisbury knows,' she said. 'Don't tell me... you killed him.'

'No. But I found him.'

'You're joking!' She put down the glass and peered at him incredulously.

'Wish I was.'

'And when you say *found* him, I'm assuming you didn't just stumble blindly upon the body?'

'Not exactly.' He related the unhappy events of the last two days, concluding with the visit from Chief Superintendent Kapoor.

'Well, that's a good thing, anyway,' she said, waving at a waiter who was wandering around with the fish and chips she'd ordered for Lucas. As soon as the meal was in front of them she asked for a Peroni for Lucas and then went on. 'It's good thing if the head honcho knows you're the real deal. I mean, he ought to know it anyway, after everything you did for them in September. But people need ocular proof, you know that.'

'Hmmm,' said Lucas, taking a swig from the Peroni bottle, ignoring the tumbler that came with it.

'It's not that, though, is it?' she intuited. 'You've found a body and tangled with the top copper in Salisbury but it's actually all about the girl, isn't it? You're in some kind of state about Kate.'

'You're very poetic this evening,' he observed.

'Stop dodging and fudging,' she said. 'This old bird ain't budging.'

'Really, I'm going to have to-'

'Kill me? Yes. Sorry. But you know what I'm saying. You've been hung up about Kate Sparrow for weeks... months. And you still haven't spoken to her, have you?'

'I told her we should talk, when she phoned me at the bungalow,' he said. 'She agreed.'

'So... set something up. Maybe bring her here and buy her dinner. You and she have got to have this thing out.'

'I don't even know, exactly, what this thing *is*,' he said, limply.

'Well, let me tell you while you eat your dinner,' she said. 'You were best friends with Zoe Taylor and Mabel Johanssen. You found Zoe's body in that quarry but you never found Mabel's. You were suspected of murdering them both. You never got charged, because you *didn't do it,* of course... but mud sticks and people can carry suspicion for a lifetime. Or until the real killer is found. So now that you've realised she knows who you are, you're wondering if Kate suspects you - even though you saved her life. How am I doing so far?'

He had a mouthful of cod and batter so he just nodded and rolled his eyes.

'And this reticence about speaking to you after everything that happened in September... you think it might be because she *does* suspect you. Even though, as I might point out again, you *saved her life*. And that other woman's. And god knows how many others if that killer had gone on with her sick art project.'

'Alright, alright,' he said, reaching for more salt and vinegar. 'Yes.'

'Not alright. You meet her again at the radio station, have a little Siddy freak out down inside your shirt, and the next thing you know, you've found a body for her.'

He blinked and put down his knife and fork. 'Are you suggesting I'm bringing her corpses like some kind of courtship offering?'

'That *does* sound more like a cat,' she acknowledged, with a rueful shrug. 'OK. Forget it. I'm not a psychologist.'

'Because I can think of better ways,' he said.

'So why don't you? Ask her out to dinner, I mean?'

'Because it's all messed up,' he said, shaking his head. 'The little sister of my... I mean, she was *ten* when I knew her before. Just a kid.'

'And now she's a grown woman,' said Mariam. 'What's the problem? Is it that you see Mabel in her and that haunts you?'

He paused and considered. 'Actually, no. They don't look that alike, apart from the blonde hair. And more than that, their energy patterns are worlds apart. Kate's nothing like

Mabel. It's just all the history, that's all. It would be like sowing seeds in poisoned soil.'

'So tell me,' said Mariam, digging into her mushroom risotto. 'I've never asked you this before and you don't have to answer... but what do *you* think happened down in that quarry?'

He rubbed his face, thinking. 'I should know,' he said. 'But I don't. Whenever I try to find the truth, it's just a blur. People say that dowsing for people too close to you, when it's *really* important, just doesn't work so well. You can't be a clean conduit for the energy to flow through - you're all twisted up with fear and love and you just scatter the frequencies.'

'So, forget the dowsing. What does your rational brain tell you?'

'That they were in the wrong place at the wrong time,' he said. 'Some psychopath came through and found them and... killed them. But I don't think Mabel died in the quarry. I think she was taken somewhere else, far away. I didn't get any sense of her anywhere after that day.'

'Did you try? After they found Zoe?'

'Did I try?' Lucas gave a dry, humourless chuckle. 'Mariam, I've never stopped trying. I have tried for years. When I went travelling it wasn't just because I was running away from Wiltshire.'

'You were searching the continent for her?' Mariam took another sip of wine, her brows drawn down. 'Bloody hell, Lucas, I never realised, I thought you were finding *yourself!*'

'Well, there was a bit of that too,' he acknowledged.

'Tell Kate,' she said. 'Fix up to see her and just tell her what you've told me. What have you got to lose?'

Lucas didn't say anything. There was *always* something to lose.

'I need a pee,' he said, and excused himself for a few minutes. He didn't actually, but he suddenly felt pinned and wriggling under Mariam's line of interrogation and he wanted it to stop. In the gents he stared at his reflection and tried to make sense of it. He had the face of a normal man; an innocent man.

But there was guilt in his eyes.

17

'I'm not a stalker!'

Finley Warner looked very affronted; baffled even. He glanced around the interview room as if he couldn't understand why he was in it.

'I'm just a fan,' he went on, his smooth face awash with hurt. 'I take them cakes. They *like* cakes. That's why I take them in.'

'But you were waiting outside the back gate in the dark for one of them... three times,' said Kate. 'Don't you think that's a bit stalkery, Finley?'

Finley folded his arms across his burgundy jumper and sat up a little straighter. 'My mother has always said the personal touch is important. How can I give the personal touch when I never get to *meet* Josh? He hardly ever comes on the OBs and he's never there in the daytime for the studio tours. So how else was I going to meet him? I had to catch him at the end of his shift.'

'By waiting at the gate in the dark?' said Michaels, raising an eyebrow. 'Would you like it if someone waited outside your house in the dark and suddenly jumped out and said hi?'

'But it's not his house,' said Finley. 'I wouldn't go round his *house*. That would be rude!'

'How often would you say you visit BBC Radio Wessex, on average?' asked Kate.

'Oh - two or three times a week, probably,' he said. 'I'm like part of the family; that's what Moira on reception says. She's nice. I like Moira.'

'Do you go into the building, beyond reception, at any time?' Kate pressed.

'Oh yes,' he said. 'I'm on the Listener's Board. We get to go on tours around the station every three or four months. I like the tech, you know. The old Studer B67s - the reel-to-reel machines they used for editing packages back in the old days - they're great. Digital editing is quicker and more precise but there's much more *soul* about a reel of iron oxide ribbon and a razor blade and splicing tape. I had a go at it. I changed British Broadcasting Corporation to British *Broadcorping Casteration*.' He grinned proudly.

'So, you know your tech,' said Kate, impressed. 'Have you ever tried to get a job at the BBC?'

'I might one day,' he said. 'But for now my mum needs me to help at home. I'd like to drive the old radio car,' he went on. 'It's got a retractable twenty-five-foot mast. It goes up with hydraulics. The new VERV ones are more efficient but the old one... it's got much more *soul*. I sat in it and put up the mast once.'

'Finley, how well did you know Dave Perry?' asked Kate.

Finley's face fell. He looked at his hands. 'It's awful what happened to him,' he said.

'What happened to him?' asked Kate.

'He got asphyixiated,' said Finley. 'On the Shrewton mast.'

Kate and Michaels exchanged glances. There was *detail* here.

'Well remembered,' said Kate. 'Do you know anything else about it?'

'It's a relay transmitter and serves about 800 homes,' he said. 'Main transmitters can't reach all areas, especially those blocked by land masses, trees and buildings, so relay transmitters receive signals and relay them on. Many of them are increasingly defunct now that the BBC and other broadcasters are using WiFi and satellite technology but they are kept in place as backup, for when the satellites fail.'

Kate suppressed a smile. 'I meant... about the murder of Dave Perry.'

'It's awful, what happened to him,' repeated Finley, his eyes down again.

'Do you know anything about what happened to him?' asked Michaels. Kate was pleased to hear the care he was taking with his tone. She really didn't need him to start playing Bad Cop with someone like Finley.

'Only what I heard on the radio,' said Finley. 'He was asphyxiated. They found him on the Shrewton mast. It's a relay mast.'

'How many times did you meet Dave?' said Kate. 'Did you like him?'

Finley looked around the room as if seeking clues or prompts. Eventually he said: 'I met him six times. Dave didn't like me.'

'What makes you say that?' said Kate.

'I used to do the Mystery Voice thing every day but Dave told them I couldn't keep doing it. I had to let other people take a turn.'

'What did you think about that?'

'Mum said he was just trying to be fair, because I kept getting it right and other people had to have a chance too,' said Finley. 'But he didn't like me. I heard what he said when he was off air but I was still connected and he didn't know. He said I should get a life. He said I was a *jock botherer*.' He glanced up at them and his brow, under a fine brown fringe, settled into a crease. 'That means someone who annoys the presenters.'

'How did that make you feel?' asked Michaels.

Finley frowned harder still. His mouth settled into a thin line and he breathed hard through his nostrils. 'Not happy,' he said, at length.

'Can you tell me what you were doing last Friday, Finley?' said Kate. 'After 8pm?'

Finley looked confused for a moment and then his face cleared. 'I was at home. I had my dinner at six and then watched TV with Mum and Dad. I went to bed at ten and I listened to Josh until I got sleepy. Then I got up at midnight, because I'd set my alarm, so I could have a shower and look nice and go and take Josh his jumper.'

'Did you go out on your own?' asked Kate.

'Yes. I took the car,' said Finley. 'I'm allowed to drive the car. I'm a good driver.'

'Are you sure it was that late?' asked Michaels. 'Are you sure you didn't go out a bit earlier and then meet Josh later on?'

'I *am* sure,' said Finley. 'Why would I go out earlier?'

'Finley, did you meet Dave Perry first - before you met Josh?' Kate asked.

'No!' Finley seemed to cotton on, at last, to what they were driving at. 'Wait! Do you think I killed him?'

Kate said: 'For the benefit of the tape, DC Michaels is showing Finley Warner a metal tin.'

Michaels held out the tin, in its clear plastic bag. 'Do you recognise this tin, Finley?' he asked.

Finley nodded.

'Finley Warner is nodding,' said Kate, feeling a sudden droop of tiredness coming over her. She really hated where this was going.

'What is it?' asked Michaels.

'It's one of the tins I used to put cake in,' he said.

'Are you sure it's yours?' said Michaels.

'Yes. There's a dent in the corner. I did that when I dropped a bottle of HP sauce on it.'

'Finley - can you explain how it came to be on the roof of Salisbury Broadcasting House today?' asked Kate.

Finley considered. 'I expect someone took it up there,' he said.

'Did *you* go up there?' asked Michaels.

'Yes,' said Finley.

18

R ob Larkhill gazed across the newsroom and let
out a long sigh. It was quiet at last. Empty. Only
the drivetime team were still in. Mike Tierney
still had half an hour left on air, straining to sound normal
when he was handling fall-out from Dave Perry while
simultaneously holding back the most shocking story the
drivetime audience might ever have heard - that a *second*
well-loved presenter had been murdered.

Rob knew it was hopeless, trying to hold off telling their
listeners about Sheila. It was only a matter of hours at best.
The news was probably already trickling out to the staff. He
was pretty sure Malcolm had said nothing - he was a solid
guy; very dependable - but the building was full of *journos*
for god's sake. They were never going to miss the sudden
switch of police activity to the roof of SBH without asking a
few questions. Initially most of them had assumed it was
part of the ongoing Dave Perry inquiry, but by the time he'd
gone down to reception and cleared all the fans out of it -
taking the Book of Condolence outside and getting one of
the receptionists to oversee the dwindling queue in the chill

November air while the revolving door was locked - questions were being asked and glances exchanged. More so when he'd asked all the freelancers and non-rostered staff to go home but keep their mobiles on, because the police would want to ask them further questions over the next day or two.

He'd spoken to DS Sparrow, while they were still up on the roof, asking whether he should keep everyone in the building like something out of an Agatha Christie whodunnit. He was very relieved when she'd said: 'It's been at least two hours since Sheila died; I think that ship has sailed. We will, of course, want to interview everyone - but practically speaking it'll be tomorrow now. Please make it clear to everyone that failure to make themselves available again tomorrow will suggest they may have something to hide.'

'Do I have to tell them about this?' he asked, trying not to look across at the body.

'That's your call,' said Sparrow. 'But I would be getting advice from further up the line now, if I were you. This has escalated from a one-off killing now. Before, Dave Perry's place of work might not have been relevant - but now it's seems clearly related to BBC Radio Wessex. I'll be speaking to our own media liaison officer in the next hour.'

'Oh god,' he whimpered. 'Are *you* putting out a press release?'

She looked tired, leaning against the doorway to the stairwell as her colleagues moved like solemn bees around the roof. 'I doubt we'll put anything out before late morning tomorrow. There's too much to do - and Sheila's next of kin will have to be informed. Of course, if it gets out anyway, we'll have to make some kind of statement to the press. You should know all about that.' She gave him a shrewd look.

It seemed her priority now, thanks to that biscuit tin, was

to speak to Finley Warner, and then to start with the staff again, first thing tomorrow. He'd had to pass on all their addresses and contact details; it looked like the police might be going to their homes this time. Rob shivered. Talking to Finley first was what he'd thought they'd do. Finley was clearly an obsessive and an obvious suspect. Hopefully he was already under arrest.

English Regions was sending down a PR person first thing tomorrow, to help him manage all the fallout. Thank god. He didn't want to handle this all on his own anymore. Being managing editor of a radio station was always a stressful thing; like being the dad of a talented but highly strung family. To make good radio seven days a week out of an array of needy, complicated presenters and producers, well - you did what you had to.

With most of his staff cleared he had finally been able, in the early evening, to get Malcolm to temporarily switch off all of the remaining employee's ID access codes to the side corridor and reception, so they could bring Sheila's body down to be taken away for the pathologist to examine without anyone else stumbling on the grim procession. He'd taken the precaution of sending the receptionists home early beforehand too. Outside, the fan queue had dried up and the rival media had gone. There was nobody to peek in and see the zipped-up body bag going through on a stretcher and down through engineering to the garage where a discreet ambulance waited. He'd stood by the old radio car, watching. It all seemed so surreal. Like in a TV crime drama. The pathologist guy was even called De'ath. Seriously.

If you'd told him, this time last week, that he'd be managing such an almighty clusterfuck, he would have found it very hard to believe. He kept seeing Sheila's face, warm and alive in Studio A - and then cold and dead on the roof. *Jesus.* If only he never had to look at another reel of gaffer tape again.

He had contacted only a handful of staff to warn them about what was coming; Mike and Lewis - just in case anything got out while they were still on air, and James and Gemma, preparing them for yet another presenter in the breakfast hot seat, then Jack and Spencer, to tell them that Jack would handle mid-morning alone and Spencer would step in to breakfast. They were all staggered at the news of Sheila's death, but also very professional about stepping up and handling the output.

'We won't run anything about Sheila until we absolutely have to... when it gets out to other media,' Rob had told each of them. 'Her next of kin haven't been informed yet - the police are trying to track down her daughter in Australia. They say they won't put out any statements until late morning at the earliest... but I will be monitoring the news through the night, just in case it gets out. Promise me you will keep this to yourself.' They all had.

When it was time to see Mike and Lewis off, he patted their shoulders as they walked to the staff exit door. 'You did well,' he said. 'Be glad you're on drive. If it gets out overnight it'll be Spencer handling the worst of it tomorrow morning.'

'Which of us is going to be next?' gulped Mike, looking sweaty and ill, while Lewis stared through to the carpet of floral tributes on the steps and shook his head.

'Nobody else from Radio Wessex is going to die,' said Rob. 'The police are going to find this killer. Soon. I'm sure of it.'

When they'd gone there was nobody else in the building. It was calm and serene; the empty newsroom bathed in the silvery light from the BBC News 24 feed monitor, which

ran constantly, day and night. Josh wasn't coming in. Rob
had called him to say that they would stay with the English
regions opt tonight, letting a Manchester-based overnight
presenter take the strain, to save him from more Dave Perry
outpourings. He didn't tell Josh about Sheila; everyone
would find out soon enough. In many ways it was good for
Josh to keep his distance from all of this. When Rob gave
him the breakfast slot, as he'd been wanting to do for some
time, it would be good for Josh to go in as a fresh face and
voice - unconnected with all the wreckage across the
airwaves this week.

Rob rubbed his face and sank into a chair by an empty
desk to watch the news feeds. Who would be a radio station
manager?

19

'He's good for it,' said Michaels, standing at the window of CID and watching Finley walk out across the lamplit car park with his mum.

'Hmmm,' said Kate, gathering her jacket and bag.

'He couldn't look either of us in the eye when he talked about Dave Perry. Did you see that?'

'I'd say he's on the autistic spectrum,' said Conrad Temple, who had observed the interview through a two-way mirror. He gathered his own coat and bag a couple of desks away. 'You can't read too much into that eye contact thing.'

Michaels snorted. 'Yeah... well, that's what everyone says, isn't it, when they're being weird? Oh... I'm on the spectrum... I can't help myself. It's a great get-out. No - it's him. We should have kept him in.'

Kate yawned, too tired to manage Michaels and his narrow world view. 'We didn't have enough on him,' she said. 'You know that. Stop being a twat and go home. We've got another early start. Team briefing and press strategy at six-thirty.'

Finley had readily admitted to going up on the roof of

the radio station. He'd described the transmitter in great detail, proud to have been able to see it, on a recent tour, with half a dozen other listeners. He hadn't, he said, been in the station earlier that day. He had come to the front steps and left some flowers when he heard the news about Dave Perry (even though Perry had been unpleasant about him) but he didn't have time to wait in the queue for the book of condolence - he had errands to do for his mum.

Kate, on a fresh tack, had asked him what he thought about Sheila Bartley.

'She's a regional radio treasure,' he said, clearly reciting from her biog on the BBC Radio Wessex website 'She's worked there for 43 years. She's got a cat called Dinky and her daughter lives in Australia. She likes Cherry Bakewells.'

Michaels had been ready to spring her death on their interviewee, but she'd wound up the interview before he could. She couldn't see the sense in it - not yet. Once it was out there, maybe. Tomorrow. Kapoor was working through the media strategy with Lucy, their press liaison officer, right now.

'You wait and see if I'm not right,' Michaels was muttering now, watching their suspect amble back across the front car park and around the corner.

'You're tired, Ben,' she said. 'Go home.'

He stomped off, giving Temple a baleful look.

'What do you think?' Kate asked the crim psych.

'I'm not sure,' he said. 'Not convinced but... I wouldn't rule him out either. Is anyone going to collect all the offerings on the steps? And the book of condolence? Our guy is probably lapping up all the drama - he might have brought flowers today, or signed that book. I'd like to get a graphologist to take a look at all the handwriting in the book and on the cards.'

Kate nodded. 'Good thinking. The manager is going to camp out at the station all night, apparently. He's hoping the news won't get out before the breakfast show. Can't say I blame him - what a shitshow to manage in front of a live audience! Kapoor says he won't do the media briefing before midday; cut the guy a little slack. Anyway... I'll get uniformed to go down and collect all the flowers and cards and the book. You can frolic through them to your heart's content in the morning. Or overnight if it takes your fancy. Me... I've got to fill in the policy book and then I've got to go home and get some sleep.'

She ran downstairs to the parade room and found a couple of uniforms willing to collect the listeners' offerings from the station steps. 'You could check in on the manager too,' she told them. 'He could probably do with it, poor sod.' They agreed and headed out immediately. She wished she could post them there all night - in theory they should be up on that roof for a good 24 hours longer, guarding the scene, but there just wasn't the manpower available right now. She'd had to make do with cordoning it off thoroughly with crime scene tape; trusting she would know if it had been tampered with. It was far from ideal, but the station was undermanned. Their new DCI was not due to arrive until February. As it was, Kate was unofficially acting DI these days. She hoped to be the *actual* DI if all went well in the next few months. Kapoor had suggested she take the inspector's exam last year and she was due to complete the second part in a few weeks and then... she *might* get that promotion.

So filling out the policy book wasn't something she was going to cut corners on, no matter how weary she was. She spent a couple of hours explaining all that had occurred so far and the thought processes behind the decisions they'd made across the past day and a half. The interview with

Gemma Henshall had been enlightening. The tech guys had found the text that had been sent and deleted. They'd sent her home soon after, looking baffled and freaked out. It could all have been an act, but Kate wasn't convinced Gemma was a contender for their murderer. Even if she'd gone loco on Dave when he'd tried it on once too often, Kate really couldn't picture her doing the same to Sheila. She mustn't rule it out, though. It wouldn't be the first time she'd encountered a clever female killer.

It was gone ten-thirty when Kate finally walked to her car and paused by the driver side door, key fob in hand. BBC Radio Wessex was a ten-minute walk from here, across the lower end of the town centre. Her brain felt clogged with the day's events; a tangled mess. She needed to freshen it up a bit. A night of quality sleep would help but she knew herself too well. Going home, stuffing a convenience meal and going to bed wouldn't work well for her. She would lie awake, dog tired but unable to switch off. There would be more plasticine action.

She needed a bit of a walk to cool her brain and she felt the urge, now, to take a look at the radio station building by night. The cold air was pleasant on her face as she walked along the flagstone pavements. She could feel her feverish thoughts cooling and relaxing. If she'd had her gear with her she would have been quite tempted to go for a run around Guildhall Square; she hadn't run for weeks.

But her townie boots and a brisk walk would have to do. She pulled a woolly scarf from her satchel, wrapped it around her neck and headed through the heart of the small cathedral city, past late night diners and boozers heading home, couples stepping out of restaurants and pubs, and knots of teenagers lurking around the Odeon. Within a few minutes she was at the quieter side of the city centre and within sight of Salisbury Broadcasting House. As she approached she could see the two uniformed officers had indeed gathered up all the listeners' cards and flowers; the steps were empty. She hoped the listeners wouldn't get upset about it, but what could she do? It was only logical to check through potential evidence. She turned down a side alley towards the BBC staff car park at the rear of the building. The wide sweep of dark tarmac was protected by high iron gates, and bathed in soft security lighting. She could buzz through from here and Larkhill would no doubt pick up on the newsroom intercom.

Go home, Kate, she told herself. She turned around and walked back up towards the main road, but, before she got there, she noticed a bin, surrounded by a thicket of low bushes. They'd learned the city centre bins were emptied daily, before nine - this was the main reason she'd not pursued searching for the biscuit tin that Josh Carnegy had dumped on the way home. But this one looked full to over-flowing. She wondered if it *had* been emptied in the last couple of days. *Go HOME, Kate!* But no... it *could* still be in there after all. Their refuse collection intel could be faulty... or there might be staff shortages at the depot.

She dug a pair of latex gloves from her satchel and let out a sharp exhalation as she realised that, yes, she really *was* going to do this. *Why can't you just ask one of the PCs?* her sensible voice demanded. *What are you UP to, Kate?*

It was probably all for nothing, anyway, but she held her breath and wrestled the bin open. It wasn't easy. Designed to be too much trouble for drunken teens to mess with, the entire outer cylinder had to be lifted off to access the bin bag liner and its contents. It was heavy and awkward but she was determined and a minute later the black plastic cara-pace was on its side in the shrubs and she was pulling the bag out and tipping out its contents. It could have been worse - most of it was fast food packaging and dribbly cartons of fruit juice or cola. She upended the bag fully, shaking out some promising weight at the base.

And there it was. A Marks & Spencer shortbread tin, right at the bottom. She picked it up and found a damp, ketchup-smeared publicity postcard of Josh Carnegy taped to the lid. She gave it a shake and something thudded around inside. Prising off the lid, she found a dozen flap-jacks. Bingo.

She fished one of her larger evidence bags from her satchel and put the tin inside it. Then, in a moment of social conscience, she put all the rubbish back in the bag, returned the bag to its inner cylinder and then put the heavy plastic covering on top. Panting from the effort, she looked around, half expecting to find a couple of her uniformed colleagues standing and staring at her with amused bafflement. Or maybe someone else. But nobody was around. It was just her, a bin, and a tin of flapjacks. *Oh, the glamour, Kate Sparrow. This is what you signed up for!*

She peeled off the gloves and shoved them on top of the other litter. Then she slid the bagged tin into her satchel, breathed out slowly, and walked back to the city centre.

This is evidence, Kate. So you're going to take it straight back to the station, aren't you?

'Yes,' she told herself. 'Of course I am.'

Because the last time you messed around with evidence you nearly got suspended, remember?

'True, but I also probably saved my own life with that action.'

Oh for fuck's sake! You're not REALLY thinking of taking this to Lucas, are you? SERIOUSLY?

Kate shook her head, as if her other self was walking

along next to her, staring her down. She hadn't decided. What did the tin tell them, anyway, even if Finley's DNA was all over it and the baked goods inside? He would happily admit to leaving that tin for Josh to find, she was sure. Her interview with him earlier had revealed that any number of the Warner family M&S biscuit tins could be lying around the BBC Radio Wessex premises. Finding one alongside Sheila's body didn't mean Finley had carried it up there, killed her, and then left it as some kind of bizarre calling card.

And she, amid all the other questions, had actually forgotten to ask about the tin left outside the gate for Josh to find. Now that she had it, she could show it to Finley in a second interview, tomorrow, along with the one found on the roof - see if the tins triggered any response.

Or you could take this one to Lucas.

Hmm. She couldn't help thinking it. Lucas might be able to pick up something straight away from this tin. Better still... *both* tins. Did she dare go back to the station and collect the other one?

Kate - stop it. You're not thinking straight. Go home, get some supper, get some sleep. Talk to Kapoor about this in the morning and ask for permission to show both tins to Lucas Henry before you bring Finley back in.

It was definitely the most sensible course of action and she would definitely have done it.

If only she hadn't then turned a dark corner and walked straight into Lucas Henry.

20

Lucas had finished a leisurely dinner with Mariam and then walked her to her car, giving her a warm peck on the cheek before heading off along the side street to find his motorbike.

'Look, dear one,' she had said, pausing as she unlocked her Beetle. 'This thing with Kate Sparrow isn't going to go away. You might as well take my advice and talk to her. Get it all out in the open.'

He hadn't argued. He hadn't agreed either. His policy, for many years now, had been simply to go with the flow. If their paths crossed again; if the patterns led him back to her... well, then he might think about it. Might see it as a sign. And they *would* meet again, of course. The inquest for the Runner Grabber case was only three weeks away; he and Kate would be in the same court room. They would *have* to see each other. He felt jangly at the thought. Good jangly? Bad jangly? As ever, where Kate was concerned, it was both. Sid buzzed with anxious static just at the thought of her. Jangly, yeah.

Twenty seconds later he rounded the corner into the

poorly-lit side street where he'd left the Triumph, and jangly suddenly peaked as he smacked straight into Kate Sparrow.

She gave a shout and raised her arms in an instinctive martial arts defence pose and then, a second later, did a kind of shocked cough, and stepped back, peering up at him, open-mouthed. Her scruffy ponytail fluttered in a sudden breeze and her wide eyes glittered. 'What the flying *fuck?*' she murmured.

'Well, yes, nice to see you too,' he responded.

'I was just... I...' She shook her head and blinked. 'Lucas... have you been following me?'

He looked past her shoulder and then back over his own, raising both palms. 'Um... is it possible to follow someone by walking *directly at them?*'

She shook her head and wiped a hand down over her eyes. 'Sorry. I'm just... really tired. And a bit spooked. I was just thinking about you and then - bang!'

He screwed up his face. 'Not sure whether I should be charmed or scared. When you start thinking about me, shit usually hits the fan not long after.'

'Oh, shit's been hitting the fan pretty much non-stop for the past thirty-six hours,' she said, leaning against a Pay & Display machine and hugging her satchel to her chest.

'Any leads on Dave Perry?' he asked, suddenly wondering about the vibrations from that satchel.

'It's not just Dave Perry now,' she said. 'There's been another one.'

'Another one?' he echoed. '*Shit.* Is Wiltshire the serial killer's county of choice now?'

She closed her eyes wearily. 'Feels like it today.'

'Who else?' he asked.

Kate opened her eyes and regarded him for a moment,

gnawing on her lower lip. 'I shouldn't say, but... it's bound to get out soon anyway. It's Sheila Bartley.'

He put his hands to his mouth, genuinely shocked. 'Seriously? No! My aunt *loved* Sheila. She met her quite a few times. *Jeezuz*. What happened to her?'

'Much the same as happened to Dave Perry,' said Kate. 'But on the antennae on top of the radio station this time. Gaffer-taped up again. Mic sock in the airways.'

Lucas felt genuinely appalled and quite personally affronted. Sheila was someone from his youth; a benign and comforting presence on the radio on days when his mum could tolerate the noise. Those were the good days. He had always associated Sheila Bartley with warmth and stability. 'Who would *do* something like that?' he muttered.

'Funny you should ask,' said Kate. She gulped and looked around.

'There's nobody here,' he said, not needing to check. 'So you might as well relax your death grip on that satchel and show me what's inside it.'

'It's evidence,' she said. 'Probably useless evidence, but still something I felt compelled to burrow into a bin for.' She opened the satchel and produced the source of some very interesting patterns that had been winding through his mind for the past couple of minutes. Inside a plastic bag he could see the red tartan and stag's antlers of a Marks and Spencer's shortbread tin.

'I think this-'

'Sshh, don't tell me,' he said. 'Wait.'

He put out a hand and rested his fingertips on the tin. As soon as the connection was made he felt a belt of shock which made him suck in his breath and blink. She was watching him carefully. 'Are you getting something?' she asked.

He stepped away and pressed his hand to his chest, flattening Sid against his skin beneath his jumper to ease down the prickles and stings that were chasing around his ribcage like static. He shouldn't know this. It made no sense. He had seen the body but he had not touched it. He had stayed *well clear* of the crime scene. All he had done was report it - he was *not* involved.

Even so.

'Whoever held that tin,' he said, 'also gaffer-taped up Dave Perry's face.'

21

J osh Carnegy was pissed off. Dave Perry was dead. It was a shocker, but nobody had liked him much. True, the guy *had* been a bit of a legend and very good at what he did. Josh had grown up listening to him. It would be hard for everyone to fully accept that The Voice of Wessex was now permanently silenced. And in such a macabre way.

But he was more pissed off than freaked out. Larkhill had dropped boulder-sized hints over the last few months that he had him in mind for breakfast. Josh had done his time on the overnight shift, charming all the oldies, the cabbies and the truckers and having next to no social life - and he really *deserved* this. But recently he'd begun to think he'd be stuck in the midnight shift for another decade - maybe two. Because Dave fucking Perry had become too much of a personality and he wasn't leaving the hot seat unless someone killed him and dragged him off it.

So now someone *had* killed him. He was gone. And who did Larkhill get to step in? Fucking *Sheila Bartley*! It was beyond belief. After all he'd done. He'd cornered Rob by the staff coffee machine after he'd spoken to the police that afternoon, and demanded to know why.

'It's just temporary,' the manager had told him, shoving coins into the slot and not meeting his eye. 'At a time like this a familiar voice... a safe pair of hands... it's what the listener wants.'

Josh would have said more, but then Gemma had been marched past them by two of the coppers, looking pale and shocked. She'd texted him later, to say she'd been released and something about a text from her phone being sent to Dave Perry on Friday night... a text she knew nothing about. He felt bad for Gemma. He knew her from their old hospital radio days and they sometimes swapped texts or calls. She had been saying for weeks how she would *love* him to get breakfast. She hated working with Dave Perry.

Josh walked through the dark towards SBH, still seething. To top it all, Larkhill had taken him *off air* tonight. Just like that! He'd phoned to say he didn't want Josh to have to handle all the Dave Perry fallout when he was alone on air - and so the station frequency had just opted over to the English Regions feed and some banal overnight guy based up in Manchester. Josh knew his fans would be furious. For a moment there, though, he'd thought Rob was going to add that he would need a good night's sleep because he was going to come in and do breakfast. *At last.*

But NO. Such. Fucking. Luck.

'Josh - your time will come, I promise,' Rob had said. 'But not like this. It wouldn't be good for your brand, showing up in the middle of all this hysteria. Trust me. We'll talk about it when everything's settled down.'

Yeah. Right. He knew he should have stayed at home but he was charged up and fizzing with the injustice of it all and Rob had given the impression he might be pulling an all-nighter at SBH so... he might as well drop in and keep the boss company. Be useful. Get him talking. Cement his position. He'd put way too much work in to let this slip away now.

He reached the building and was surprised to see all the flowers and cards had disappeared from the front steps. Hmm. The listeners wouldn't like *that.* He guessed it might be the police, trawling for clues. As if the killer would be dumb enough to show up with a bunch of evidence tied up in a ribbon or written in a card.

He took the side road to the back gate, pulling his ID out of his jeans pocket and dragging its elastic out of the yo-yo clip so he could buzz in. The sensor beeped and flashed green in response and the tall iron gate clunked as the electronic lock disengaged for three seconds. He pushed it and entered the car park. The lighting was very low and he found himself shivering involuntarily, as if someone was crouching in it, watching him. Ghosts, maybe. There ought to be a few around here.

Then there was a thud and a metallic rumble. Instinctively he pressed himself back into the dark alcove of the staff doorway, watching from the shadows as the heavy duty security shutter across the garage began to rise. A thin strip of light began to grow fatter across the tarmac as the garage revealed itself. The two VERVs were parked inside it, along with a couple of BBC Radio Wessex liveried pool cars, still and dark. But at the far end, the old radio car was starting to move, pulling out of the dock, its headlights sweeping across the far brick wall and arcing around.

What the *hell?* It was gone eleven. Who would be going out to do an OB at this hour? Maybe it was Malc, driving his beloved broadcasting antique home for some engineer's TLC.

But as the car swung out and past him, still pressed, invisible, into the alcove, he could see it wasn't Malc in the driving seat.

Josh gaped and felt chills sweep over him.

What the *actual FUCK?*

22

Kate left Salisbury Police Station with a large bump under her jacket; as if she'd been suddenly and speedily impregnated by an alien. The motorbike helmet she was hiding had been borrowed from Traffic. It wasn't a bad fit and she didn't think anyone would notice it was gone. It had been up on a shelf in there for months, gathering dust.

Lucas was sitting astride the Triumph in a side lane a minute's walk away, waiting for her to climb on and ride pillion with him. She had tried to get him to travel in the Honda with her, but he'd been adamant.

'No. Not a chance. One - I'm not getting into another police vehicle unless I'm tasered into it.' He'd shot her a dark look and she'd smiled guiltily - his recent adventures with tasers had been partly down to her. 'And two - the bike is going to be much better. We'll be going off road.'

'How can you possibly know that?' she'd said.

He touched his chest and his head and shrugged. 'I just do. So get on the back.' He'd indicated the motorbike, parked just behind her.

'I've got no helmet,' she'd protested.

'Live a little.'

'No - we're way more likely to get stopped if one of my colleagues spots me without a helmet on!'

He conceded it was a fair point, so she'd left him to bring the bike to an agreed rendezvous and made her way back to the station to get that helmet. She was mightily relieved that she hadn't encountered anyone else after slipping in through the staff entrance around the side.

She rested the helmet on the back of the long leather seat and pulled her hair out of its scruffy, drooping ponytail. Let loose, it allowed for a better fit. She put on the black protective shell, clipping it under her chin. She was happy it was a nondescript civvy helmet and not a police one which would flare up like a beacon in passing headlights.

'It's a good look on you,' said Lucas, raising his eyebrows. Taking the piss. 'If you keep your bag tight between your front and my back, it'll help. I'll be in contact with the tin that way, more or less, while we're riding.'

She nodded and did as he suggested, getting astride the seat behind him. She was glad of the barrier between them; having to wrap her arms around his waist was quite intimate enough without pressing her chest and belly up against his spine. He glanced back at her, through his lowered visor, to check she was ready. She tucked her feet up on the rests and held up one thumb and then the engine throttled up and they moved, sedately, away. It wasn't like they'd roared off into the night like a scene from Easy Rider, but she still felt a tremendous surge of excitement as they picked up speed through the darkened streets. She had no idea where Lucas was taking her and a large part of her was scared. Really scared. Because she strongly suspected she was going to be meeting a killer this night.

Assuming she hadn't already met one.

———

LUCAS WAS in a state of extreme flux. The dark frequencies emanating from that tin reached out into the night, tracing down through Sid in a strong silken thread, diffusing through his chest and then shooting out somewhere around his solar plexus to throw surging tendrils and arrows across their route. It was hard to simply describe it as a mind-map - this kind of navigation seemed to suffuse his entire being. He was being guided to the west of the city and out into the countryside. Had he been alone it would have been intense enough. He would have zoned completely into the dowsing state and followed his instincts without too much analysis. Not thinking *too* hard was often the key to the most efficient dowsing.

But wrapping her hands around his waist was DS Kate Sparrow and *that* threw a whole load of conflicts across his dowsing state. He should probably have left her behind and gone alone... but there was no way she was going to hand that tin over to him if she wasn't coming along too. He supposed he should be glad she hadn't radioed for back up and brought the whole cavalry along with her. She was bending the rules again - which must mean she had some level of trust for him. Maybe he was wrong in his suspicion about her suspicion about him..?

Stop it. Focus.

Sid was right. More important matters were at hand. Because as well as a strong essence of the person he was increasingly certain had killed two BBC presenters, Lucas was picking up a quickening dread that more death was coming. The last time this had happened, he'd been proven spectacularly right, as the woman riding pillion with him could testify.

The energies weaving through him and plunging ahead into the dark November night had more dimensions than he could explain, one of them being time. Sometimes they could reach their probing fingers backwards for years or even decades... and sometimes they reached out and brushed the near future, warning him that time was not on his side...

23

F inley could not believe his luck. He had dreamed about this moment for years, ever since he'd first shown up at the Wiltshire Show with Mum and Dad when he was nine. It had been a sunny August day and the show was full of farm animals and fairground rides. There were exhibitions of dog agility, falconry and even some scaled-down Motocross in one of the penned fields.

There were marquees full of arts and crafts and food; cheeses and honey and home baking. You could bring your pet along and enter it into the Best Pet competition and he'd brought his guinea pig, Gloria, in a travel cage. The smell of the hot grass and straw, the canvas and the candy floss, he remembered it still.

But his most golden memory was the moment they encountered the BBC Radio Wessex outside broadcast unit - a caravan with open sides revealing walls hung with poster sized images of the station and its presenters. And, on its burgundy carpeted floor, a desk at which two *real life* presenters sat, with big headphones on and microphones, clad in grey spongey windsocks, positioned in front of them.

To one side of this mobile studio sat the radio car, its mast reaching up high above the crowd that had gathered there to put the faces to the voices they were all so familiar with.

Finley was amazed to discover that the presenters - Dave Perry and Sheila Bartley - were actually broadcasting *right now!* Across three counties hundreds of thousands of people were listening to every word they said, thanks to the microphones and the little desk with buttons and faders, and the mast which had travelled up and up into the sky like his telescope back home, Mum said, only much, much longer.

He had been absolutely entranced. Mum and Dad wanted to go on to the pet show and in the end Mum had taken Gloria along on her own, because it was too hot for the cavy to be cooped up in her carrier out in the sun. Dad had stayed with him right until the end of the radio show, which concluded with shouts and applause from the audience, egged on by Dave Perry getting to his feet and waving his arms in the air.

But while most of them wanted to queue to talk to Dave Perry and Sheila Bartley, and get signed postcard pictures of them, Finley really had eyes for the tech. He was mesmerised by the radio car and what it could do. Dad took his hand and they wandered across to speak to a man with a beard. Finley later learned this was Malcolm Bright, the station's chief engineer. Malcolm was very nice to him and had allowed him to press the button which brought the mast slowly down, folding steadily into itself like a series of connected, tubular Russian dolls.

When it was down, Finley had begged to be allowed to send it back up again. Malcolm had laughed and said *OK, but only once.* They had to pack everything up soon and get back to the station. So Finley had held the button, on the passenger side of the Ford Focus dashboard - keeping it pressed because if you stopped, the mast would stop too - until the whole thing had risen up again, taking its umbilical loops of wire with it. Finley could - quite literally - have pressed the up button and then the down button all day, but Dad said they had to let the radio guys get on.

Finley knew he had to move along. He couldn't expect them to let him go on playing with the radio car all day. But when he left, he took something with him. A new and abiding passion for the workings of local radio began to burn in him from that day forth. He had to know *everything* about it. *Everything.*

Mum and Dad thought it was a passing fad, like his thing for helicopters and, before that, his thing for old vinyl record players. But they were wrong. This was to be the love of his life. He started listening on an old transistor radio in his room, wearing out the batteries regularly because it was the constant soundtrack to his life. He got to know every presenter, although it was difficult to get to know the mid-morning and mid-afternoon guys, because most of that time he was at school. On the weekends and in the evenings he could listen in as much as he liked... except when Mum or Dad told him he *had* to go to sleep. Even then he would sometimes wake in the night and sneak the radio under the covers with him so he could hear the whispering tones of the midnight shift guy. Back then it was someone called Gavin Fletcher, who was nice, but nowhere near as nice as Josh Carnegy.

Of course, he got on air whenever he could, going in for quizzes and talking about any topics that a school kid could, charming the producers and researchers over the phone until *Finley from Laverstock* had become a regular on air. Sometimes they wouldn't let him on, though, and Mum had to explain that they had to be fair and let other people have a go.

He'd had his first station tour at the age of thirteen and found it electrifying. Especially the behind the scenes stuff with the engineers, who showed him the radio car again and let him sit in it. They showed him the old Studer reel-to-reel machines, too, which presenters and reporters used to use back in the nineties, to edit audio they'd recorded in studios or out on the road with small reel-to-reel recorders called Uhers. The Uhers had a leather shoulder strap and weighed a tonne. Not a literal tonne, but something that *felt* like a tonne, one of the reporters had explained.

When he was older, on another tour, he even got the chance to use the sticky tape and razor blades to do some editing with those silky ribbons of red-brown oxide, in special metal grooves. You used white chinagraph pencils to mark the places you needed to cut. You had to sign a form beforehand, because of the hazard.

But even though he often dreamed of it, part of him always knew he'd never get the chance to *work* at the station - to be the guy running the outside broadcasts and talking to other kids about how the radio car mast went up and down. He was too awkward around people. Even though he tried really hard he could never seem to work out what was *too much* and what was *not enough*. He was as smart as most men his age but he just couldn't seem to get a hold on the way other people operated. He was always being either *too much* or *not enough*.

Now, though, it seemed everything had changed. Today had been terrible. He'd been interviewed by the police and accused of being a stalker. He really hadn't expected that. It was awful. But what had happened since was wonderful. Just look what he was doing *now*! He was driving the BBC

Radio Wessex car to an extra special outside broadcast - *in charge* of the vehicle of his dreams. He could have got into one of the VSAT Enabled Reporter Vehicles but the VERVs didn't have the *soul* of the old radio car.

When he reached his destination, with the very special passenger he was carrying, there was going to be a really important live broadcast and it would be down to him to make sure it got out on air. It felt as if his whole twenty-three years of existence had been preparation for this moment. He was *getting a life.* Dave Perry, if he wasn't dead, would have to *eat his words.* For a moment, Finley almost wished he *wasn't...*

————

ROB LARKHILL WAS in a state of shock. He could smell the gaffer tape as he and Finley Warner sped through the dark, away from the city centre and towards the rural roads. Who would have guessed it would come to this? Finley Warner of all people? Sweet, annoying, childlike, psychotic Finley Warner. Of course he had already thrown a little suspicion on the guy because, with that stalking business, he *was* suspicious, wasn't he? Obviously not suspicious enough because he'd been interviewed but not arrested. What the hell were the police even *for*?

Honestly, he hadn't seen this coming until tonight. He'd been so wrapped up with the death of Dave Perry and then Sheila Bartley. He had thought - hoped - maybe it was all over.

Then Donna had said on the phone: 'It'll never be over, Rob. Not until they arrest and charge someone. I don't know about you, but I'm never going to be able to relax again until that happens.'

Rob had agreed. This whole thing was taking such a toll on him. Coming back to Radio Wessex had been fantastic, even with all its challenges. He was really beginning to make his mark, shaking up the scheduling and getting fresh blood in. Getting back together with Donna was also wonderful... but Dave fucking Perry just *had* to get murdered.

And then Sheila had to join him. Christ. What a week. What a brain-melting, nerve-shredding week. He'd always known the job would eat him alive, but not like this. Now he was on a journey into the dark, swallowing his fear, putting on a good show, but understanding that it was all going to end in another death. He breathed that gaffer tape stink again, felt the adhesive against his fingers, and tried to stay calm.

24

Kate felt her phone buzzing in her inside pocket as the bike sped on. She was in no position to answer it. She realised she had been due to arrive home hours ago and Francis might have started worrying. Although they had their own flats and were meant to be living grown-up, independent lives, her younger brother had taken to checking in on her much more since the dramatic end to her last case. Finding out she'd been moments away from being murdered by a psychopath had shaken him up a bit. He'd lost one sister already.

It was sweet but also a bit annoying, having to worry about him worrying about her.

Did he have just cause tonight, though? His sister was currently clinging to the leather-jacketed waist of a man who was riding through the Wiltshire backroads, almost certainly above the speed limit, following the directions of a lump of glass on a chain around his neck... which was getting *its* intel from a tin of flapjacks.

If that didn't sound batshit crazy enough to at least

mildly concern an anxious sibling, she didn't know what would.

She had no idea how long this journey was going to take. Part of her was enjoying it, though, if she was honest. She'd not done much biking in her time but had always loved the sense of freedom it gave her. She understood why some of the traffic guys stuck with their two-wheeled steeds for years - decades, even. There was a thrill in getting to the scene of a crime or accident when you could speed past slow traffic without having to clear your path with blues and twos first.

Another part of her, though, was getting uncomfortable and weary. It would have been easier, she had to admit, if that bloody shortbread tin hadn't been jammed under her boobs. Even through the thick canvas of the satchel it dug into her ribs and held her away from the natural curve of Lucas Henry's back. She longed to flip it around over her shoulder and fit herself properly against him. It would be warmer, too. The misgivings she'd felt earlier about this level of closeness to someone she was so conflicted about had vanished. She was too tired to care now; she just wanted to get comfortable.

She sensed that they were slowing down and wondered if they were close to the killer... or another victim. Soon she realised it was for a different reason entirely. In a lay-by just ahead of them was a roadside disco of red and blue flashing lights. *Shit!* Not a spot check, *please!* It was past midnight by now and this was the time of year when her colleagues in traffic started ramping up their pre-Christmas drink and drive campaign. A patrol car she recognised from Salisbury Traffic was parked up, its door already opening.

Lucas continued at a sedate pace and then, sure enough, an officer stepped out and raised his hand, his fluorescent jacket gleaming in the headlight, and waved them in to the lay-by. *Shit, shit, shit!* This was all she needed. To be caught out on the back of Lucas Henry's bike was going to be mortifying. And worse - it could mean they would lose their connection with the Gaffer Tape Killer.

Lucas slowed to a halt, tilting the bike a little as his boots found the cold tarmac. She hopped off the back as he kicked down the stand and switched off the engine.

'Good evening, sir,' said PC Bob Hartnett. She recognised his thickset build, his greying beard and his extreme chirpiness.

Lucas took off his helmet and said: 'Is there anything wrong, officer?'

'Not that we know of, sir,' went on Bob. 'We're just doing the drink and drive spot check lottery between now and Christmas and you're lucky enough to have won a party blower.' He held up a black unit with a white tube protruding from it. 'Have you had a drink in the last twenty minutes, sir?' he asked, cheerily.

'No,' said Lucas.

Kate hung around behind the Triumph, arms folded over her satchel and the helmet still on. She hoped and prayed Bob wasn't feeling too officious tonight and wouldn't ask her to remove her headgear and take a test too. As a passenger she shouldn't necessarily have to, especially if she stood there looking as sober as a judge and not suggesting she might be a danger to traffic.

'Had a smoke, sir?' went on Bob, taking the plastic wrapper off the tube.

'Not any more,' said Lucas, with a sigh.

'Tough to give up, isn't it?' empathised Bob.

'You should see my Twix habit these days,' said Lucas. He sounded remarkably chilled out.

'Just blow in here please, sir.' Bob held up the breathalyser and Lucas blew. Kate steeled herself. She had no idea whether Lucas had been drinking. He'd been out for the evening when she met him, so he could have been half-cut for all she knew.

Bob peered at the result and said: 'So you have had *something* to drink, then.'

'Yes - I had a bottle of Peroni about two hours ago,' said Lucas. 'Within the limit, isn't it?'

Bob peered for a bit longer, dragging out the drama, and she held her breath, praying he wasn't about to turn to her next. And then he *did* turn to her next. He peered at the helmet, narrowing his eyes. Oh *shit!* The helmet! The fucking helmet! She had literally taken it from the shelf above Bob's desk half an hour ago.

'Nice helmet,' he said, finally.

She patted it and nodded. 'Does the job,' she said, affecting a northern accent in a moment of wild improvisation. If she turned around right now he would catch sight of the little neon green sticker he must have put on the back and there would be an interesting conversation.

'I've got one just like that,' he said. She was about to northern up another response but then he turned back to Lucas and said, 'You're good to go. Keep it to the one bottle next time too and you'll have no arguments from me. Have a nice evening.'

Thirty seconds later they were pulling away and PC Bob Hartnett was waving them off with no obvious recognition of the helmet she'd stolen from him. She hoped to god he wouldn't catch sight of the sticker and give chase.

———

FINLEY TURNED the car off road and began to bump along a farm track, the headlights picking out the rutted route between high hedgerows; a few late insects flitting across the beam.

'Will he be here?' he asked. Robert Larkhill nodded. He'd promised that Josh was sorry about calling Finley a stalker, and that he was going to make it up to his number one fan. Josh and Finley were going to run a very special OB in the last hour of the overnight show. The manager had fixed it all up. All the way here they'd listened to some other guy in Josh's slot - someone based up in Manchester who was presenting to various parts of the south of England where radio stations didn't have their own overnight guy. He was *nowhere near* as good as Josh. It was quite offensive having to listen to him.

But Finley understood that everyone at BBC Radio Wessex had had a really bad day and that Josh needed a break. So he was just going to do this one little outside broadcast, opting into BBC Radio Wessex in the last hour. Normally Finley would be listening to the last hour in bed, drinking cocoa from his BBC Radio Wessex mug. Tonight he was out here in the wilds of Wiltshire, getting ready to play his part in the most important OB ever.

He drove on up the hill until the track ran out and it was just grass. This was where Josh would meet them; he'd been quite specific about the location. He seemed really keen to get there, according to the texts on Larkhill's phone.

I'm on my way. Don't do anything until I get there!

As if. This was all about Josh, wasn't it? Finley had always known they were meant to be together. His mum and dad hadn't believed him. Dad had said he needed to 'see someone' about his obsession; that it was unhealthy. If only they could see him now!

Finley stopped the car and put the handbrake on carefully. He was going to have some cocoa now. Here in the dark in the middle of nowhere, with the manager of BBC Radio Wessex. Did it get any better than this? Yes! After the cocoa, he was going to get the mast up.

———

JOSH SHOULD REALLY HAVE GONE HOME to bed. He should be getting an early night so he could go in again in the morning and speak to Larkhill about what he'd seen.

Why he had decided to come over all private eye and get into the pool car, he really didn't know. Maybe it was because he'd suffered so much anxiety about Finley Warner and now he had a chance to take back some kind of control - find out what was going on in that nutjob's head and get him to answer for it. How the fuck had he managed to steal the radio car? How did he know where to find the key?

Malc kept all the keys in a cupboard in the engineers' room. Everyone on station knew about it; you had to get your key from it when you took a VERV or a pool car; you signed a book to say you had the key. Malc usually locked the cupboard at the end of the day.

Except not *this* day. When Josh had run into the building, he'd failed to find Rob Larkhill there - or anyone else. He'd checked the cupboard and found it open, the radio car key missing, of course. He tried Rob's mobile but it just went to voicemail. Josh took a deep breath and dug out the card he'd been given by that blonde detective - the good-looking one called Kate Sparrow. He called the number and left a message: 'Um... DS Sparrow? This is Josh Carnegy from Radio Wessex. You said to call if I thought of anything... suspicious. Well... I've just *seen* something suspicious outside. Finley Warner... the guy who's been kind of stalking me... he just drove out of here in the radio car. I think he's taken it off on some kind of... I dunno... joy ride? I think he might be going to the Wiltshire Showground, out near Devizes. He's got a big thing about that site because that's where he first saw the radio car. I'm going to follow him in a pool car. You might want to send someone.'

She hadn't called back. It made him feel slightly foolish. With a *murder* investigation going on that week, maybe a car theft wasn't a big deal. Maybe Finley was just driving it round the block and would arrive back in five minutes to sheepishly park it. Still didn't answer the question of how he'd got into the garage in the first place, with no ID pass. Perhaps he'd stolen one from someone...

It was then that Josh decided to drive out to the show ground... check out his hunch. It would take about twenty or thirty minutes at this time of night. He wasn't entirely sure what he was going to do when he got there, but he was too wide awake, too wired to just go home and go to bed. If he saw Finley and the radio car up at the showground he wouldn't even get out of the car. He'd just call Kate Sparrow again and if she didn't pick up he'd dial 999.

And if he didn't see anything, he'd just drive the pool car back, report everything and go home to bed. He collected the key from the unlocked cabinet and headed down to the garage. He started up the beaten-up old Peugeot, shoving the seat back - whoever'd driven it last was clearly a midget - and shot out of the garage, giving the roll-down shutter a click from the pool car key fob, so it would lower automatically, in case Eileen from Old Milton decided to drop by next, and take a VERV for a midnight spin.

The gate opened automatically for him and he hoped someone back in the security hub, somewhere in Swindon, would take note of the activity down in Salisbury and maybe look into it. He doubted it though. He'd long since reached the conclusion that the remote security system was manned by a Miniature Schnauzer called Derek. Or someone just about as useful.

'Come on Carnegy,' he said as he turned left and gunned the 1.6-litre engine sluggishly up the hill towards the ring road. 'Let's see if the jock botherer's gone back to his birthplace...'

25

I t was dark out here. Countryside dark. Behind them was the pale glow of the city and ahead was nothing but an inky tree-lined horizon and starlight. There was a moon, but only a crescent. Lucas pulled up into an off-road track and brought the Triumph to a halt. Kate hopped off the back, relieved to be able to stretch. She couldn't see anything except a rutted farm track ahead of them, picked out by the headlamp on the front of the bike.

Lucas put down the kickstand and dismounted, switching off the engine but allowing the light to play out over the ground. He took off his helmet and shook his messy dark hair off his face.

'Are we lost?' asked Kate, flipping up her visor and inhaling the scent of cold earth and dying leaves. Not far away a male tawny owl called to its mate and got a mournful reply.

Lucas shook his head. 'I just need to take a moment,' he said, unzipping the leather jacket and snagging the pendulum out on its chain.

'What does Sid say?' she asked, pulling one heel up to her buttock and stretching through her stiff thigh muscles.

Lucas turned away from her and let the glass stopper drop and swing. She couldn't see much of what he was doing but as she did the other heel and thigh she caught glimpses of the chain, links glinting in the pool of headlamp light. She shivered as the thought occurred to her that she was out here in the dark, in the middle of nowhere with a man she barely knew; a man whose actions as a teenager had caused a great deal of doubt over his innocence. *Oh, stop it,* she told herself. *If you really think he's dangerous, why the hell are you here, risking your bloody career again?*

'Sid says this way,' he finally answered. He pointed along the track.

'Should I call for back up?' she said.

He shook his head. 'We need to go in quietly. I think we can ride a bit further but soon we'll have to leave the bike behind. We'll need to go in on foot.'

'Coppers do *know* about stealth,' she said, feeling she ought to defend her colleagues, although she saw his point.

'When we know what we're looking at,' he said, 'then you can call whoever the hell you want. It's just that... there's more than one pattern I'm picking up here. They're tangled. They're connected but they're coming from different places. We need to be careful.'

'I'm always careful,' she said. 'Let's go.'

He nodded, putting his helmet back on, and they both remounted the bike. He pulled away, taking care not to allow the engine to rev too loudly.

———

FINLEY GOT out of the car and looked around the field. He wished it wasn't so dark; he would have liked to see the scene he was about to create more clearly. He put the handbrake on and looked at his passenger.

'It's time, isn't it?' he asked.

He got a nod and he killed the engine, but left the headlamps on, carving a white channel through the midnight gloom, picking out grass and thistles waving in the breeze. He opened the door and stepped out, using his phone torch to check the sky above him for overhead lines. You never put up the mast near overhead lines.

But all he could see was a fathomless dark picked out above him; no power lines. No trees either. With a grin he reached back into the car and across to the console in front of the passenger seat where he found the big red button. He pressed it up and felt elation trip through him as the old motor immediately kicked in, driving the first stubby section of antennae up out of the roof of the car. It hummed its loud and purposeful song for a good thirty seconds until the mast was up at its highest height, reaching for the heavens, ready to bounce its signal from here to Shrewton or Tisbury or even across the Solent to Rowridge on the Isle of Wight - and then back to base, through the antennae up on the roof of Salisbury Broadcasting House.

He loved this thing. He knew it was just machinery but he loved everything about it. He'd sign away his soul to be its owner; *had* signed in fact.

He went around to the passenger door and opened it, grinning and shaking his head at the wonder of it all.

'Best bit comes next,' he said.

———

Rob Larkhill had managed to get a message out, quietly, when Finley was out of the car, sending the mast up, too excited to notice. He'd made the call using Siri. Now help was on the way.

'I know where you are,' said Donna, sounding much more together than he would have guessed she could be in the circumstances. 'I'm getting in the Jeep now. Don't worry. I'll get there in time... and I'll be prepared. I'll bring the twelve-bore.'

Now he just had to stay calm and keep Finley talking for as long as he could. As if his life depended on it. Which it very much did. The door opened and Finley's fanatical face swung down towards him. 'Best bit comes next,' he said.

Rob gulped. 'Take it easy, Finley, eh? Let's just have a little talk first.'

'OK,' said Finley. 'How about some brownies from the tin while we talk? And some more hot chocolate?'

———

The farm track was rutted and bumpy and Kate had to grab handfuls of Lucas's leather jacket so she wouldn't be pitched off into the undergrowth. The tin of what must by now be sticky oat granola jarred against her through the satchel and she began to wish that she'd just taken it to the evidence room and gone home to bed. What time was it now? It had to be past midnight. She wasn't sure how far they'd travelled because it had been pretty stop-start, what with the traffic boys and then the pendulum consultation.

She wasn't at all sure where they were, either. She'd felt as if they were heading west at first but it was long past the point where she had any bearings at all. They could have driven to the Cotswolds for all she knew. God, when would they ever get there? When could she take some kind of action... or find out this was all a wild goose chase and get Lucas to take her home?

She was startled out of her inner grumblings by a sudden flare of light throwing long shadows ahead of them. She felt Lucas start and he glanced in his handlebar-mounted mirror before turning to peer back over both their shoulders.

She glanced back with him and saw two bright, full beam headlamps heading up the track behind them. What the hell? Who would be out here at this time of night? Squinting, she could make out that it was some kind of four-by-four - a farmer's vehicle? Oh hell. What if they were just about to be accused of sheep rustling? She'd heard of thieves on bikes taking a whole flock away in a single night. It was the kind of thing her more rural colleagues were called out to deal with from time to time.

She could tell that Lucas was trying to decide what to do... speed up or pull over? But there was no room to pull over. The track was wide enough for a tractor but overgrown thickly on either side with hedgerows. The car, though, wasn't slowing down. If anything it was getting closer to them. Dammit. Some furious farmer was on their tail. She would have to get off the bike and get out her ID; talk him down. Maybe get his help.

She tapped Lucas on the shoulder, trying to shout this at him, but Lucas seemed to have other ideas. He was speeding up; the engine roaring up through the seat and bumping them harder over the ruts, ridges and potholes.

'Lucas! Shit! Slow down!' she yelled as her teeth jarred with each brutal landing.

But he wouldn't slow down. And nor would the vehicle behind them. It was suddenly coming for them at great speed, the bouncing headlights growing bigger as it gained on them, its engine growling. *Shit! This was getting serious!*

Lucas yelled back 'HANG ON!' and the bike suddenly lurched forward at full throttle, knocking the breath out of her for a second. She flung the satchel to one side and pulled in to him, anchoring her arms tightly around his waist and pressing her cheek to his back while her eyes rolled sideways, taking in the frightening acceleration of the vehicle on their tail.

It wasn't going to bump them, was it? Seriously? She couldn't believe a farmer would do that but she'd met a few on her patch and they could get very worked up. It was a stressful job, farming. Even so...

She let out an involuntary shriek as the metal grille of the four-by-four suddenly surged towards them, so close that the Triumph's red rear light was reflecting in it.

She turned around to wave a furious arm and shriek: 'GET THE FUCK AWAY!' at the driver.

Lucas swerved violently to the left and then to the right, trying to dodge the oncoming menace but finding nowhere to go. The undergrowth was thick, prickly and unforgiving; there was no way off this track - and no way to slow down and try to negotiate with this psycho driver because he was already nipping at the rear wheel and they were flat out now. Lucas must be doing seventy - maybe more. She could feel her loose hair flapping madly around her chin. If she had only been armed she could have turned around and unleashed a volley of bullets through the windscreen, but she was a British copper and she didn't think a stern warning was going to save them.

'HOLD ON!' screamed Lucas and suddenly they were slewing sideways towards a blur of twigs and leaves and thorns; some of them whipping against their shoulders. He must have found a way off this deadly track. It wasn't quite in time, though. Even as she spotted the dark break in the foliage zooming towards them she felt the massive jolt of the four-by-four striking the rear of the bike and sending its back wheel into a skid. She screamed as the full beam-lit night began to whirl around her, spinning her up and over and hurtling onward and downward and into an oblivion that could only end with a

CRUNCH

Yeah. That.

26

Lucas had no idea how long he'd been there. He awoke wrapped around the base of a slender tree trunk, his face in a prickly pillow of leaves and sticks, one leg pinned underneath the cooling engine of the bike. It was dark. Something liquid was running across his chin.

Light flashed. A torch beam. A rescuer?

No. Stay still. Stay completely still. Be dead.

The torch beam flailed through the dark, lighting twigs and shrivelled leaves for a second as it passed. Lucas thought about Kate for the first time. Where was she? Was she dead? If she wasn't dead, would she have the instinct to pretend to be? Because there was no rescuer out there; just someone hoping they were a pair of corpses.

The light faded; darkness reclaimed him. Then someone was touching his face.

'Lucas! *Lucas!*'

He felt her warm breath on his mouth as she leaned in to check whether his own was ever coming out again. He groaned something like: 'I'm here.'

'Stay still,' whispered Kate. 'Stay quiet. I don't know if they've gone yet. I was playing dead.' He felt her grab his wrist and run her fingers across his pulse point, double-checking.

There was a rumble of an engine and a distant red glow as the tail lights of the four-by-four moved on up the track and then the light faded out altogether and they were in pitch darkness. Whoever had run them off the road seemed to be satisfied that they were no longer a problem. They might very well be right. He wasn't sure he could move. He might be in a bad way; he couldn't feel his left leg at all.

'I'm going to lift the bike off your leg,' said Kate. 'Try to stay still, OK?' There was a sudden beam of mobile phone torchlight. 'I've tried to call for back up,' she said. 'But I can't get a bloody signal - not even for 999.' She rested her rectangle of light against a tree and moved across to the bike.

He heard her grunt and shift and then felt the weight lift away. More grunting followed as she tilted the whole thing up and over, so it fell onto its other side, with a crackle of torn undergrowth. There was a sudden warm surge of extra light as she found its headlamp switch and turned it on again; the crash must have knocked it out. He hoped the maniac driver was long gone and wouldn't notice.

The feeling was coming back into his leg. Spitting out leaf litter, he rolled over carefully, wincing at a belt of pain. 'Shit,' he grunted. 'Shit. Fuck. Bollocks.'

'Are they OK?' Kate was back at his side, her hands on his shoulders.

'My bollocks?' he asked.

She nodded, grimacing. 'Classic bike crash injury. Scrotums catch on handlebars. I'd hate to think there'll be no little Henries in the future.'

He checked. 'All present and correct,' he muttered. 'Leg hurts like hell, though. How about you?'

'Probably going to have whiplash tomorrow,' she said. She held up one bleeding hand. 'And I'll never play the cello again.'

'You play the cello?'

'Not since primary school,' she said. 'By the fourth lesson my mum made me promise to stop.'

He laughed, slightly hysterically.

'Let me take a look at that leg,' she said. 'And your head. How is your neck - your back?'

He sat up and moved his shoulders and head.

'Shit - stay still!' she said. 'You could have a spinal injury!'

'He took off his helmet before she could stop him. 'It's OK,' he said. 'It's my leg that took the biggest hit. I put out my foot to slow us down; I don't think I'm concussed.'

'But you're bleeding,' she said, kneeling in front of him and touching his jaw.

'A scratch from a branch,' he said. 'And you're bleeding too. If it's not a big deal for you...'

'The point is - can you get up?' she said. 'Just in case psycho driver decides to come back. I kept my eyes open, staring like a corpse, and I think that fooled him, but he didn't get to look at your face, did he?'

He struggled to stand up in the low cave of branches and found that although his knee was complaining bitterly, he could put some weight on that leg. 'I think I'm just going to have a nasty bruise,' he said. 'A bit of tendonitis maybe. It'll be worse tomorrow. But right now, yes, I can walk. Where to, though?'

'You're the pendulum guy,' she said. 'And we still have a killer to catch.'

He nodded and felt around for Sid, panicking slightly when he couldn't feel the old stopper under his jumper and then calming again as he realised it had worked around and was hanging down his back. He hooked it out and did what he could to steady himself.

'Biscuit tin,' he said, holding out his hand.

Kate passed him the satchel. 'You might as well put it on,' she said.

He did and immediately felt the connection again and a very strong frequency pulling him further west, higher up the farm track. He'd half hoped to find nothing; no connection left. Sometimes that could happen and a glitch like that would have given both of them an excuse to get the hell out of here. He really did want to get the hell out of here, with Kate, and get to somewhere safe. Because everything he was dowsing told him that one hell of a tangled up clusterfuck was awaiting them, half a mile up that track.

He sighed. 'Do we have to be heroes?' he said.

'If we know we can be,' she said, patting his shoulder. 'Or give up and lose all self-respect.'

He nodded, wearily. 'Let's get going then.'

'Is the bike any good to us?' she asked.

He stared at the fallen Triumph with an ache in his heart. 'It's not too bad but the noise of it - and the light - we can't afford that. We'll have to go on without it. On foot we stand a better chance of getting close enough to Clusterfuck Central to have some idea of what's going on. We get back on Hugh, and Psycho Driver will be coming after us again.'

'Hugh?' she queried, picking a twig out of her hair.

'It's a Triumph Bonneville.'

'I never had you down as a *Downton Abbey* fan,' she laughed, carefully making her way back to the track.

'It's more his *Paddington Bear* oeuvre that rocked my world,' he said.

27

The hot chocolate was all drunk before Donna made it to the radio car. Rob didn't think he could hang on much longer.

The headlights suddenly swung across the back window. Finley leapt out of the car before Rob could say anything. In the rearview mirror he could see Donna getting out of the Jeep; the interior light flicking on and casting her face into golden highlights and shadow. God, he loved her. She had come. She would do *this* for *him*.

Finley ran straight for her and then stopped dead as she got the twelve-bore out of the car and raised it, levelling both barrels at him. The shocked reaction of the jock botherer was palpable even from here, as he slowly raised his hands. Rob put the empty mug and the reel of tape down in the footwell and slowly got out of the car. This was going to be tricky. They would have to be very, very careful if they were to have any hope of a happy life after tonight.

He walked across the springy turf, taking long, slow breaths as Donna - a farmer's daughter with nerves of steel - held Finley in a horrified trance.

'Mr Larkhill..?' Finley burbled. 'What's going on? Why is Donna pointing a gun at me? Is this... is this part of the OB thing?' The wobble in his voice betrayed that he didn't believe that slim hope.

'It *is* part of the OB thing,' said Rob. 'You need to play along, Finley.'

'But... isn't Josh coming?'

'He's on his way,' lied Rob. 'Isn't that right, Donna?'

'He'll be here as soon as he can,' she said. 'And in the meantime, Finley, I'm going to need you to go back to the radio car and climb on top of it.'

Finley glanced back over his shoulder at Rob, as if seeking his permission. As if being held at gunpoint was genuinely part of a remote outside broadcast set up. Seriously - what a cretin. 'Do what she says,' Rob said. 'Get on top of the radio car.'

Finley turned around slowly. 'Can I put my hands down now?'

'Sure,' said Donna. 'Just keep them where I can see them.'

Finley stumbled a little on the uneven field and then made a beeline for the vehicle of his dreams. At least that was something, thought Rob. At least he was doing something he loved.

'Climb up,' said Donna, marching up behind, the gun lowered but at the ready with a second's notice.

'Um... OK,' said Finley. He scrambled onto the bonnet of the Ford and then reached up and across towards the base of the antennae. 'Is it safe?' he asked. 'I mean...'

'It's fine,' said Rob. 'Get up on the roof and sit yourself right up against the mast.'

Finley planted his lace-up boot on the windscreen, his face puckered with concern and confusion. However deluded he was, it was clear he was finally picking up that this night's adventure wasn't panning out quite the way he had hoped. No favourite presenter making a surprise OB appearance on air, alongside his all-time number one fan. No chance to be the assistant tech op, making it happen. Instead, he was up on the roof of his beloved radio car, well away from that big red button and the other smaller buttons and backlit dials he had been so diligently learning to use.

Rob walked around to the passenger side, reached down into the footwell and retrieved the reel of gaffer tape that his gloved fingers had been clasping, on and off, for the past couple of hours. 'Take this tape, Finley, and tape up your legs.'

'What..?' Finley squinted at him, his confused face uplit by the Jeep's headlamps.

'Tape your legs together,' repeated Rob. 'Around the ankles and then around the knees. Make it tight.'

'But... but I can't get down again if I do that,' said Finley, with a break in his voice.

'He's bright, this one, isn't he?' said Donna, raising the shotgun again. 'Do as he says.'

Finley's teeth were beginning to chatter. He bit his lips together and nodded, taking the heavy reel of silver-backed tape and pulling out a stretch. He wound it around his ankles and then ripped the tape off at the reel end.

'Good,' said Rob. 'Now around your knees.'

Finley wordlessly wrapped his knees three times and ripped the tape off again. Then he looked up at them both, realisation dawning over his simple features. 'You... you killed Dave Perry,' he gasped. 'I heard he got taped up like this.'

'Focus, Finley,' said Rob, 'I want you to wind the tape

around the base of the mast *and* around your waist, until you're nice and secure.'

'Why?' Finley asked, incredulously. 'Why do you want me to do this?'

'Because I don't want you to fall off the car when I start driving it,' said Rob.

'But,' squawked Finley. 'But... you can't drive the radio car with the mast up. An alarm will go off!'

'True,' said Rob. 'An alarm *will* go off, strongly advising against driving the radio car with the mast up. But you *can* actually ignore the alarm. It doesn't immobilise the car.'

'But it's dangerous,' said Finley.

'So's this,' said Donna, levelling the shotgun at him. 'Better hurry up.'

Finley began to wrap the tape around the mast and his waist, passing it from hand to hand, back behind him, in awkward loops.

'Keep going,' said Rob. 'Three or four times, nice and tight.' He walked across to Donna and said, in a low voice, 'What kept you?'

'I had a bit of a problem on the track, on the way up,' she said.

'What kind of problem?' He felt a surge of fear. As if this night wasn't stressful *enough*.

'Two people coming up here on a motorbike,' she said.

'Shit! Who?'

'I don't know, but don't worry; they're not a problem any more. I ran them off.'

'What?' He felt a pulse of amazement at what this woman was capable of. 'You mean..?'

'They're deep in the undergrowth,' she said. 'They're not coming out again any time soon. If at all. Problem solved.'

He shook his head and let out a shaky breath. 'This time

tomorrow, we can forget about all of this. Put all of this behind us once and for all.' He turned and saw that Finley was now fully taped up to the mast.

'Did he sign?' asked Donna.

'He did,' said Rob. 'I made him sign all kinds of stuff; said he had to so he could have clearance to drive the radio car. He didn't waste a second checking anything, stupid bastard.'

'Show me.'

He pulled an envelope from his pocket and extracted a piece of paper. On it, printed in Times New Roman, were the words: *I'm sorry. I just wanted to be part of the BBC Radio Wessex family. But Dave Perry laughed at me and called me stupid, so I killed him. I killed Sheila Bartley too, because she said I couldn't be her friend and she didn't want my cakes. But now I'm sorry. I can't stop feeling sorry. And I can't take it any more.*

At the foot of the paragraph was Finley's big, scrawly signature.

'That's brilliant,' she said. 'And it's got his prints all over it, yes?'

'I got him shuffling the papers around a bit,' said Rob. 'His prints will definitely be on it.'

'But not yours?'

'Gloved up all the way,' said Rob, waving his vinyl-clad fingers.

'One thing I've been wondering,' she said. 'How could he have put the mast up when he's taped to it? That's a dead man's switch, isn't it? You have to press and hold or it stops.'

'There's a remote, too,' said Rob. 'It's in the car. We'll put it into his hand afterwards.'

'It is a really cool way to do it,' said Donna. 'If that bloody radio car was the centre of my world I might do the same.'

'I'm done!' called Finley. 'What's going to happen? What is all this about?'

'Are you going to tell him?' Donna asked.

'I might as well,' said Rob. 'Poor little shit deserves to understand it, considering he's taking the fall.' He walked up to Finley and took the diminished reel of tape from him.

'Finley, would you believe me if I told you it's all about love?' he said.

28

'Shit - my battery's down to six per cent,' groaned Kate, waving her phone in the air. 'If I can keep it alive a bit longer, we might get high up enough for a decent signal. Bloody hell - there should be at least ONE provider covering 999 on this patch!'

'Haven't you got a radio?' asked Lucas, limping along as fast as he could, beside her.

'No. I'm off duty. Signed it back into the charging bay back at the station before I left.' She waved the mobile a little higher, groaning with frustration.

'Forget it,' said Lucas. 'Your guys won't get here in time anyway.'

'How can you *know* that?' asked Kate, tucking the phone away in her pocket and leaving Lucas to use his - equally hopeless for signal - for the torchlight. 'I mean - I thought dowsing was just about finding stuff... or people. I didn't think it could tell the future!'

'It can't,' he said. 'But... the patterns... the frequencies I pick up, they all vibrate in a way which tells me things. I can read extreme emotions in rocks and bricks and trees, even, if something violent or just really intense has happened there. I can also pick up a sense of... I don't know... velocity, I guess you could call it. A sense of how fast something is travelling or unravelling. I can read trends and patterns like a weather forecaster... or like a doctor, reading symptoms.'

He stumbled in a muddy pothole and she put her hand out and grabbed his arm, doing a bit of her own reading at this point. He was in pain. A lot of pain. God, she needed back up. Why the hell had she jumped on the back of a motorbike with him? She should have brought a team with them.

But Lucas would never have gone for that. His talent was seriously blunted by the presence of those coppers, who still hated his guts for embarrassing them back in the autumn. In truth, this *had* been her only option. It was going to be very difficult to explain at the morning briefing, though. If she ever reached the morning briefing.

She wasn't too great herself. The bike crash had left her feeling woozy and shivery. Regaining his balance, Lucas pulled his arm away from her, steadier now, as they journeyed on up the dark track, and she instinctively put her hand into her jacket pocket and found the smooth lump of plasticine. Digging her nails deeply into it gave her a faint sense of control. She let out a long breath and pushed on. 'We must be close, surely, by now,' she said. 'This track has to end somewhere!'

'There,' said Lucas, pausing to point to a pale glow on the horizon.

'That looks like headlights to me,' said Kate. 'Is Psycho Driver waiting up there for us?' Before he could answer there was a burring in her pocket. She whipped out her phone. 'There's a bar!' She waved it in the air. 'I've had a message come through!' She accessed the screen with her thumb print and opened the voicemail.

A familiar voice rang out of the speaker. 'Um... DS Sparrow? This is Josh Carnegy from Radio Wessex. You said to call if I thought of anything... suspicious. Well... I've just *seen* something suspicious outside. Finley Warner... the guy who's been kind of stalking me... he just drove out of here in the radio car. I think he's taken it off on some kind of... I dunno... joy ride? I think he might be going to the Wiltshire Showground, out near Devizes. He's got a big thing about that site because that's where he first saw the radio car. I'm going to follow him in a pool car. You might want to send someone.' The call ended.

Kate and Lucas stared at each other. 'Is this the showground?' Kate asked.

Lucas nodded. 'It's just fields... but yeah, it could be. A lot of farmers rent them out for events in the summer.'

'Was *Finley* our psycho driver?' asked Kate. 'Did he just try to kill us? Shit! I didn't have him down as a killer. I really didn't. Fuck, fuck, *fuck!* Michaels was right, I should have kept him in overnight and we wouldn't b-'

'Stop it.' Lucas grabbed her wrist; his fingers cool against her skin. 'Your instincts are good. Don't assume anything. We need to get over to that light source and then we're going to find out.'

'Wait - I've got a signal now,' said Kate. 'I can call for back-oh *shit on a stick!*' She nearly threw the useless chunk of metal and glass into the bushes as the whole thing conked out, battery spent. 'Why now? *Why?!*'

'Kate,' said Lucas, clasping Sid against his chest with one hand and pressing on. 'We don't have time for this. We really don't.'

She hurried after him, dread tying a knot in the pit of

her belly. For the second time in an hour, she wished she was an American cop, carrying a gun. Although she had no desire at all to see the UK go the way of the States, with a gun-toting vigilante in every street of every town, at times like this her martial arts prowess seemed woefully inadequate. She would love to be packing a Glock or a Beretta right now.

The track was reaching its summit and broadening out into a field. Although her eyes had grown accustomed to the dark it was still difficult to make out much about the land around them, especially as the bright source of light, a two or three minute run across the field, was throwing everything else into deeper shadow. There were headlights - two sets of them - and a warmer glow spilling from inside the vehicles. The sky above was almost purple and she could just about make out hills on the horizon and the looming shape of a pylon in the distance.

Lucas broke into a limping run. 'This isn't good,' he puffed. 'This isn't good at all.'

'Wait! We need a plan!' she called out, running to catch him up. He didn't reply but kept moving, lurching along determinedly, in spite of his injury. 'Where are you *going?*' she hissed, catching up with him. Because he wasn't heading towards the headlights. If she wasn't mistaken, he was running at a wonky, painful, full pelt for the distant pylon. What did he plan to do? Climb up it and get a better view?!

But no. Suddenly he stopped dead. 'Here,' he said.

'What - *here*?!' she gasped, skidding to a halt. 'There's nothing here!'

'No...' He spun slowly around, suspending Sid by an inch of chain between his knuckles. 'There's nothing here *yet.*'

'DAVE PERRY WAS A SHIT,' said Rob Larkhill.

In spite of everything that was happening, Finley was still shocked at the language. BBC personnel didn't talk like *this*.

'He was a shit from day one,' went on Rob. 'Right back at the start of his career. I started my career at Radio Wessex too, you see, all fresh-faced and idealistic, straight from university. I adored radio, every bit as much as you do, Finley.'

Finley nodded, dumbly. He didn't really know what to say. The roof of the radio car was cold and damp through his jeans and he was deeply confused about why they wanted him to be here, all taped up to it.

'I was a BA... you know, a broadcast assistant,' said Rob. 'But I knew that I was going to go a lot higher than that. I had big plans. I did all the usual stuff, planning shows, jacking guests, recording packages, doing the What's On bullies. I took the listener calls in tele-in, I went along as a gopher on the summer roadshows, I learned the radio car and did OBs in the middle of nowhere. I loved it all.'

Finley nodded again, vigorously. *He* would love all of that too.

'I even got together with a girl; someone I really loved,' said Rob.

'You're so sweet,' said Donna. She wasn't holding the gun up any more. She had broken it so that it folded over like she wanted to reload it. Although she had no need to because she hadn't fired it. Finley was glad she hadn't fired it.

'And she liked me, too,' said Rob. 'We were getting on just fine. Apart from Dave Perry. She worked on his show...

he was the afternoon jock back then. I used to do packages for it and sometimes help in tele-in. I had a s-stammer back then,' he said. Finley wondered if he'd just stammered on that 's' deliberately. It hadn't sounded like it.

'He would take the piss out of me all the time; rip my packages to shreds if I got the tiniest thing wrong... He'd point out all the edit points; he was always going on about how he could hear an edit in any package. He said I edited like a sh-sh-sheep. Really baaaa-aadly. He'd even make jokes about it on air. He'd say: "And that was another Lanky Larkhill offering for you. Hey, Rob, don't worry. We didn't notice the joins!" and other crap like that. *To the listeners!* And I just had to take it. Because he was this big shot presenter, you know? So full of confidence and already being lined up for the breakfast show.'

'He... he was a shit to me too,' said Finley, trying to build a bridge with a word he'd never normally use.

'He was a shit to everyone,' said Donna. 'But some of us got special treatment.'

'He loved the ladies,' said Rob, rolling his eyes. 'He seduced Donna.' Donna shrugged and looked at her feet as if she was sorry. 'I didn't blame her. He was *Dave Perry*. Why wouldn't she be bowled over? He took her off me. And anyway... it was worse for her in the end.'

'What... what happened?' asked Finley, trying to stop his teeth chattering so loudly.

'He got me pregnant and then dumped me for a newer, cuter researcher,' said Donna. 'And then, when I told him I was having the baby, he said he'd spread stories about me shagging the entire sports team and say it wasn't his. He started calling me Kleenex. He said I was just something men used and chucked away. So I had the baby aborted.'

Finley blinked. It all sounded horrible. Nothing like the

BBC was meant to be. Was he supposed to feel sorry for Donna? He supposed he did... but he just didn't understand what all this had to do with him.

'So - twenty years later I come back,' said Rob. 'And this time *I'm* the one calling the shots. I'd gone off to other stations - Solent and Berkshire - and learned everything I needed to. Rose up through the ranks to take the managing editor job at Wessex. And there he is... still the same piece of shit, *The Voice of Wessex,* for fuck's sake. All chummy and matey, now I'm the boss - like we'd been best friends back in the day.'

'Why didn't you just sack him?' asked Finley. 'Because, like, I would.'

'I would have loved to,' said Rob. 'And his RAJAR figures aren't so hot. I might have done it in time.'

'But..?' asked Finley.

'I got back together with Donna,' he said, reaching out a hand and squeezing her shoulder. 'We'd both been through a lot and we found each other again. We've been together for the past six months and we've been really happy. We might even get married.'

'So... you did OK in the end, didn't you?' said Finley. 'Um... I'm getting really cold up here. Can I get down now?'

'We did OK?' echoed Rob. 'You think? Because, *I* don't. Not really. We want kids, both of us. Donna's only thirty-eight - it's not too late. Except... a week ago we found out why she can't. You want to know why? Because of Dave fucking Perry. Aborting his kid destroyed her ovaries and now she can't ever have another baby.'

Finley looked at Donna, who was staring at the ground again. 'Oh,' he said.

'Even twenty years later he's still having the last fucking laugh!' said Rob, his voice rising and choking.

'Um, OK... so...' said Finley.

'So? SO? So I KILLED HIM,' said Rob. 'It was me who grabbed him and took him out to the Shrewton mast and made him tape himself to it - and then I choked him with his own mic sock. And he fucking deserved it. He got what he had coming. For Donna, for me... for all the women he was feeling up whenever he got the chance. If anything, his death was too easy. But it was good to make him finally shut up.'

There were a few beats of silence. Finley began to think about the TV shows he'd seen where the killer confesses everything to one person, usually in a deserted warehouse or up on the roof of a tall building. The person getting the confession quite often ended up dead. Finley gulped. *Keep him talking.* That's what they'd say on the TV show.

'So... why am *I* here?' he asked. 'I don't understand.'

Rob and Donna looked at each other and then back at him. 'You're a bit dim, really, aren't you, Finley?' said Donna. 'You really haven't worked it out yet.'

Finley shook his head. He thought he maybe *had* worked it out, but he didn't want to say it out loud. If he didn't say it, it might not be true.

'You're taking the blame for the murders,' she said. 'For Dave Perry and Sheila Bartley.'

Finley's throat clogged up. He felt sick. 'Sheila Bartley too?' he whimpered.

Rob sighed and shook his head. 'That was a pity. Sheila just said the wrong thing. She told me she saw me near the murder scene on the night I killed Dave. I knew if she told the police that, they'd trace it back to me sooner or later. We had to stop that happening. The police found her gaffer-taped to the aerial on the roof of Salisbury Broadcasting House a few hours ago. We didn't want to do it like that but we realised it had to look ritualistic. Do you know what that means?'

Finley nodded. 'I watch TV,' he said.

'Because we knew we had to get the police looking somewhere else and you - I'm afraid - with all your station visits and your calls and your endless bloody tins of cake, were always going to look guilty. Especially when you started stalking Josh in the dark, you fuckwit.'

Finley felt wounded. He'd done those things to be accepted. Because he cared. Everyone had always been so lovely to him when he went into Radio Wessex. Except Dave Perry, of course. He sniffed. He'd loved Sheila. He felt tears welling up in his eyes when he thought of her, taped up to the aerial, cold and dead. Suddenly he went very still, realising *he* was the one taped up to an aerial now.

'But... wait,' he blurted. 'This doesn't make sense. If you kill me like you killed the others, how can they think it was me who killed *them*?'

Rob laughed. Actually *laughed* like one of those TV psychopaths. 'I won't be killing you, Finley,' he said. 'You'll be killing yourself.'

'But...'

'OK - enough with the backstory,' said Donna. 'We need to get this thing done. Get in the car and follow me down the hill. I'll show you where to go.'

'What? Wait! What are you doing?' Finley squawked. 'You can't drive the radio car with the mast up! It's dangerous!'

'Yep - it is,' said Rob. He took the remote out from the car, held it up, and pressed it. The aerial started to vibrate and Finley stared up in panic. He was taped to it. He could get caught up in it!

But only the top section, just a metre in length, sank into

the cylinder below it before stopping. It was still at nearly full height when Rob got into the driver seat, slammed the door and started up the engine. The mast up warning alarm went off immediately, but Rob ignored it.

Donna got into her Jeep and began to drive down the hill. Rob turned the Ford around in a slow circle and Finley stared out across the field in horrified silence as he was carried across the sloping grass, his head jarring against the metal pole behind him with every bump and dip. He flung his hands up and gripped the mast just above his head. He should be ripping the gaffer tape off but, as the car picked up speed, he was too scared to let go. What were they going to do? He just couldn't work out what was going on. None of it made sense.

The car rocked and swayed as it rolled down the hill, unsteady with its centre of gravity thrown out by the mast, like a top heavy boat on a grassy sea. Finley wondered if it was too late to get his phone out and dial 999, but then he remembered his phone was in the car, in the cup holder where he'd left it. He was sitting at the base of an incredibly powerful transmitter but he could do nothing to make contact with anyone.

29

‘They're coming this way!’ Kate grabbed Lucas's arm. ‘We've got to get out of sight!’

Lucas looked up and shook his head. ‘This is not good,’ he murmured. ‘This is really not good.’

‘Come *on!*’ she said. ‘They're heading straight for us. The lights are going to find us any moment and then...’

Lucas seemed to finally get the message. He turned and ran with her, stumbling across the dark turf as the car headlights painted shafts of brightness through the night air. Thankfully the beams missed them by a couple of metres as they ran. Lucas took hold of her hand. ‘I can't use the torch,’ he hissed. ‘I'm dowsing our path. Stick with me.’ Sid was really putting in overtime tonight. Lucas suddenly angled them away to the left and then said ‘Stop - wait - slow down. There's something here.’

She could just about make out a dark bulky shape. She put out her hand and found what felt like a rough panel of metal. Feeling up and over it, she encountered the slap of cold water.

'It's a drinking trough,' said Lucas. 'For cattle. Get on the other side of it. Fast.'

They pulled themselves along and around its chilly lip, hand over hand, and dropped into a crouch on the compacted mud at the far side. Here they had a barrier to hide behind - and not a second too soon. The car headlamps flooded through the air above, casting a black block of shadow safely across them. She leaned out carefully to peer around the edge, her face screened by some high, scraggy weeds growing at its corners. Her heart pounded crazily; she tried hard to get it under control, grabbing the plasticine in her pocket again and mashing it between her fingers.

The cars rolled to a stop at what looked like the precise place she and Lucas had been standing thirty seconds ago. His dowsing forecast had been spot on about that. It made her shiver to think of it. But why? Why did they want to stop right there? There was nothing but grass.

The drivers got out of their vehicles. It looked like a man and a woman. In the light of their headlamps she could just about make that out. She was squinting and trying to study their features when Lucas nudged her and whispered 'Look at the car on the left. On the top.'

She did so and was shocked to see a third figure up on the roof. Her eyes travelled up further and she made out the pale gleam of a mast, rising high above the vehicle. 'Shit - Josh was right - it's the radio car! What the hell is Finley doing?'

'Finley's doing nothing,' said Lucas. 'He's the one on the roof.'

'But what's he up to?'

'Nothing. He can't get down. He's been taped there.'

Kate went to get up but Lucas grabbed her arm and

pulled her back down. 'No,' he said. 'Unless you're packing a gun under that jacket. Which you aren't.'

'Those other two... they're just about to stuff his airways with grey foam and choke him to death!' she hissed. 'I'm not letting that happen.'

'They're not going to do that,' he said.

'How the hell do you *know?* You're just a dowser, Lucas, not a bloody clairvoyant!'

'I don't need to be a bloody clairvoyant,' he said. 'Just look at where they are. What they're doing. If they wanted to gaffer him up and choke him to death, they didn't need to drive down the field. They wanted that precise location.'

'Why?' she asked, her eyes locked on the figure on the car roof.

He sighed. 'Look *up.*'

She shook her head. 'It's *the sky!*'

'No. Look *again. With your actual bloody EYES.*'

She took a deep breath and tracked her eyes up the mast and then further up to the purple-black sky above. She could see nothing except a handful of the brighter stars piercing the canopy of thin, high cloud. And then... suddenly... she *could* see something. A long, thin, black line. Next to it, another long, thin, black line.

'Ooooh fuck,' she murmured, as realisation dawned. 'Overhead power cables. They've parked it directly under overhead power cables. Why the hell would they do that?'

'It's time to think of something,' said Lucas. 'Fast.'

Kate dug out her phone and reminded herself it was dead. 'How much juice is in your mobile, Lucas?' she asked.

'I told you before - there's no time to get your guys here, even if we could get a signal.'

'We don't need a signal. Just a torch beam,' she said. 'And a shitload of bluff.'

———

'I WANT TO GO HOME,' said Finley. He sounded so sad. So pathetic. He wished he'd paid more attention when Dad had said 'Finley - you need to focus on some other things in your life. Not just the radio station. You're wasting your time. You could be doing so much more.'

Dad had been right. He had been stupid, stupid, stupid. Now he was going to get murdered and it was all his own fault for being so stupid. Once they had parked he looked up into the sky and understood what was going to happen. He started tugging at the gaffer tape, desperate to get off the roof, but Rob and Donna were back and she was pointing the rifle at him again.

Rob said: 'Stop struggling, Finley. It's too late. Don't worry about it. You won't feel a thing.' He had a remote controller in his hand and he held it up. 'I'm going to take the aerial fully up. It'll hit the power cable and you'll be dead before you know anything about it.'

'It's wrong! It's not fair!' he cried, sounding like a little kid. He thought he might wet himself too, like a little kid, he was so scared. 'I didn't kill them,' he wept. 'Don't say I killed them. I liked Sheila. She was kind to me.'

'It won't matter,' said Rob. 'Once this is done it's all over. We won't need to kill anyone else. I'm going to make Josh the breakfast show presenter - the main guy. You should be glad about that.'

'He... he was never coming tonight, was he?' said Finley, tears tracking down his face. 'There was never going to be a special OB. You cheated me.'

'Oh, for fuck's sake, hit the button,' said Donna. 'Let's get it done.'

Rob nodded. He pressed the button and the aerial began

to vibrate and hum and the top section started rising up. In spite of the gun levelled at him, Finley began to scrabble at the tape, but he already knew it was too late. He had about ten seconds before he was electrocuted. He thought about Mum and all she'd done for him... and hoped she wouldn't believe their lies.

───────

Rob Larkhill was wired and nervous. Donna was so impressive, standing there with her rifle raised, not a tremor to be seen. He wasn't really cut out for this, though. With Dave Perry he'd been so full of hate and anger he had *made* himself into a killer. Although it was definitely premeditated, it was still a crime of passion.

Without Donna helping, he wasn't at all sure he could have killed Sheila. Donna had hatched the plan to get Radio Wessex's local treasure up on the roof once she realised that Sheila could bring the police to their door. 'She's always going on about her stargazing saddos,' Donna had said, in his office, yesterday morning. 'Tell her she can take them all up on the roof for the next alignment or meteor shower or whatever. I'll take her up to scope it out, then I'll give her some hot chocolate with a bit of Rohypnol in it. She'll be totally gaga by the time you get up there. She won't even notice when we tape her up. She'll go quite peacefully. It's not like she's got much to live for, is it? Just that stupid cat. Her only daughter's on the other side of the bloody world.'

He had no idea how Donna happened to have Rohypnol, but he didn't ask. It had made perfect sense and, amazingly, in the midst of all the pandemonium around the station, with the fans piling into reception and the staff crowding the newsroom and getting their police interviews done, they'd pulled it off.

He'd even found another of those M&S biscuit tins from Finley to place at the scene, covered in his DNA and fingerprints. Just like the one he'd put outside by the gate for Josh to find the night before. It was clever, like using Gemma's phone to send that text to Dave last Friday and getting him to show up in the darkened BBC car park, thinking he was going to score sex with someone less than half his age; the fucking pervert. That had been Donna's idea. Yes, they had been very clever.

And now, the final scene. Finley taking his own life, in the ritualistic way he'd killed the others, overcome with remorse. Again, his prints and hair and skin cells were all over the car, while Rob Larkhill, wearing his peaked cap and ever-ready gloves, had left nothing significant. And even if some of his DNA *was* picked up - so what? He was the station manager. He had been showing some visitors that radio car only last week.

Along with the signed suicide note, this was surely a done deal. When he reported the radio car missing the next morning, and the police saw it leaving on the security camera footage (he'd been careful to sit too low in the passenger seat to be seen) then it was only a matter of time before they found Finley's body, the remote control dropped from his dead hand, and his note in the car. It would make one hell of a story. When it all hit the nationals and network, BBC Radio Wessex was going to be massively on the map. On the dial, too. RAJAR figures were going to soar as casual listeners tuned in, riveted, to find out how the presenters were managing this tragedy live on air.

So when he finally pressed the button on the remote he was certain it was for the best. For everyone. For him, for

Donna and for the station. Even the listeners. He'd done a lot of people a massive favour and only a handful would suffer for it.

He counted down the final seconds of Finley's life, backing away a little, with Donna, in case of sparks or leaping electricity from above. He wondered if he would get to ten.

"STOP! POLICE!'

'DROP THE GUN!'

'DROP THE REMOTE!'

Rob jerked around, his thumb falling off the remote button and pausing the raising of the mast. He couldn't see anything except a torch beam waving in the air further down the field. The voices were loud and authoritative. He thought he recognised DS Sparrow... but the male voice he didn't know. He was suddenly sick with terror, his blood pressure roaring in his ears.

'DROP THE GUN!' yelled the woman, again. He realised that Donna had swung around and was pointing the rifle in the direction of the torch light. 'YOU ARE SURROUNDED BY ARMED POLICE!' went on the voice. 'IF YOU DON'T DROP THE GUN *RIGHT NOW* YOU *WILL* BE SHOT!'

'*Fuck!*' breathed Donna. 'Alright!' she yelled, holding the rifle above her head. 'I'm putting it down. Slowly...'

'DO SO - AND THEN RAISE BOTH YOUR HANDS!' yelled the policewoman.

'THROW THAT REMOTE DOWN!' yelled the male officer. 'THEN RAISE YOUR-'

But he didn't finish the sentence because Donna had suddenly darted sideways, behind the Jeep, taking the rifle with her, and started running away into the darkness. Rob stood frozen to the spot. He was aware of a tearing sound off to his left. Finley was trying to get away. Out of pure, perverse, anger Rob dropped to the ground and held the remote to his chest, pressing the button once more.

'STOP!' shrieked the female officer and he could hear panic in her voice. He guessed the police snipers would be tearing into him at any second but he didn't care. He wouldn't go to jail, at least.

The aerial was rising again and Finley was screaming. He couldn't have more than five seconds left. He'd taped himself up so securely - always so very happy to please the BBC - he wasn't going to make it off that roof.

There was a crunch as someone landed heavily on Rob, forcing the wind out of him, and smashing the remote out of his hands. A man with wild dark hair and a beard punched him hard in the face and he just had time to see the top of the mast stop, less than a hand's width from the overhead cable.

He howled with rage. He'd come so far. He'd *so nearly* pulled off the perfect crime. For Donna. He'd done it all for Donna. Where the fuck *was* Donna?

30

The woman with the shotgun had vanished into the darkness and Kate was aghast. She had no idea where she had gone. Kate flared the torch around in all directions and caught the momentary gleam of the heel of a boot as its owner legged it up the field.

'STOP!' she yelled again, tracking wildly with the torch but unable to find the escapee again. She guessed the woman, who'd been dressed for the farm, knew this spot well and could dodge and weave through it with ease. Even so, she gave chase, trying not to think of the loaded shotgun. 'YOU WILL NOT ESCAPE!' she bawled. 'WE'VE SET UP ROADBLOCKS AND A CORDON!'

But she knew her words were paper thin. Anyone could glance around this cold, dark valley and work out that not a single other glimmer of torchlight, reflective vest or whirling flash of red and blue was out there, signalling any back up at all. There was no helicopter chopping the air overhead and sending down a searchlight. There was no two-way radio chatter. Her fakery had rested on two loud voices and one mobile phone torch.

She tripped on an unseen root and landed face first in the thistly grass. With a curse, she rolled over, realising that her torchlight was now doing nothing more than picking her out as a target for some shotgun practice. She switched it off and held still, trying to quieten her heavy breathing and listen. Behind her she heard scuffling noises as Lucas dealt with the man he'd floored. There was no electrical crackle or bang, so she guessed they had at least stopped Finley Warner's death by electrocution.

The gunwoman would have to be hunted down later. Her partner in crime would probably give her up eventually - and Finley might well be able to identify her. Better still, the car she'd driven in, assuming it was the Jeep and not the station's radio car, would lead them to her. Kate got carefully to her feet. It was time to call it a night.

She turned back to the pool of light between the two vehicles, noting that Lucas had the man well under control, down on the grass, while Finley appeared to be tearing at the tape around his waist. With luck there would be a decent signal near that transmitter mast, or perhaps on a mobile somewhere in one of the vehicles, and she could finally call in the back up she'd invented. This could all be tied up within hours.

There was a click and something cold came to rest on the back of her neck. 'Don't say a fucking word,' growled a female voice. 'Don't move. Just lift your hands up where I can see them.'

Kate realised, too late, that in standing up she had turned herself into silhouette against the light of the cars. Keeping equally still, watching in the dark, the gunwoman had easily found her. 'Who are you?' Kate said, quietly, raising her hands, Lucas's mobile in one of them. 'I recognise your voice.'

'Shut up or I'll blow your head off.' The cold nose of the gun slid up to the base of her skull. 'Turn around slowly.'

Kate turned, and as she did so her contact with the shotgun remained unbroken; her adversary was turning a wider circle, keeping the barrel tight against her skull. Kate considered dropping suddenly and dashing left or right into the darkness, but she sensed that this woman was too sharp for that and the chances of getting a bullet through her skull, her shoulder blade or her spine were better than good. So when the woman growled 'Walk', she did just that.

'Drop the phone.'

She did; hearing her last contact with the outside world thud into the grass.

'Keep walking. Don't turn around. Don't make any noise. I am seriously fucked off at you and I'm *that* close to pulling my trigger.'

Kate didn't say anything. She just kept walking; her misty little dream of wrapping up this murder case in a matter of three days evaporating into the night. She only hoped Lucas would get Finley away and go for help. There was a further three or four minutes of silent walking, during which she stumbled twice and fully expected to be shot when her captor assumed she was doing a runner. But there was a dim light throwing her shadow ahead and she realised the shotgun sight must have a torch attachment, meaning the woman wielding it could see that her stumbles were genuine.

Eventually a dark shape loomed ahead of them... some kind of barn or shed. Kate was marched up to it and instructed to push against a lichen-furred wooden door. She did so and it gave after a couple of shoves, held shut only by its rain-swollen frame. Inside it smelled of damp straw and diesel. There was a click and a single dangling lightbulb in a cage lit up the room. It was a large shed, rather than a barn - perhaps twice the size of the average double garage. The floor was compacted mud and straw. There were sacks of feed along the far wall and an old Kubota tractor in one corner, its shovel nose resting on the ground.

'Sit against that,' said the woman, whom Kate was beginning to recognise.

'Donna..?' she murmured. 'Donna Wilson? Really? It's *you?*'

'Shut up and sit down,' said Donna. Her hair was tucked into a woollen beanie hat and she was wearing a padded Barbour coat, jeans and wellies, but her smooth, well-preserved features held the same control and reserve that Kate had seen in Rob Larkhill's office.

Suddenly, Kate realised who the man with her was. As recent memory flashed past she recognised the thinning hair and the slightly stooped gait. It *was* bloody *Rob Larkhill!* Sinking to the ground against the tractor she felt quite stunned. She had not seen that coming. A reel landed by her feet. 'Tape up your ankles,' said Donna. 'Tightly.'

'No,' said Kate.

'What?' Donna waved the gun at her.

'No. I won't. Because then you'll just suffocate me,' she said. 'You can shoot me instead. It'll be much harder to cover your tracks that way, though.'

Donna stood staring at her for a few seconds, looking furious. As she opened her mouth to speak again, Kate grabbed her moment, picked up the heavy reel of tape and threw it. It struck Donna hard on the jaw, eliciting a shriek, and then Kate was on her feet, hands raised. She struck out with a high kick, aiming to dislodge the shotgun. She didn't miss - the gun spun out into the air and sailed across the shed. Donna shrieked again and dived for it and Kate got a kick in to the other side of her face. Donna jerked sideways and hit the ground with a loud grunt of pain.

Kate ran for the gun but Donna was already scrambling for it. She would never have reached it in time if Kate hadn't tripped on some rusty iron chains coiled on the floor, hidden in the shadow of the tractor. Tipping through the air, she let loose her own shriek of fury as Donna grabbed the gun, twisted up onto her knees and drove the butt in a sharp jab towards her foe's head.

Kate felt the impact for a moment and had enough time to curse herself again, before she lost consciousness.

———

LUCAS SPOTTED a reel of gaffer on the turf within easy reach of his squirming, whining captive. He grabbed it, flipped the man onto his front and snagged both his hands together, glad of his strong fingers and enough angry momentum to get the tape wound tightly around the man's wrists before he could break free.

Once done, his captive sagged onto the ground, face in the grass, and fell silent.

Lucas paused, sorely tempted to kick him in the head for what he'd just seen him attempt to do, but then a whimper from the roof of the radio car caught his attention. The young man by the mast was still pulling at his bindings, tears tracking down his face, shock permeating through his energy patterns. Lucas realised he needed to free the guy and get him inside the car and wrapped up warm, or he was going to go into shutdown. 'Come on,' he said, striding across to the car. 'Let me help.'

It wasn't easy. The tape was wound around the mast and his waist several times and locating the end of it was impossible in the dark. Lucas reached into his pockets, trying to locate his Swiss Army knife. 'Finley... is it? What the hell happened?' he asked, as much to keep the young man talking as to find out the answer. *Where was that bloody penknife?*

'I... I don't really know,' said Finley, through chattering teeth. 'They wanted to k-k-kill me.'

'Who are they?' asked Lucas.

'They're from the BBC. That's Rob Larkhill - the station manager - and the woman is Donna, his secretary. They... they wanted everyone to think I w-was a murder-er-er...'

'OK,' said Lucas, still rummaging. 'Breathe... deep and slow. You're going to be OK.'

'Oh, he's really not.' There was a click and Lucas closed his eyes. Well, he hadn't dowsed *that*, had he? The return of Shotgun Bitch had eluded Sid.

'Step away from the saddo on the roof,' said the woman. 'Hands up.'

Lucas was all out of moves. He recognised the confidence with which she held that weapon - and read the cold determination in her patterns. It didn't take a master dowser to work out that she meant business. He stepped away and raised his hands.

'Now, slowly, bend over and - keeping one hand up - pick up that tape,' she said. Lucas did. 'Now tape up his wrists. Properly.'

Lucas let out a long sigh, holding up the reel. 'What's the point of all this, really?' he said. 'You must know it's just got way too complicated for you to pull this off, whatever the hell it was you thought you were doing.'

'Shut up and do it.'

'Your best bet now is to do a runner,' he said.

She suddenly swerved around him and pressed the barrel of the shotgun right up against Finley's temple. 'I am SO done with all this,' she said as Finley squeezed his eyes shut and bit his lips together in a compressed white line. 'And I am *this close* to blasting his face off. So do up the FUCKING TAPE or his brains will be all over your nice leather jacket. Followed shortly by your own.'

Lucas did as he was told. She was too far away to risk lunging for that shotgun. He could only play for time and hope that Kate would come back to intervene somehow. She'd vanished with his phone. She might finally have found some signal and called in that legendary back up she'd been promising all night.

But Kate did not come back. He finished taping Finley, giving his joined hands a sad little squeeze which was not going to be any reassurance and then stepped back. 'Done,' he said.

'Good,' she said. 'Finley... just stay put like a good boy and I'll be back soon. Rob,' she called across to the man on the floor. 'Hang in there, babe, I'll be back for you too. I can't risk dropping the gun to release you just now.'

'It's alright,' grunted Larkhill, still nuzzling the ground. 'Just hurry back, OK?'

'I will,' she said. 'I'll sort out these two jokers and then we'll carry on as planned. Don't you worry.'

She marched Lucas up the dark hillside, the barrel nudging between his shoulder blades. He stumbled once or twice but she was locked on to him and he couldn't sense a moment to get away. The patterns around them both signalled that his odds of doing a successful runner were slim... and he was also picking up that this woman had put

Kate somewhere. He needed to know where. Whether she was OK.

They walked towards the outline of a door sketched in electric light. He recalled he had vaguely sensed an outbuilding off to his left when they'd first entered the field.

'Push open the door and go in,' he was instructed. He did so, stepping into what turned out to be a shed containing a load of feed sacks, a tractor and the body of Kate Sparrow.

For a second his heart seemed to ricochet around his chest and he felt suffocated with horror... but then his dowsing sense elbowed the personal panic away and informed him that she was still breathing. She lay on her side, eyes closed and blood dripping out of her hairline. Her feet were tethered to the tractor with more of that fucking gaffer tape and her hands were bound in the same way, behind her back.

'Take the bag off and drop it.' He shrugged Kate's satchel off and dumped it. There was a central post in the shed. The gunwoman made him sit down with a leg on either side of it and then tape up his ankles. Then she paused. How was she going to get his wrists secured? She would have to put the gun down. It was a two-hander. 'Right,' she said. 'Attach one wrist to the post. Now.'

'Jesus. Have you got shares in Duck Tape?' he muttered. But he did as he was ordered and then, managing to keep the gun cocked and pointed at his face, she did a fair job of taping his free wrist to it too.

She stood back and then checked the satchel, finding only a few papers and the biscuit tin inside it. She chucked it all into a corner and then stood and looked at him. 'Don't go anywhere,' she smirked, and then left.

'Kate!' he called, as soon as she'd gone. Kate didn't reply. 'Detective Sergeant Sparrow!' he yelled.

She stirred and groaned. Her eyelids flickered apart and she struggled to focus. 'What..?'

'Sorry,' he said. 'I'm a bit stuck up.'

She lifted her head, wincing. 'Where's Donna gone?'

'To rescue lover boy, I think,' he said. 'She'll be back.'

'She's the Terminator in wellingtons,' mumbled Kate.

Their captors returned five or ten minutes later. Larkhill was still picking gaffer tape glue off his wrists as they stood in the shed doorway, planning what to do next. Kate looked dazed and only half aware and Lucas thought it best to say nothing.

'We can still make this work,' Donna said, walking straight over to him and searching his jacket pockets. 'Bingo!' she said, holding up the remote control he'd wrestled off Larkhill. 'OK. Finley's still in place. All we need to do is now is get that mast up as planned. Nothing's changed there.'

'But what about these two?' said Larkhill, glancing from Lucas to Kate as if they couldn't hear him.

'I know her - DS Sparrow, isn't it? But who the hell is he?' said Donna.

'I think it's the dowser guy who was on Louella's show this week,' said Larkhill. 'Lucas something. Helped solve the Runner Grabber case.' He glanced at Lucas as if for confirmation. Lucas stared stonily back at him.

There was an upended crate near the door. Donna sank onto it, looking tired. 'Well, as much as I'd like to shoot them, it's better if I don't.' She broke the shotgun, leaned it against the crate, and took a small leather cartridge bag off her shoulder, dropping it next to the twelve-bore. 'It'll be too easy to trace back to me. No... dead in the bushes is where they belong. I thought they *were* dead. My bad. I should've checked properly.'

'OK - so we get them back to the bike crash site - but how do we..?'

Donna looked at Lucas, narrowing her eyes speculatively. '*He* was going too fast, trying to impress, when he lost control and killed himself and his girlfriend.' She turned to look at a stack of metal farm implements in the corner near the door. 'A spade to the head will look a lot like blunt force trauma from a bike crash, won't it?'

Lucas saw Larkhill gulp and nod his head, flicking his beloved a glance which was a mixture of love, admiration and fear. 'Same for her?' he said, staring down at Kate who now seemed to be unconscious again.

'Better,' said Donna, pulling a small plastic bag from her Barbour pocket. 'She looks out of it but you can't be sure. I've got Rohypnol left over from the Sheila thing - we can get that into her. It'll look like he tried a bit of date rape drug on her and convinced her to go out on a ride with him.' She shook the white powder inside the bag. 'There's enough here to finish her off.'

Larkhill rubbed his face. 'It's all a bit close to the site of Finley's suicide though, isn't it? Won't the police make a connection?'

'I don't *fucking know*,' snapped Donna. 'Maybe they will. Maybe they'll think the pair of them were chasing Finley... maybe they'll think this Lucas guy drugged her first and then they saw the radio car and went on a jolly to catch up with it. Honestly? Who gives a shit as long they don't connect it to you or me? And let's be honest, Wiltshire Police aren't exactly ace criminologists, are they? Look how long it took them to solve the Runner Grabber case? Probably never would have if it hadn't been for dowser boy, here.'

'Hmmm. And maybe they won't find the bodies of these two for a while,' mused Larkhill. 'How deep into the undergrowth did their bike go?'

'Deep enough,' she said.

Larkhill looked at Lucas warily. 'It's going to be heavy work... getting him all the way to the crash site... it won't be easy. Bodies are dead weight. And I'm worried about tyre tracks. If the Jeep tracks are noticed...'

'Or for god's sake, it's fine,' said Donna, rummaging in the corner. 'We'll drug them both. Then, when they're off their heads, we can just lead them back there like a pair of sheep, bash him on the skull, top her up to a fatal dose and put them back in the bushes.'

'Jesus Christ on a bike,' said Lucas, unable to stay quiet any longer. 'Do you have any idea how insane the pair of you sound? You're never going to pull this off. You're not criminal masterminds. You're just a pair of overexcited am drams with a BBC email.'

Which was probably the wrong thing to say because three seconds later Donna hit him in the face with a spade.

'I've stunned him,' he heard her say as he drifted away. 'We'll do the Rohypnol plan; get it down his neck now while he's out of it.'

He felt them move his head, tip his chin upwards, then drop some powder into his mouth. He groaned and jerked his head away. The plastic bag fell onto the floor and Donna cursed. 'Shit. Half of it's spilled. We're going to need more. I'll give the copper a bit of what's left - make sure she stays under. Then I'll have to go back to the car for some more. Shouldn't take too long.'

'Donna... how do you come to have all this Rohypnol..?' Larkhill asked, a touch of anxiety in his tone.

'My old dad used to have insomnia,' she said, crouching

down over Kate. 'He got it on prescription. I found shed-loads of it in the bathroom cabinet after he'd died last year.'

'It's for insomnia?' queried Larkhill, going very quiet as Lucas began to slip further away.

'Well, that's what he told me. He could have been drugging and murdering women for the last decade his life, I suppose. Wouldn't put it past the nasty old bastard...'

31

P ool cars were meant to be kept topped up with fuel at all times. It was a rule. You went out on a job and then, on your way back, if the needle was even a hair's breadth lower than half a tank full, you had to take it to the local garage and fill it up on the BBC tab. Malc would give you a seriously hard stare if you failed in this; Josh remembered this from his early radio car days.

That's how it *should* have been, but of course, on this night of emergency, Josh found the bloody thing running on fumes. So only fifteen minutes into his hair-raising midnight adventure, he'd been forced to pull in to a garage. Still, it was probably for the best. With any luck he would arrive at the showground just in time to see Finley Warner getting helped into the back of a patrol car.

It was as he filled up the tank that Josh finally realised *Finley* was Dave Perry's killer. *Shit!* It was obvious! The cops wouldn't just be picking him up for car theft... it was *murder* too. Maybe the police already knew from DNA and so on. He felt a frisson of fear and excitement as his fantasy arrest scene went up a gear - a flood of blue flashing lights and Finley Warner getting slammed up against the side of the radio car, frisked and restrained by armed officers.

All *he* would need to do was lean against the Radio Wessex Peugeot, hands in pockets, and wait for that hot detective to come over and thank him for the tip-off while they drove Finley off to the slammer. He imagined the attention he would get at work the next day when he rolled in mid-morning and everyone knew he'd got the police onto the psycho jock-killer and had been there at the end of the chase. 'Look, I was just at the right place at the right time when I saw him drive off,' he would shrug, nonchalantly. 'You would've done the same.'

But would they? Who else would jump into a car and go off in hot pursuit? Well... maybe not exactly *hot* pursuit, because he was now a good twenty or thirty minutes behind Finley and really more in lukewarm pursuit. This was more reccying than chasing. Following a hunch. He reworked his speech. 'Look... it's no big deal. I just remembered where Finley first fell in love with the radio car - god knows he's told me often enough - and then decided to go and check it out.'

Yeah. That was better.

He overshot the turning to the West Wiltshire Showground; the sign was small and it was very dark - then U-turned on the deserted B-road, and located the entrance. It was only after he'd been bumping along the narrow track for three or four minutes that he began to feel a sense of misgiving. Perhaps this wasn't such a great idea. Maybe he should just go home and call the police again. Problem was, he couldn't turn around on this track and by now he was too far along it to back up. It would take him all night to navigate those ruts and potholes in reverse. No. He needed to reach the field, turn around, and go home. Have a bit of common sense.

Another three or four minutes and at last he could see where the track opened out into the top end of the field. He realised he could see it quite well; there seemed to be some source of light up there. His insides clenched. Had he been right? Was Finley *actually* going to be here with the radio car? Murdering someone? Maybe he was choking Judy Goodson from traffic and travel because she hadn't liked his biscuits, or Rebecca Barker off the gardening show because she'd dissed his homegrown carrots...

Don't be ridiculous, he told himself. But that was before he saw the lights down the valley and recognised the shape of the old Ford Focus and the long slick gleam of the raised mast. What the holy *fuck?!* He stopped the car dead and switched off the headlamps. Pulling out his mobile, he hit redial on DS Sparrow's number. No good. No signal. He tried 999 instead, beginning to hyperventilate. Shit! Something really *was* going down in the Wiltshire wilderness.

At this point a shaft of light opened up in the darkness off to his left and he saw two people emerge. His was dimly aware of his jaw hanging like a broken piñata as he recognised *Rob Larkhill* and... what the actual *fuck?* Donna?!

Josh stared at them and then down at the mobile in his palm, which was singularly failing to dial 999 for him, his brain whirring. What did it mean? He had heard rumours that Rob and Donna had something going on, but were they both hot enough for each other to want to go out in the dark and have a shagfest in a shed or a barn or whatever? No. They weren't teenagers. Something was seriously fucked up about this.

Although part of him was itching to jump out of the car and run after them to ask what was going on, another much more astute part of him cautioned silence. Stillness. To simply sit and wait and see. He knew, with the pool car's dark burgundy livery and no lights, he was pretty much invisible in this darkness. Even so, as the pair of them walked down the slope towards the radio car and some other vehicle, its headlamps lighting the scene, he took the handbrake off and let his ride roll on a little further towards some sprawling hedgerow, masking his presence further still. Once it had nosed as far in as it could, he put the handbrake on again, took the key out of the ignition and waited until they were far enough away not to notice the weak courtesy light as he got out.

After maybe thirty seconds he exited the car, closing the door swiftly and quietly. He walked carefully across the grass, trying to decide where to go next - to the shed, where dim light was still showing around a closed door, or down the slope towards the cars?

He could have gone to the shed but instinct called him down the slope of the field instead. As he approached could hear something in that direction. It sounded like someone crying. A soft, forlorn weeping. Was it Donna? Were she and Rob having some kind of row? Because he could make out their shapes, faintly picked out by the interior light of what looked like a Jeep. No - the crying wasn't coming from inside the Jeep. Josh felt the hairs prickle across the back of his neck. He should get back to the pool car and get out of here right now. *Right now.* But... the crying. It was so pathetic. He shone his phone torch down low in the grass, just to mark out his path and then switched it off again, still wary of getting noticed. As he got closer he could hear the crying more clearly. It was heavy sobs, like a child in a real state; distraught, not stroppy.

Nearing the radio car he realised the sobs were coming

from above it. He made out a shape on the roof, up against the extended mast, and felt a cold sweat break out across his skin as he crept around the far side, out of sight of the Jeep parked nearby, and shone his phone's torchlight up.

Fucking hell! 'Finley?' he hissed. 'Jesus! Finley - is that *you?*'

But Finley couldn't answer. There was tape across his mouth. Josh's mind swam as he swiftly recast Finley from killer to victim. He was about to reach up and untape the guy when some instinct made him pause, snap off the torch, and duck down, out of sight of the Jeep. The fact that Rob and Donna were a few metres away, sitting in their car while Finley was stuck to the mast and bawling his eyes out... well, it raised a few questions, didn't it?

Josh felt waves of unreality washing over him as he crouched against the mud-spattered front tyre of the Ford. He literally pinched his arm to double-check he was awake. Because if not, this was the weirdest dream he'd had in years, *including* the one about Darcey Bussell and the emu... He felt the pinch, which left him with the unhappy certainty that he was indeed out here in the middle of the Wiltshire wilderness with Finley Warner stuck to the radio car mast and his boss and his boss's PA sitting in a nearby vehicle, enjoying the view.

But surely *they* couldn't be..? His mind wouldn't even allow him to form the words. It was just too bizarre. There *had* to be a logical explanation. Above him Finley was still sobbing, but more quietly now. 'Stay there,' hissed Josh, ridiculously. 'I'll get you down... just wait...'

Then light flared across the grass as the Jeep door opened and he heard Rob and Donna get out, talking so casually you would think they were wandering through SBH with a mug of coffee, planning staff appraisals.

'We can still do this,' Donna was saying. 'Oh shut *up*, Finley, for fuck's sake.'

Finley shut up at once, allowing Josh to hear the conversation more clearly, despite the bash-bash-bashing of his panicked pulse in his ears.

'I'm still worried it leaves a confusing narrative,' Rob was saying. 'I mean, yes, he could have spiked her drink, but they'll find Rohypnol in *his* system too and wonder why.'

'The guy's a weirdo - all that twig waving,' said Donna. 'He could be into all kinds of druggy fetishes. The police hate him anyway; that's what I heard. My friend's brother-in-law works at Salisbury cop shop and apparently Lucas Henry led them all into a bog back in September and then did a runner, leaving them stuck there, looking like a bunch of pricks. They won't take much convincing that he killed their colleague.'

'Alright,' said Rob, still sounding worried. 'Let's just get this done. Dear god - it's nearly 2am. I've got to get back to the station before the breakfast crew get in. *And* I've got to get all this bloody mud off my shoes. I'll have to go home first. You'll have to get the Jeep washed too.'

'Fine,' said Donna. 'We'll get those two drugged up and back to the crash site, finish them off, then get back to Finley. At least *he's* not going anywhere. Check his tape, will you?'

Josh shrank tightly against the side of the car, holding his breath, as the man his radio career depended on walked across and looked at Finley.

'He's not getting out of that,' he said, after a pause and a fresh whimper from their captive. 'Come on. Back to the shed. I've really had enough of this business, you know.'

'Well, you started it,' said Donna. 'And if you're going to start something, you've got to be ready to finish it.'

The pair of them wandered back up the field. Josh sank onto the grass and wondered if now would be a good time to put his hands over his eyes and starting singing *lalalalalalala*.

———

THERE'S GOT *to be a way out of this*. Kate knew she was concussed; she just didn't know how badly. The motorbike crash hadn't helped and the blow with the butt of the rifle and a sprinkling of Rohypnol was quite the cocktail. She had been more awake than she had let on, though, when Donna had tried to drug her. Kate had managed to keep most of the powdery residue in her cheek, diluting it with saliva and dribbling it down across her chin. She knew she'd been affected by it - but not as badly as that blow to the side of the head.

She had heard most of what was said as Donna and Rob had discussed their masterplan, allowing herself to peer between half-closed lids as Donna settled on the crate, broke her twelve-bore, and set it down by her feet. She'd watched the woman take a small leather cartridge bag off her shoulder and dump that on the floor too.

When Donna had got up again, Kate, still peering through the letterbox of her eyelids, saw she had taken the rifle, but, in her eagerness to go and collect some more date rape drug, had left the bag of cartridges behind. The ammo wasn't much use to anyone, of course, without the rifle. It wasn't like she could throw a cartridge *really hard* at Donna's face, even if she could get her hands free. Shove it down her throat... yes...

'Kate! Are you awake?' She could dimly make out Lucas, working hard to pull against his tape, but not making much headway. She found she didn't have the resources to reply beyond a vague grunt, because she was focusing hard on her own bindings. She was very woozy. Very hot. Sweat was running off her, making her cotton shirt stick to her skin, trickling between her breasts and her shoulder blades. Sweat was good, though. It was even pooling between her wrists, gummed up in their sticky sheath of tape. She twisted them back and forth and found that the salty moisture she was exuding was making her skin slippery. The cut on her hand started stinging and bleeding too. Yep. That'd help.

Go gently, she told herself. *Don't pull it too tight.* Because the more you pulled and twisted on gaffer tape, the more it worked itself into a kind of tortured cord, even harder to break. If you were gentle and left it as a cuff you could more easily get at its joins and pick them open. The blood and sweat continued to pool and she began to gently work her palms against each other, up and down, rubbing like a miser, slick with perspiration and A positive, vaguely aware of Lucas trying to say something. She began to tilt and rock her hands so that the moisture travelled up the sides and onto the backs until finally, finally, the skin was so wet she was able... oh so carefully... to slide one hand out.

This should have been the moment when she leapt up, unbound first herself and then Lucas and got the pair of them away. That's exactly what should have happened. What happened instead was she lost consciousness again.

———

LUCAS HAD WRENCHED at the tape so fiercely it had twisted into an unbreakable cord. He wanted to headbutt the post he was attached to, from sheer frustration. But why bother when Donna was going to come back and do the job properly with that spade?

The drug they'd managed to get into him was having an effect. He felt waves of sleepiness rolling over him and had to keep shaking his head to keep it at bay. He *must* stay awake - he was no use to Kate in a stupor. He felt Sid thrumming on his chest and wished he understood what his dowsing senses were trying to tell him. Problem was, he was too fucked up to remember his own name, let alone devise a way out of this.

'Kate! Are you awake?' he burbled, his words thick through swollen and bloodied lips. Kate only groaned in reply. Damn. Damn. Damn it. This was *not* how they were meant to end. There was so much more he needed to say to her. He rested his forehead against the post and said: 'Kate... there are things I need to tell you. About Mabel... about that day in the quarry.'

Kate made another moaning sound. Could she understand him?

'I want to say... I'm sorry,' he said. 'About what happened. It was me who...'

Kate suddenly sat up. In the light overhead she looked red and flushed, her blue eyes bright and feverish. Then she raised one shaking, bloody hand before slumping over sideways again. 'Shit,' she grunted. 'I always knew...'

———

KATE CAME to enough to hear Lucas mumbling away again, apologising. Like it was *his* fault. She sat up with a velocity that made her head swim, but she still couldn't move her legs properly thanks to her feet being stuck to a bloody tractor. She fell over sideways with a thud.

'Shit. I always knew,' she said. *That she shouldn't have got him involved. That sooner or later she would wreck his life again.* He was probably actually going to die this time and it was all her fault. She wanted to apologise but her mouth wasn't working properly and her words weren't making much sense. Still... she had her hands free now although one still had a cuff of grey tape stuck around it. She turned over and reached across the packed earth and straw towards the leather cartridge bag. When Donna came back it might help if there was no extra ammunition available. She could hide it.

She faded again and then found herself snoozing on the bag, using it like a pillow. It was thin. There were actually only six cartridges in it. Were there still two in the gun? Had Donna already shot them into someone else? Maybe into *her*? She was losing herself. Panicky waves kept coming for her. Was she in a shed? Or was she in a basement, naked and about to be killed by a deranged nurse who believed herself the next Damien Hirst?

Kate knew she needed to get those cartridges out of the bag. She could try to hide the bag but in her present foggy state, she didn't think she was really capable of it. She didn't have the oomph to throw it to the far end of the shed and just lying on top of it wasn't much of a plan. She might not even be conscious when Donna came back for her ammo. Getting the cartridges out and throwing *them* around the shed was a better idea. She got up on one shaky elbow and tried to extricate them... but she couldn't get them out of their tight little pockets. Her blood and sweat-smeared fingers kept slipping and sliding and she just couldn't make the pinching shape she needed to tug them out. She slumped down again, dazed and defeated, panic roaring somewhere in the distance. Panic wasn't going to help.

Panic. There were ways to manage it. She remembered Joanna, the counsellor, and reached one hand into her jacket pocket, squeezing the plasticine, feeling it give as her fingers forced ridges into it. That was better. She brought some out with her and massaged it between her fingers. She needed to do something soft and calming before she tried to sit up and attack the tape on her ankles. Something slow, soft, squidgy and calming.

'Kate? Can you hear me?' That was Lucas. Probably. He wasn't dead yet, then. She felt vaguely glad before she fell asleep again.

32

It would have been hard to untape Finley at the best of times, but here in the deep chill of a November night, trembling with shock, Josh was making a pig's ear of the job. Finley had at least stopped crying at last and was listening to Josh's whispers and fixing him with wide, wet eyes.

Josh had found the skinny pen torch on his keyring. After disconnecting it he was now holding it between his teeth, shining a beam the size of a teacup onto the tape around Finley's wrists. It had been wound around clumsily, in haste, so it was fairly easy to find the edges. Josh went to work on it, aware that he should probably be ungagging Finley first, but afraid that doing so might unleash a torrent of panicky words which would bring Rob and Donna running back down the field.

'Don't worry - I'm getting you off there,' he said, with difficulty, his teeth clenched around the torch.

At last he found a decent amount of edge and started tugging the tape back against itself. It made horrifyingly loud tearing noises, but there was no sudden beam swinging back down the field. He tugged and ripped and at last Finley's hands were free. At once the young man ripped the tape off his mouth, gasping.

'Ssshhhh!' hissed Josh. 'Whatever you want to tell me - wait! We mustn't make any noise or they'll come back.'

Finley gulped audibly and they both went to work on the tape, Finley on the thick grey gaffer cummerbund around his waist and Josh on the broad ribbons around his knees and ankles. It took another couple of minutes and at any moment Josh expected to hear a shout from Rob or Donna.

A perverse part of him *wanted* them to come back; wanted to scream 'What the FUCK do you think you're doing?' He still could not fully believe what he was seeing; what he had heard them say. Although he hadn't heard anything about Dave Perry it seemed increasingly likely that they'd killed his fellow presenter too. What the actual *fuck*? He had a vague memory of some psychologist on Radio 4 talking about how many psychopaths there are in the world... around one per cent of the human race, apparently... and how many of them make it into the top tiers of politics and big business. He guessed that had to apply to the BBC too. He knew that his contemporaries in local radio were incredibly passionate and competitive and there was a rich smörgåsbord of personality disorders among them, no question... but he hadn't really expected to find *two* psychopaths at SBH. Who knew? The psychologist was right.

At last Finley was free and Josh helped him to slide across the roof and jump down, on the darkest side where he had hidden. Finley's legs gave way immediately. 'I'm sorry,' he whimpered. 'They're not working right.'

Josh pocketed the pen torch and put an arm around

Finley's shoulders. 'I'm not bloody surprised,' he said. 'But you can do this. Come on. Let me help you up. We've got to get away from here. I've got the pool car at the top of the slope.'

Finley staggered to his feet and together they began to make their way through the darkness. Josh kept his eyes fixed on the light showing around the edges of that shed door. He guessed whoever the other two were, they were being held in there. Did he dare go and look? Maybe try to help them? No. He had to get Finley into the pool car and get the hell away from here. Then maybe find a high point and a signal for his mobile so he could finally dial 999 and scream blue murder.

'They tricked me. Made me sign a suicide note,' Finley said. 'Saying it was *me* who killed Dave and Sheila.' He started crying again and Josh stopped and stared at him.

'Sheila? They killed *Sheila?*'

———

LUCAS DRIFTED for a while and then he was aware of Kate getting up again and struggling with her bound ankles. He heard a ripping sound and thought that was probably a good sound to hear. He couldn't be sure because the room was doing a long, wallowing spin at that point and he was pressing his forehead against the post, trying hard not to fall off the floor.

'Fuck it,' he heard Kate say. And then he heard another rip and a whisper of 'Yesss.' Then she was close to him; he could smell her breath and her sweat and was suddenly assailed by the most intense, bizarrely-timed, desire for her. *It's the drug,* some part of him suggested, but most of him didn't pay it attention. Sid was hot against his chest and he felt the distinct and perplexing stirrings of a hard on. Maybe it was because he knew he would be dead soon. He'd heard men got erections when they were hanged; the doomed body having its last ditch attempt at leaving a little seed behind. *Bloody hell!* He didn't want to be thinking this way. The room had stopped spinning, though, and Kate was pulling at his taped wrists. 'Sorry,' she said, close to his ear. 'I... can't really... co-ordinate. Bastards have drugged me I think.'

'Me too,' said Lucas.

'It's getting to be a habit for me,' she muttered. '*Shit.* Fucking hate gaffer tape.' She tugged at it ineffectually and he could sense her energy dipping dangerously low.

'Stop,' he said. 'Try my jeans pockets. There's a pen knife in there. I'm sure of it.'

And then she was digging her hot hands deep into his pockets and his subsiding erection was suddenly ready to party again. He felt hollow with embarrassment. What if she noticed? Of all the times...

'Well, what do we have here?' she burbled, drunkenly.

'I'm sorry - I can't help it-'

'I bloody love the Swiss!' she said, holding up the shiny red gadget with its reassuring silver cross shield.

His reassurance was short-lived. He could sense their enemies returning even before he heard it. 'Quick!' he said. 'They're nearly here.'

But she was right, her co-ordination *was* still shot. She couldn't get the blades open. And now he could *hear* them approaching the door. 'Just give it to me!' he whispered, urgently. 'Then play dead, OK. Wait for your moment!'

She grunted her agreement, shoved the pen knife between his clumped fingers and sank back down into the same position she'd been in before, pulling her hands in behind her back and closing her eyes. Lucas could see she was breathing heavily from the last few minutes of exertion, but hoped their captors wouldn't notice. The element of surprise was all they had against a loaded shotgun and a lot of motivation to see them both safely dead.

He pictured the two of them being dragged into the bushes and elaborately posed to depict a fatal bike crash. Would they put his helmet back on before or after they got to work with the spade? He shuddered and worked the penknife between his constrained fingers, trying desperately to prise out a blade when his wrists and palms were so tightly bound. Sid told him he had about ten seconds to pull off quite a trick. The only upside to this new level of panic was that his cock had settled down again.

In fact, they stood outside for a good couple of minutes, talking in low voices before they moved on with their plan. As they reached the door he could clearly sense their inter-twined energies; the man was scared - and the fear made him desperate and dangerous. The woman was much colder and very determined. He got the feeling she had no qualms at all about ending their lives; while her partner in crime was feeling it all much more sharply. He was wishing he'd never started all this.

'Don't overthink it,' said Donna. 'Ready?'

'Ready,' said Larkhill.

The shed door opened and they came in on a draught of cold air and even colder intent. 'Right,' said Donna, handing her lover a teabag-sized plastic bag and holding up one of her own. 'About half of this should keep them docile. They'll stagger a bit but we should be able to keep them walking. It's only about five minutes down the track, anyway. You do him - make sure he swallows it. We can pool the rest to finish her off when we get there.'

'OK,' said Larkhill, sounding nervous.

'Don't worry - they're both pretty dopey already,' she said. 'Just get it done.'

Lucas kept his eyes half closed as Larkhill approached. He had rested his forehead on the post and he stayed there in a semi-recumbent pose, allowing his mouth to hang open a little as if he was asleep. He laboured his breathing. Larkhill leaned in and tipped the plastic bag, shaking the white powder inside it towards the edge. He gingerly held it out towards Lucas's mouth and Lucas gave a snort and breathed out hard, sending a cloud of the stuff into Larkhill's creased face. 'Shit!' the man said.

'Get it *done,* Rob,' said Donna.

Larkhill tried again, pushing the bag close up to Lucas's drooping lips. Then several things happened very fast. Lucas snapped his teeth shut on the man's fingers, like a Rottweiler, hanging on grimly while slicing the blade he'd finally unsheathed through the tape and releasing his hands.

While Larkhill screamed in shock and pain, trying vainly to pull away, Lucas heard Donna give a shriek. As he grabbed hold of Larkhill by both ears and rammed the man's face against the post he heard further commotion across the shed floor; a scuffle and a crack.

And then the deafening bang of a shotgun going off.

33

J osh didn't fumble with the keys. They weren't grabbed from behind as they scrambled to get in. The engine, still warm, started up like a dream. The only jarring moment was when Karen Carpenter started singing: '*Such a feeling's coming over me...*' through the stereo which Finley must have smacked on with his elbow.

Josh smacked it off again, shouting: 'Fuck OFF, Karen!'

As he hit the central lock button and heard the doors clunk, Josh knew he and Finley were going to get away safely. The plan had worked. The two people in the shed would have to take their chances while he and his number one fan got the hell out of there and tried to get the signal for the emergency services call.

Then he heard the shotgun blast. He stalled the car. Finley was gaping towards the shed. 'That guy,' he murmured, in a strangled voice. 'He tried to save me. Him and the policewoman. I think they're killing them.'

Josh flung the car into reverse. Nearly every instinct was screaming at him to get the fuck out of this hellhole. *Nearly* every one. Just one was screaming '*They KILLED SHEILA!*'

Finley was crying again. 'I don't want them to die,' he wailed.

'Put your seatbelt on!' said Josh.

'It's on,' sobbed Finley.

Josh put his own on. 'Hang on tight,' he said. He swung the car around and saw the shed door was open, the light shafting outside. He couldn't quite believe what he was about to do.

———

KATE HAD TAKEN a dark pleasure at the way her elbow had connected with Donna's face. She had held her pose beside the tractor, waiting for her moment as the woman leaned in to tip more poison into her. Her dopiness was being shoved aside by adrenaline and this was a great help when she abruptly flung herself forward like a human mantrap, swinging her legs around and sending her knee hard into Donna's kidney while pistoning her elbow upwards. The white powder puffed into the air in a tiny mushroom cloud while Donna fell sideways with a shriek. A few steps away Larkhill was screaming as Lucas bit into the man's hand while simultaneously smashing his enemy's face against the wooden pole with such force that the whole shed was shaking.

Kate leapt up, going into her defence pose and readying herself for a kick to Donna's head as soon as the woman got to her knees. She didn't, however, reckon on the effects of recent concussion combined with a modest dose of Rohypnol, and suddenly staggered sideways as her balance went. She was steady again in a second but not before there was an ear-splitting bang and Donna was standing up, holding the smoking shotgun. Kate froze, glancing to Lucas, who was still holding Larkhill's head against the post but no longer pile-driving the man towards oblivion. He didn't appear to have been shot and Kate was pretty sure she hadn't been either... although that could change at any second.

'Let... him... go!' growled Donna, waving the gun back and forth between Kate and Lucas. Lucas disengaged his teeth from Larkhill's bloodied fingers and released his grip on the man's ears. Larkhill staggered backwards, groaning, blood gushing from his nose.

Kate suddenly felt fully alert. She understood why. This was her last chance. Life was about to be punched out of her by a shotgun slug at point blank range. Or maybe Lucas would get it first. She couldn't bear to think of either option but grim reality was staring her in the face. Oh, poor Francis. How would he manage with *all* of his womenfolk dead and gone?

'It won't work, you know,' she heard Detective Sergeant Sparrow say. *Calm voice. Neutral tones. Speak to the common sense of your potential attacker - connect with them.* Hmmm. Kind of hard to get a rapport going with someone whose jaw you'd probably just dislocated. 'Right now you might just about make it through this. You will be caught but so far you've not killed anyone, right?' The look that passed over Donna's face told her this guess was wrong. Donna was fully complicit. Bugger. 'Even if you have,' she went on, 'you could be out again before you're old. Shoot a police officer and you've got no hope. You'll die in jail.'

'I know this land,' said Donna, in a voice chillier than the plains in January. 'I know where to leave your bodies so you'll never be found.'

She lifted the gun, settled it against her shoulder, aimed at Kate.

And then flew abruptly up in the air as a maroon Peugeot 208 smashed through the shed wall.

34

The impact of the car against the shed was terrifying. Finley screamed in harmony with Josh as the front of the car ploughed through the old timber with a deafening bang and a bone-shaking crunch. Splintered wood and nails thumped the windscreen, cracking a star shape across Josh's side of the glass but not shattering it. The seat belt cut brutally into his chest as he lurched forward and the passenger seat airbag went off in Finley's face, knocking him back against the headrest with a grunt.

It wasn't over. There was another resounding bang as the bumper struck something behind the wrecked shed wall. Even through the steering column and the juddering chassis Josh could sense that the collision was with something softer than a crate or a wheelbarrow; something dense but with *give*. He hoped it was Rob or Donna.

This whole thought process took place in a matter of three seconds and ended as he stamped on the brake. He'd never intended to drive straight through the shed and out the other side - only to smash into the wall and somehow stop a murder. Truth was, he hadn't really thought it through at all. He'd been acting on pure, dumb, instinct. A moment later and here he was - staring, dumbfounded, through a cracked windscreen and a pile of broken planks, at the back of Donna Wilson's head. She lay against the windscreen as if she was having a little power nap. He recognised the black of her bobbed hair and, on her flung up wrist, the gold charm bracelet which she often wore to work .

He might have just killed the woman who organised his multi-signed card and Marks and Spencer birthday cake last month. It hadn't been a gesture of much consideration. She'd overlooked the note on his staff file that he was coeliac. He'd left the cake in reception for Moira to take home. *Just goes to show... you should pay more attention to the overnight guy, Donna.*

————

THERE WAS a hiss of silence - like dead air - for a few seconds after the crash. Kate found she wasn't breathing. Her chest was hitching but her throat was shut. The wing mirror of the Peugeot was an inch away from her right hip. Inside the car sat Josh Carnegy, gaping through the windscreen, and next to him was the dazed face of Finley Warner, evidently rescued from the radio car mast and recently punched catatonic by an air bag.

Donna lay back across the bonnet, looking quite peaceful for someone whose lower legs were pinned against the unforgiving flank of a tractor. Her eyes were open and unfocused and her chest was rising and falling at great speed. Kate hoped she was in a deep enough state of shock not to notice that everything below her knees was missing in action. Permanently.

The slow ticking of the stalled engine found its way through the silence, ushering in more sounds, slowly increasing in volume, as if the radio presenter at the wheel was bringing up a fader. The driver side window was gently powering open. Larkhill was whimpering 'Donna! Donna! Oh, Jesus Christ, Donna...' Lucas was ripping the tape off his ankles and getting to his feet, white-faced and breathing heavily.

Kate heard a sudden sucking sound and realised her throat had reopened for business and she was breathing again. Hard and fast. 'Josh - Finley,' she called out, trying for *commanding* and achieving *feeble*. She coughed and did better with 'Are either of you injured?'

'I don't know,' said Josh.

'Carefully... move your arms and legs. Tell me what you can feel,' said Kate.

Her head was sharpening up, thank god. She glanced at Lucas and he gave her a small, reassuring nod; he was OK. Not great, but OK. She returned the nod as Josh said: 'I think everything's alright, but I might have pissed my pants.'

'Finley?' she asked.

Finley turned his gaze slowly around to her. 'I feel a bit sick,' he said. Then he pushed the passenger door open and threw up noisily on the floor.

'Robert Larkhill, I am arresting you for the murder of Dave Perry and Sheila Bartley,' said Kate, suddenly finding her full detective sergeant voice and reaching to the back of her belt to find her station issue handcuffs. 'And the kidnap and attempted murder of Finley Warner, Lucas Henry and... Kate Sparrow. You do not have to say anything-'

If she had been expecting Rob Larkhill to go quietly -

and looking at him, sagging against the far wall in a state of horrified shock, it wasn't an unreasonable assumption - she was wrong. Larkhill suddenly leapt across the room and out through the broken shed wall and fled into the darkness.

Lucas immediately gave chase, as if sprung from a trap. 'Oh no you don't, you little shit!' he bellowed and vanished into the darkness too. Kate was left with a quandary. Her instinct was to give chase with him, and bring Larkhill to the ground with as much accidental violence as she could get away with. But she was faced with managing Donna Wilson, lying critically injured on the bonnet of the BBC pool car and two witnesses who might also be about to go into shock.

'Have either of you got a working phone?' she asked Josh and Finley.

Josh got out of the car, keeping his eyes away from the victim on its bonnet, and dug into his pocket. He retrieved a small iPhone. 'Couldn't get a signal, though,' he said, inputting the security code and passing it to her with a shaking hand. 'I tried earlier.'

'My phone's still back in the radio car,' said Finley, wiping his face and getting to his feet with a fearful glance at Donna before slumping down on the crate next to the bit of wall that remained standing.

Kate checked Josh's phone and held it up. Then, averting her eyes from the point where it connected with a Peugeot 208 and some human limbs, she clambered up on top of the tractor and lifted the device to the rafters. 'There's one bar!' She hammered out 999 but couldn't get the call to connect. *Calm. Stay calm.* 'I might at least be able to get a text out,' she muttered, tapping out an emergency back-up request to her colleagues, along with the best directions her tired brain could summon. Then she clicked *send* and prayed she wouldn't get a bounce back message. She held the phone high above her head, eyes riveted on the message she'd written. After five seconds there was nothing to suggest it had failed. Maybe she had finally caught a break.

Finley was starting to shiver uncontrollably. 'I think you need to get back in the car,' said Kate. 'Try to keep warm.'

He shook his head. 'I can't look,' he said.

'Me neither,' said Josh. He edged along and around the Peugeot to sit next to Finley on the crate.

Kate got down from the tractor and gingerly reached for Donna's wrist. It felt cool, but she could just detect a pulse. 'We should probably get something over her - keep her warm,' she said.

'Should I back the car up?' said Josh, looking sick at the thought.

'No,' said Kate. 'There's a lot of damage to her legs and I think moving her could make it worse. Her blood pressure would probably crash and she'd die. We just need to hold on until the ambulance crew gets here.' She checked the phone again, reflexively. There was no answering text.

'I think there's a first aid kit with a foil blanket in the boot,' said Josh. He got up and opened it, digging around. 'Shit,' he gulped. 'I really didn't think I'd mash someone's legs up tonight. *Shit*.'

'You saved my life,' said Kate. 'And Lucas's. No question. Thank you.'

'He made me do it,' said Josh, glancing at Finley. 'I would have driven off otherwise.'

'You saved *my* life too,' Finley told her, shivering harder. 'You and that guy.'

'If there's more than one foil blanket you need to get one for Finley and yourself, too,' said Kate. 'You need to keep warm. I think there's some sacking over here.' She walked to the back of the tractor and found the damp material. She picked up a bundle, shaking away any creatures and turned back just as Finley shrieked 'No, no, NO!'.

She had half a second to register that Donna was sitting up before she was shot.

35

Lucas skidded on wet grass and glanced left and right, trying to locate Larkhill. Sid, thrumming against his skin, told him to go right. The radio car and the Jeep were down to the left and he would have guessed the man had headed that way if it wasn't for the patterns he was picking up. Neither of them had a torch, it was obvious, but Lucas had a dowser's frequency map vibrating helpfully across his third eye and picked up a seething, panicked blur of energy stumbling towards the western end of the field. He increased his speed, determined to get the guy before he vanished into the trees that lined the perimeter.

But then Larkhill zig-zagged a little and headed back to the cars. He'd obviously worked out his best hope of escape now lay with one of them. Lucas doubled back too, not chasing but finding a path that would intersect with the man before he reached his escape point. He tried to keep his breathing quiet and not thud too heavily; better to let Larkhill think his change of tack was undetected. Lucas reckoned, though, without the distraction of his damaged knee which suddenly kicked off with a surge of intense pain, leaving him breathless and staggering. He fell onto his side and groaned mutely as the agony ripped through him. He had to get up. He *had* to. It took him time, though, shakily getting onto his good knee and placing the foot of his injured leg carefully on the turf. It howled, but it was still just about usable.

Meanwhile Larkhill had reached the cars and was getting into the Ford. He slammed the door and the head-lamps brightened as he gunned the engine. Then the car moved a few metres before coming to a halt with the harsh beep of an alarm signal. As he limped across the grass Lucas could see Larkhill opening the driver door and half getting out, while pressing on something inside. A motorised hum cut through the air and the mast began to descend at a slow and steady rate, which had to be purgatory for the escaping murderer. 'Shit, shit, *SHIT,*' Lucas heard him curse. 'Come ON!'

But the mast was not designed to *come on.* It was designed to retract at a steady, sensible pace. Just steady and sensible enough to allow Lucas to cover the ground between them and hurl himself at Larkhill. He grabbed the man by the lapels of his winter coat and threw him to the ground. Larkhill shrieked and bucked and clawed up at his face.

'Stop it, you little shit,' said Lucas, punching the side of his head. 'I'm arresting you on behalf of the Wiltshire Constabulary, for murder and kidnap and for *really pissing me off.*'

He wasn't sure what he was going to tie the guy up with. He didn't carry cuffs. There would probably be rope or something in the radio car and maybe some more of that godforsaken gaffer tape, but right now he didn't dare let Larkhill go. The man was fighting back hard. Lucas realised he might be wearing the only thing he could use right now - the chain around his neck. It was made of stainless steel and its links were strong. Strong enough to have saved his life once, when he was just about to slide off the roof of a tall building in Paris.

So he rolled the guy again, onto his chest. He managed to pin Larkhill's wrists together once more and then whipped a hand up and pulled Sid out of his jumper and flipped the chain over his head. He was about to loop it tightly around Larkhill's wrists when he heard a gunshot ring out across the field. *Shit! Kate!* He glanced up in shock and Larkhill took his chance to twist around, kick against his bad leg, and leap up. Crying out in agony, Lucas slumped back against the driver door, knocking it shut, and Larkhill came at him, trying to drag him away.

Lucas found Sid singing in one hand, the looped end of the chain in the other. As Larkhill came for him he lassoed it around the guy's neck and jerked him sideways. Then he was up again and shoving his adversary against the windscreen. Larkhill kicked and hissed, elbowing Lucas in the face until he released his grip, and then scrambled up the windscreen and onto the roof. There he wrapped both arms around the lowered stub of the antennae to steady himself while he kicked out repeatedly against Lucas's face. Lucas felt a surge of rage as he saw Sid now swinging wildly around his enemy's neck.

The muddy sole of Larkhill's boot abruptly connected with his brow and Lucas slumped against the car door as his leg gave another almighty howl of pain. He found the driver's side window was wound down and he reached inside it to grab the key from the ignition; he could at least prevent Larkhill from driving away. He felt another kick to the base of his skull which made him spin and grasp blindly around the dash. His fingers encountered another ignition point on the far side of the steering wheel - a red rocker switch which he knocked in passing. At once the motor of the mast began to hum again and the antennae started to rise up. Taking another kick to the face, he bashed the button again to stop it. But the motor didn't cut out. It just hummed on.

Again Lucas went to get the key and turn all the electrics off but another vicious boot strike to his brow beat him back out of the car and onto the grass. He looked up in time to see Larkhill grimacing murderously down at him for around three seconds before the man suddenly jerked up and away. There was a gurgling cry. For a second Lucas wondered if Kate had arrived and seized the guy by the throat from the far side of the car, but no. It wasn't any human intervention.

Lucas scrambled across the grass on his backside and elbows, and stared up into a sky which was slowly growing lighter with the approaching dawn. His mouth fell open as the tower of metal and cable travelled relentlessly upwards, the outline of a man struggling, choking and gasping against it. Larkhill was now standing to his full height, up on his tippy-toes, his hands scrabbling vainly at the hydraulic mechanism he was snagged on.

Lucas finally worked out what was happening. While Larkhill had been hanging on to the low level antennae and kicking his foe repeatedly in the head, the steel chain around his neck must have looped across the top of the mast. And now that mast was rising up, taking the strong chain and the struggling man with it, his back to the mechanism, his fingers at his throat and his legs kicking out wildly.

———

KATE WAS surprised it didn't hurt more. The punch of the lead pellets as they struck her spun her around 180 degrees and she found herself face-planting the rear wheel of the tractor. She rolled over on the ground, her hand reaching for her right shoulder, hot moisture meeting her fingers. She could dimly hear Josh and Finley shouting and she could see that Donna had scooped up the bag of cartridges from somewhere amid the wreckage of wood, metal and her own limbs and was now rummaging in it so she could reload the gun.

'You're... not... going... anywhere,' panted the woman.

'Josh... Finley... run,' Kate yelled, although it only came out as thin gasps.

The bag opened and Donna broke the shotgun and went for her ammo with the slick motion borne of decades of farm girl experience. Then she paused, staring into the bag in confusion. 'What the fuck?' she said, as stringy blobs of plasticine came away on her fingers.

Two seconds later Finley threw the crate at Donna's head and the shotgun, the ammo bag and its neat little row of plasticine-smothered cartridges scattered to the far corners of the broken shed.

Finley and Josh came into view, leaning over her. Finley pressed his scarf firmly to her shoulder and held it there. 'I trained in first aid,' he told her. 'I have to use pressure to stop the bleeding. Sorry if it hurts.'

She watched them for a while, unable to speak, until eventually the sides of their faces went blue and red and blue and red and she passed out.

———

LUCAS DID everything he could to save Robert Larkhill. He got into the car and bashed around all the buttons on its dashboard, randomly switching on the stereo with a blast of BBC Radio Wessex jingle and a familiar swell of easy listening music. He took the keys out of the engine but it didn't make any difference. The mast power source was obviously running on a different battery to the one under the bonnet and the red rocker switch seemed to have fused itself in the UP position. Hammering it with his fingers didn't have any effect. He shoved the key back in, in case that might help but all it did was start the stereo again.

As Lucas attempted to get up onto the roof of the car and lift the guy off the aerial he realised it was too late. The man's body was still going up, snagged firmly to the top of the antennae by the chain around his neck. Larkhill was no longer struggling, but hanging limply, his eyes wide and fixed.

Lucas didn't need to be a dowser to know the man was dead. He sagged back onto the grass, his knee screaming a shrill note of agony and his badly-kicked head throbbing along to the melodic strains of *Lifted* by Lighthouse Family.

36

Getting loaded into an ambulance by her work colleagues was becoming a habit. Kate was happy to see the paramedic, though, because the wound in her shoulder was hurting like a bastard by the time they'd walked her out of the shed, leaving another medic to work out what the hell to do with Donna Wilson who was still, amazingly, in the land of the living. Wiltshire Fire & Rescue trucks were on their way with rescue equipment.

Further down the field a circle of lights had been set up around the radio car and the Jeep and from her seat in the ambulance, wrapped in a blanket, bandaged and finally getting the benefit of some intravenous morphine, Kate could see the limp body of Larkhill slowly descending as someone at last worked out how to get that mast down.

Michaels emerged through the pre-dawn light, looking shell-shocked. He sat next to her. 'How are you doing, boss?' he asked.

'I'll live,' she said. 'What's happening down there?'

'Your boyfriend's getting his leg strapped up and then I'm going to be asking some questions.'

'I've told you what happened,' said Kate, a wave of immense weariness stealing over her as the paramedic put a blood pressure cuff on the arm below her uninjured shoulder and began to inflate it.

'Yeah - at your end - but what happened down there is another story. Looks like Henry decided to be judge and jury and hang Robert Larkhill.'

'He wouldn't do that,' she said. 'He was just trying to stop him escaping. If he says the mast thing was an accident, that's what it was.'

'Yeah, well, we'll see,' muttered Michaels and Kate realised there were so many ways still open to Wiltshire Police to wreck Lucas Henry's life. She could only hope forensics would bear out what Lucas said. Certainly the injuries on him would tell a lot of the story.

She drifted away for a while and then drifted back, finding herself under a blanket on a gurney in the ambulance. Lucas Henry was lying across from her, similarly blanketed, blood and bruises all over his face. Two medics were securing them both with straps across the blankets. 'We're about to take you in,' said the woman nearest to her, smiling reassuringly. 'You've lost a bit of blood and you'll need topping up.'

'What about Lucas?' asked Kate.

'He'll be OK,' said the guy tending to Lucas.

'They won't let me have Sid back,' mumbled Lucas.

'Who's Sid?' asked the man, but Lucas was out for the count.

'Who's Sid?' the man asked Kate, looking worried. 'Another casualty?'

'No,' said Kate. 'Sid's a bit of glass.'

'I think she's delirious,' said the female medic.

Kate thought she was probably right.

37

'Good morning, you lovely people! Great to have you here with me for my very first breakfast show on BBC Radio Wessex! It's just gone six and we've got a lot to pack in over the next three hours, including news, sport, weather, traffic updates *and* Wiltshire's own top psychic and spoon bender Davy Gatward *On The Couch,* but first, here's a little Neil Diamond to start your day...'

It caused Kate a great deal of pain to hit the volume switch on her radio fast enough to block out the opening bars of *Sweet Caroline,* but it was worth it. Afterwards she sank back on the sofa with a sigh of relief. She would turn the sound up again in a couple of minutes when Neil had safely belted out his final chorus. She wanted to hear how Josh was getting on. It was quite amazing that he was taking over the old Voice of Wessex slot just a couple of weeks after the events at the show ground. A lesser man would still be too traumatised after everything Josh had been through.

It was no less amazing that the listeners were adapting so fast. After the shock of Dave Perry's death came the even greater shock of the murder of Sheila Bartley just the next day, which had hit the news, locally and nationally, roughly twelve hours after Kate and Lucas's ambulance had bumped them painfully down the farm track away from the West Wiltshire Showground.

Sheila's untimely end prompted a condolence book signing queue three or four times the length of Dave Perry's and a media circus unseen in Salisbury since the Novichok poisonings of 2018. Most shocking of all for the regular listeners was the news that the station manager's personal assistant had been arrested and charged with the murder of Bartley and the cover up of the murder of Perry, as well as the attempted murder of Radio Wessex's number one fan Finley Warner, a local motorcyclist *and* a Wiltshire police officer. More staggering still, that she would have been jointly charged with station manager Robert Larkhill, had he not expired before he could be arrested.

Kate knew the full facts of the case would blow the collective mind of the Radio Wessex listenership when it all eventually came out. For now, she was merely an anonymous copper who'd helped to bring the surviving murderer into custody, sustaining a serious injury for her trouble. By the time this came to court she would already be renowned for her testimony on the Runner Grabber case. The thought of such notoriety was even less comfortable than her slowly healing shoulder.

Of course, had Donna died, it would have been a shorter, simpler inquest rather than a full-blown prosecution. If she was pleading guilty it wouldn't be so drawn-out, but the word was that Donna - now a double amputee - was pleading innocence, claiming that coercive control by Rob Larkhill had terrified her into being his unwilling accomplice. *Yeah.* She'd looked so *unwilling* as she'd tried to reload that shotgun and have another go.

Kate knew she was lucky to have come away from that shed without a much worse injury. The slug had torn through flesh and grazed her scapula but missed the vital junctions of her shoulder joint. It still hurt like hell, though. The slow-healing pain wiped her out, siphoning off her energy and forcing her to rest at home when she was longing to get back to work. The high dose painkillers were quite effective, but they gave her vivid and unsettling dreams, repeatedly taking her back to the shed and Donna's legs crushed against the tractor, Lucas biting Larkhill's fingers, Finley up on the car roof, about to get electrocuted... some nights she didn't get there in time to stop it.

If that wasn't entertainment enough, some dreams were an imaginative mash-up of the Radio Wessex Murders *and* the Runner Grabber case. And a little amusing side dish was Mabel, her long lost late sister, occasionally wandering through the mayhem, her golden hair floating in the breeze, amid the sun-bleached stones of the quarry whilst somehow simultaneously strolling through the midnight horror of the strangled man hanging from a mast.

It was disconcerting the way the truth floated around the dreams and the dreams floated around the truth... until she wasn't sure what was real memory and what was just the drugs and her own dark subconscious. It might take a while - and a bit more therapy with Joanna - to tease it all apart.

'Tea?' Francis leaned in her doorway. He had taken to dropping in to check on her so often he might as well just live here in her bit of the house.

'Early up or late to bed?' she asked, easing up the radio volume now that Neil Diamond had stopped reaching out and touching sweet Caroline.

'Late to bed,' he said, with a stretch and a yawn. 'Did you sleep?'

'..ish,' said Kate, shrugging.

'Heard any more from Lucas?'

She shook her head. Lucas was, as far as she could find out from her work colleagues, also recovering steadily from his injuries. The motorbike crash had done worse damage than the fight with Rob Larkhill; his knee had needed surgery. She had seen photos of the bruises all over his face. They had a distinct boot sole pattern which would help confirm the defence that Larkhill had been stamping Lucas to the ground when the rising mast had snagged him by the neck and finished him off. The chief engineer at Radio Wessex had also confirmed the glitch with the hydraulics on the mast. Forensics would probably be able to bear out exactly how Larkhill had died, but until then Lucas was once again under a cloud of suspicion. He had to be getting used to it by now.

Francis brought tea and digestives. 'I like the dragon,' he said, settling down next to her and putting the tray on the coffee table beside her small sculptures.

Kate nodded, picking up her creation in bright green modelling clay and teasing its tail upward. She was finding the plasticine therapeutic; perhaps even more so now. It had probably saved her life, slowing down the ammo retrieval from the bag and giving Finley a few more seconds to hit Donna with the crate. And now it was helping to keep Kate's mind off things. Lucas was among those things. She hadn't spoken to him - apart from a couple of texts - since that night when they'd both come so close to being murdered at the bike crash scene. She'd asked if he was OK. He'd texted back: **Yeah. OK. You?**

She'd responded: **Doing alright. Painkillers help.**

Gotta love Voltarol, he'd texted back.

And that was that. All the official stuff, like taking his photos and his statement, was being handled by her colleagues. Lucas and she were destined to meet again, of course. They would see each other across *two* courtrooms now. It would all come to a head over the next few months and she knew she *would* see him again. All in good time.

So why couldn't she stop thinking about him? Especially that time in the shed when they were both so out of it. Something had been going on... something he said. Or maybe it was just a *feeling* she had. She'd felt so... intense. Like everything in her world was about Lucas Henry and something he was telling her.

But that was hard to get into by text and she wasn't supposed to be talking to him. Kapoor had been to see her at home, checking in with genuine concern. He'd brought an impressive pack of plasticine. Word had obviously got out about her murderer-thwarting habit. He also advised that she and her dowser friend should maintain some professional distance while the facts of the case were established.

He'd looked tired as he got up to go. She'd said: 'Guv... are you OK?'

He'd smiled and said: 'I'll be fine. I'm taking a few days off, though. I need a small procedure.' She knew that was all she would get in the way of detail.

———

'GOOD MORNING, you lovely people! Great to have you here with me for my very first breakfast show on BBC Radio Wessex! It's just gone six-thirty and we've got a lot to pack in over the next couple of hours, including news, sport, weather, traffic updates *and* Wiltshire's own top psychic and spoon bender Davy Gatward *On The Couch,* but first, here's a little Neil Diamond to start your day...'

Josh Carnegy triggered *Sweet Caroline* and took down his mic fader. He sucked in a deep, deep breath and reached for his mug of coffee.

'You doing alright in there?' Gemma buzzed in his headphones.

He nodded and put a thumb up, grinning to her through the glass window to tele-in. She beamed back at him and put both her own thumbs up before keying the button to add 'You've got this, Josh.'

He knew she and James were totally behind him. They would protect him from any callers intent on dragging up the events of the last couple of weeks. Although his presence at the location of the police arrests had got out, nothing further had yet surfaced about exactly what had happened that night. The British judicial system was a godsend; he literally *couldn't* talk about any of it until he was testifying in court. Not publicly, anyway. So any caller being put through was getting a firm warning from the production team that they must not ask about Dave Perry, Sheila Bartley or Finley Warner.

'Josh will be in contempt of court if he responds in any way,' he'd heard Gemma say on the phone, two or three times already this morning. 'Anyone who brings up the case with him will get cut off immediately, OK?'

Of course, once it got to court it was all going to come out and there would be no escaping the morbid fascination. He just hoped his fledgling career would survive it and not be defined by it. He also hoped Finley would survive it and not be defined by it. He guessed he would find out soon enough how his number one fan was coping. He smiled at the Tupperware tub of macaroons next to his coffee mug. The note stuck to it read: *Congratulations and good luck! You'll be the best breakfast show presenter EVER. F*

Despite his high adrenaline, he reckoned he could get maybe half a macaroon down before the end of the track.

————

'GOOD MORNING, you lovely people! Great to have you here with me for my very first breakfast show on BBC Radio Wessex! It's just gone six-thirty and we've got a lot to pack in over the next couple of hours, including news, sport, weather, traffic updates *and* Wiltshire's own top psychic and spoon bender Davy Gatward *On The Couch,* but first, here's a little Neil Diamond to start your day...'

Lucas crushed a peppermint teabag in a mug of boiled water. He was longing for a coffee but his nights weren't too great and maybe that was down to the high dose painkillers not mixing well with caffeine.

Yeah, right.

He was missing things. He was missing sleep. He was missing Sid. He was missing bits of memory, thanks to that bloody Rohypnol... and he was missing Kate. A couple of texts weren't much after everything they'd been through. He could have used a support group, even if Kate was the only other member.

He took his mug of mint tea and a hunk of granary bread and butter and sat down at the kitchen table. He ate breakfast, wondering if was better to just leave Sid in the Salisbury nick evidence locker.

He was about to turn up the volume on Josh's first show when his mobile rang; number withheld. He steeled himself and picked up the call.

'Lucas?'

He recognised the voice but was puzzled by the informality. 'Chief Superintendent?'

'I'm off duty. You can call me... Kapoor,' was the response - only semi-detached from formality after all.

'Oh - well - OK then.'

'I'm sorry. I've just realised how early it is. Did I wake you?'

'No. No, I was up. What can I do for you?'

'I wanted to thank you,' came the reply. Lucas began to see patterns drifting around the visualisation of his ally and adversary. He sensed Kapoor was reclining. And connected to a machine.

'I acted upon your advice to get my kidney function checked,' went on Kapoor. 'It turns out I have been hosting a small tumour on my left lower lobe for the past year.'

'Oh,' said Lucas. 'That's... not good.'

'It could be worse,' said Kapoor. 'I don't think I would have known about it for some time. I *was* tired, but I had put that down to the stresses and strains of the last few months. I had no idea there was an underlying problem. The nephrologist says that in another two or three months it might have been a much more serious situation. As it is, the tumour has been removed and has, I am told, not spread. I am very lucky.'

'That *is* good news.' Lucas breathed out, nodding his head to nobody. He never intentionally dowsed people's state of health. It was way too much of a minefield to get involved with. He only ever mentioned anything if Sid picked something up in passing and then got quite insistent. He was very glad his little glass helper had pushed him past his annoyance with Kapoor. It would have been easy to let that one pass.

'The chain that cut off Robert Larkhill's air supply is still being held for evidence,' Kapoor went on. 'I can't return that to you. But you should receive the pendulum. The pathologist agreed with me that it was not relevant to our enquiry. I asked for it to be sterilised before they posted it to you.'

'Thank you,' Lucas said. 'I appreciate it.'

'Extraordinary,' said Kapoor. 'Just... extraordinary. Lucas... would you be happy to be on our register of consultants?'

Lucas took a deep breath. 'Let me think about that,' he said.

'Of course - quite right. Well... no doubt we will meet again soon. In the meantime, please don't speak to DS Sparrow.'

Chance, thought Lucas, would be a fine thing.

After the call he turned the radio back up. Josh sounded great - much brighter and sharper and wholly less annoying than his murdered predecessor, whom Lucas had occasionally heard when seeking traffic and travel updates before a journey. There weren't many upsides to recent events at BBC Radio Wessex but this was one of them.

His mind kept drifting from the broadcast, even so. His patchy memory was unnerving him. There was something about that time in the shed with Kate, when he'd thought they were going to die. Something he'd said to her. Or thought he'd said. Did he say it? Did he actually make his full confession... *out loud?* And did she hear it if he did?

———

FINLEY'S SMILE was every bit as wide as it ever had been when Josh met him in the BBC canteen, sitting with a mug of tea, wearing his guest ID on a lanyard and drumming his fingers on the table.

Something was different about him, though. Not surprising, considering what had happened to him. Josh still felt appalled and guilty about it. He sat down with the half-empty tub of macaroons and his half-drunk coffee and smiled back. 'Those macaroons were the best I've ever tasted,' he said. 'And I'm not just saying that because my former boss tried to murder you.'

Finley's smile deepened to a grin and Josh realised suddenly what it was. Nothing about the young man had really changed; it was just that *he* was seeing Finley differently. There was warmth in that smile. No creepiness or fanaticism; just warmth.

'You know I don't actually *bake* them, don't you?' said Finley.

'Shit. Are you telling me you've been ripping off Mr Kipling all these years?'

Finley laughed. 'No! My mum makes them. She's a brilliant baker. She's won prizes at the WI.'

Josh shook his head in wonder. 'How are you doing?' he said.

Finley's smile faded a little. 'OK, I guess. A bit... nervous sometimes.'

'You getting nightmares?'

'Yeah. Are you?'

'Yup. I suppose it'll take a while to settle down.'

'You saved my life,' said Finley. 'I will never be able to thank you enough.'

'And you saved the other two,' said Josh. 'Don't forget that. If you hadn't said what you said I would have just driven us away. I wouldn't have crashed into that shed. And you wouldn't have been there to smash that psycho bitch

Donna over the head with a crate and stop her killing DS Sparrow.'

'Yeah, well... DS Sparrow saved me too,' said Finley, with a shrug. 'And that Lucas Henry guy. If they hadn't shown up it would have been game over well before you got there. You'd have just found me all crisped up on the radio car. You'd have read that fake suicide note and you'd have thought I killed Dave and Sheila.'

'That was some seriously fucked up night out we had,' said Josh. 'But we got through it. We were a total *team*.'

Finley was grinning again now. 'Yeah. We were, weren't we?'

'There's this new person in charge here,' said Josh. 'Her name's Jocelyn Pearson. English Regions rushed her down here the morning after our wild night out. She's the acting station manager but I think she'll probably get the job permanently when everything's settled down.'

'Yes, she was at BBC Radio Oxford for five years as manager and worked as a senior broadcast journalist for BBC Radio Leeds for three years before that,' said Finley.

Josh laughed, shaking his head.

'I read *Ariel*,' explained Finley. 'Moira prints off the on-line articles for me.'

'Of course you do,' said Josh. Only Finley could charm a staffer into handing over print outs of the BBC's internal newspaper. 'Anyway, there are some trainee opportunities going, for the technical side of broadcasting,' he said. 'Not here - up at Berkshire. She says she thinks you should go for it.' He slid a card across the table. 'This is the number of the chief engineer up there. He's expecting you to call. What do you think?'

Finley looked transfixed. 'You mean.... I could actually *work* in radio? At the BBC? Me?'

'Why not you? You already know loads about the network and the radio cars and the broadcasting tech. What's stopping you?'

Finley sat up straight, turning the card over in his fingers. 'Nothing,' he said, his eyes aflame. 'Nothing at all...'

'Y ou know, don't you? You know the truth about him?'

Kate rolled over on the sofa, where she'd dropped into a mid-morning doze in front of *Homes Under the Hammer*.

Mabel sat on the tractor in the shed, staring down at her with that long-suffering expression she had always worn when Mum made her take an annoying little sister along to hang out with her and her teenage mates.

Kate was lying on the ground with a hole in her shoulder and Lucas was still taped up to the wooden pole, muttering something she couldn't quite hear. 'I... I don't know,' she burbled up at Mabel. 'What truth?'

'Listen!' said Zoe, her cold, blue hand reaching out from underneath the broken shed wall.

'I want to say... I'm sorry,' said Lucas, swinging Sid on his chain. 'About what happened. It was me-'

'You see?' said Mabel. 'Do you *see*?'

Kate jolted awake, her mobile buzzing. A text had arrived. From Lucas.

I know we're not allowed to talk, so this is a one off, it read. **Just want to say I'm thinking about you.**

Kate felt slightly sick.

She thumbed back: **I'm thinking about you, too.**

ACKNOWLEDGMENTS

Grateful thanks go, as ever, to my top editing team Beverly Sanford and Nicola Sparkes, and police procedural guru Sarah Bodell, who between them save me from making a total idiot of myself. There's every chance I'm still making a partial idiot of myself, but it could be so much worse.

Also huge appreciation to Mia Costello, Rebecca Parker and Malcolm Baird at BBC Radio Solent, who updated me on the workings of a busy regional station - because it's been a few years now since I was let loose on the faders.

And ongoing warm hugs to Simon Tilley, for championing my Henry & Sparrow odyssey, sorting out all the clever stuff and offering tea.

ALSO BY A D FOX

HENRY & SPARROW
book 1:

THE DYING DOLLS

available on Amazon now

For a free copy
of the Henry & Sparrow prequel novella

UNDERTOW

go to www.adfoxfiction.com

ABOUT THE AUTHOR

AD Fox is an award winning author who lives in Hampshire, England, with a significant other, boomerang offspring and a large, highly porous labradoodle.

With a background in newspaper and broadcast journalism, AD would like to point out that nobody she ever worked with in BBC local radio was anything like Dave Perry. Dead Air is all fiction. Apart from the radio car. That radio car always was a *beast!*

Younger readers will know the AD alter ego as Ali Sparkes, author of more than fifty titles for children and young adults including the Blue Peter Award winning Frozen In Time, the bestselling Shapeshifter series and Car-Jacked, finalist in the national UK Children's Book of the Year awards.

For more on AD Fox, including blogs and updates, visit www.adfoxfiction.com.

Printed in Great Britain
by Amazon

58955134R00161